Praise for Aimée Carter and The Blackcoat Rebellion

"Corrupt leaders, graphic violence, rebellion, and first love, this title has it all... Carter (the Goddess Test trilogy) has created an engaging heroine to root for in Kitty and a page-turner full of twists and turns. Readers will look forward to the next book in the anticipated trilogy."

—*Booklist* on *Pawn*

"The tempo is brisk, the tension is deeply felt, the protagonist is a great reader's proxy, and the villains are smooth and terrifying. Kitty is a brash, imperfect hero, and readers will root for her every step of the way as she makes tough decisions."

—*School Library Journal* on *Pawn*

"Well-paced and readable."

—*Publishers Weekly* on *Pawn*

"*Pawn* is an intriguing political thriller that readers will want to finish in one night.... Filled with scheming, subterfuge, and the threat of being shipped off to Elsewhere, Carter has crafted a suspenseful mystery that will necessitate the purchase of the sequel."

—*VOYA*

"The plot twists and turns, with red herrings and a dynamic pace that will keep readers guessing. With even more political maneuvering, suspense, and romance, fans of the first book will not be disappointed."

—*School Library Journal* on *Captive*

"Readers will race through this and count the days until the final book is released."

—*Booklist* on *Captive*

"Carter's writing is smart; readers will feel as if they're really in Elsewhere experiencing Kitty's anguish, but these descriptions never take away from the rapid-fire plot. If you loved *The Hunger Games* and want your next dystopian YA fix, try this series now."

—*RT Book Reviews* on *Captive*

**Also by
Aimée Carter**

The Goddess Test Novels

in reading order:

THE GODDESS TEST
"The Goddess Hunt" (ebook)
GODDESS INTERRUPTED
THE GODDESS LEGACY
THE GODDESS INHERITANCE

The Blackcoat Rebellion

PAWN
CAPTIVE
QUEEN

CAPTIVE

AIMÉE CARTER

If you purchased this book without a cover you should be aware that this book is stolen property. It was reported as "unsold and destroyed" to the publisher, and neither the author nor the publisher has received any payment for this "stripped book."

Recycling programs for this product may not exist in your area.

ISBN-13: 978-0-373-21159-3

Captive

Copyright © 2014 by Aimée Carter

All rights reserved. Except for use in any review, the reproduction or utilization of this work in whole or in part in any form by any electronic, mechanical or other means, now known or hereinafter invented, including xerography, photocopying and recording, or in any information storage or retrieval system, is forbidden without the written permission of the publisher, Harlequin Enterprises Limited, 225 Duncan Mill Road, Don Mills, Ontario M3B 3K9, Canada.

This is a work of fiction. Names, characters, places and incidents are either the product of the author's imagination or are used fictitiously, and any resemblance to actual persons, living or dead, business establishments, events or locales is entirely coincidental.

This edition published by arrangement with Harlequin Books S.A.

For questions and comments about the quality of this book, please contact us at CustomerService@Harlequin.com.

® and TM are trademarks of Harlequin Enterprises Limited or its corporate affiliates. Trademarks indicated with ® are registered in the United States Patent and Trademark Office, the Canadian Intellectual Property Office and in other countries.

Printed in U.S.A.

To Carli Segal and Veronica O'Neil

I

FADING

Somewhere nearby, Benjy was waiting for me.

I could feel his stare as I made my rounds through the grand ballroom of Somerset Manor, greeting each new face with a smile that was becoming harder and harder to hold. They buzzed around me, vying for a few moments of my time, but we all knew they were only here because of my name and face. I was Lila Hart, the niece of the Prime Minister of the United States and one of the few VIIs in the entire country—which, in a roomful of VIs, made me more powerful than them all.

But I didn't want power or fame. If I had my way, I would be tucked away in my suite with Benjy, stealing as many moments alone together as we could. Instead, I was stuck celebrating my birthday with a roomful of my so-called closest friends, led around by a fiancé I didn't even particularly like, let alone love.

Except it wasn't my birthday. These weren't my friends. And Knox Creed was most definitely not my fiancé.

My name wasn't Lila Hart. It was Kitty Doe, and on my real seventeenth birthday in September, I'd been kidnapped by the

Prime Minister and surgically transformed into his spoiled, rebellious, and supposedly dead, niece against my will. He'd given me a choice: pretend to be Lila or wind up with a bullet in my brain. I wasn't an idiot, and even though it had meant giving up everything I'd known and everyone I'd loved, I'd chosen to live—and to fight. Three months later, after discovering a lifetime's worth of political conspiracies and secrets that should have stayed buried, here I was, with Knox clutching my arm as he led me through a crowd of people who would kill me if they figured out who I really was.

I glared up at him and tried to subtly twist my arm from his grip, but he hung on. I didn't care that he was handsome and tall, with dark hair and even darker eyes, and that most girls would have killed to be in my shoes. They didn't have to deal with his endless stream of instructions on how to impersonate a girl I hated, nor did they have to pretend to love him in front of the entire country when we spent most days in a constant tug of war.

Besides, I was extremely happy with the boyfriend I already had, thank you very much—a boyfriend who, with his infinite patience, had been waiting over an hour for me to slip away from these people. If I didn't find a way soon, the night wasn't going to end pleasantly for any of us.

"We had a deal," I whispered, leaning into Knox so only he could hear me. "I play nice for a couple hours and leave at nine. It's now almost eleven."

"Sometimes plans change," he said, his fingers tightening around my elbow. Even though he was speaking to me, his eyes scanned the ballroom. "Relax and try to enjoy yourself."

The only times I'd enjoyed myself in the past few months had been those stolen moments with Benjy. "Lila would have never stayed this long. Every minute I hang around, the more suspicious it looks."

"I know," he said quietly, bending down to brush his lips against my ear. The heat of his breath reminded me just how cold it was in the ballroom, and I shivered in my flimsy silk dress. "But sometimes even Lila had to do things she didn't like. Incoming."

I turned around in time to see a portly man amble up to us. Minister Bradley, one of the twelve Ministers of the Union who worked under the Prime Minister. I didn't know many of them on sight, but Minister Bradley's handlebar mustache was burned into my brain, along with the way my skin crawled whenever he was nearby.

"Lila, my dear, you look ravishing." He leaned in to bump his dry lips against my cheek, and it took every ounce of willpower I possessed to keep myself from shuddering. "After all you've been through, I expected something less..." He made a vague gesture, his eyes locking on my chest.

I didn't bother to smile this time. "Minister Bradley. I'm surprised to see you here. I thought your wife was sick."

He chuckled, and his gaze never wavered. "Yes, yes, well, I would never miss a chance to see your beautiful face."

"In that case, you might want to look up here instead," I said, and Minister Bradley turned scarlet.

"I'm sorry, Minister," said Knox quickly, and he hooked his elbow with mine. "Lila's had a bit too much to drink tonight. If you wouldn't mind, darling, I need a quick word with you."

He led me away, and I clutched my glass of champagne. We both knew I hadn't taken a single sip. I couldn't afford to drink, not when I needed every wit I had to survive the night.

Weaving through the Ministers and their families, along with several of the most prominent VIs in Washington D.C.,

Knox led me to a table laden with food and cloth napkins folded into the shape of peacocks. The people lingering nearby began to move in, but Knox shot them a look of pure poison, and they scattered.

"You know how important tonight is," he said quietly, once we were alone. He handed me a small plate from the end of the table. "Do you really think insulting Minister Bradley to his face is going to make this any easier on you?"

"He was staring down my dress," I said. "Why do you expect me to smile and let him when Lila would've—"

"Right now I don't care what Lila would have done," he said. "I expect you not to cause a scene with one of the most powerful Ministers of the Union and make us another enemy we don't need."

"Everyone in this place is an enemy." I turned away and began to pile my plate with bite-size desserts.

"I'm not."

I hesitated, my hand hovering over a piece of pink cake. I was here because I trusted Knox more than I trusted most people, but some days I wasn't so sure he cared about me more than he cared about why he needed me in the first place. "If you don't want me to think you're an enemy, then stop treating me like a prisoner."

Knox sighed. "I wouldn't have to if you quit acting like you don't know how to behave in public. It's been months. You should know the rules by now."

"How can I when you keep changing them on me?" At the next table over, I spotted little bites of steak wrapped in a fluffy puff pastry, and my mouth watered. I hadn't eaten red meat since October. By now I was almost used to it, but there were days I would have given my right arm for a cheeseburger. Today was one of them.

If it was wrapped in a puff pastry, no one would notice, I decided. Edging toward that table, I tuned out whatever lecture Knox was whispering in my ear and casually picked up a piece. One bite. That was all I wanted.

It was half an inch from my lips when Knox's fingers closed around my wrist. "Lila, darling, that has red meat in it."

"Are you sure?" I said innocently, trying to tug my hand away, but his grip was too strong.

"Very."

I dropped the pastry onto his plate, and the last of my patience went with it. "If you'll excuse me, I need to pee." *And find Benjy before he gives up on me.*

"You need to freshen up," corrected Knox in a low voice.

"Minister Bradley is staring at me like I'm some prize pig," I said. "I *need* to *pee*."

Without warning, Knox wheeled me around toward an antechamber nearby, his fingertips digging into my arm, and he didn't say a word until we'd passed through the doorway. "Do you realize who's here?"

I glanced over his shoulder. Now that we had left, suddenly the buffet had become the most popular corner of the room, as Ministers, their families, and the clingiest social climbers in the District of Columbia milled around, waiting for us to emerge. They all had VIs tattooed on the backs of their necks—the highest rank we could earn after taking an aptitude test on our seventeenth birthday. The same one that decided the rest of our lives, including our jobs, where we lived, how many children we could have, and how long our lives would be. Their VIs meant endless privilege and put them at the top of the food chain. The III hidden under my VII had earned me a one-way ticket to cleaning sewers for the next four decades, if I'd managed to live that long with the few cruddy resources

I would've been granted by our gracious government. "Yeah. Every bottom-feeder in Washington."

"Enough." Knox glared at me, and his carefully crafted facade finally dropped. He shut the door. "You can either play nice, or you can explain to Daxton why the entire country suddenly knows who you really are. Because those people out there aren't idiots, despite what you seem to think, and if you keep talking like this where they can all hear you, they *will* figure it out. Your choice."

"The only thing that's going to make them figure it out is if I act like I'm perfectly happy out there, pretending like I care about any of this," I said, my fake nails digging into my palms. "Lila wouldn't have stuck around this long."

Knox grimaced. Glancing at the door, he took a step closer, lowering his voice. "I know, Kitty. I'm sorry about that, I am. But if we slip away now, someone will come looking for us, and that's the last thing we need tonight, all right?"

"Then you should've told me that to begin with instead of playing this ridiculous game," I said. "I'm not completely unreasonable, you know. If you'd tell me these things—"

"I tell you as much as I can."

"You treat me like an object, Knox. Right now, in that room—I'm your prop." I shook my head, torn between seething and breaking down. All I wanted was to go upstairs and be alone with Benjy. With the only person left in the world who still cared about the person underneath Lila's face.

"You're not my prop," said Knox, his tone softening. "I'm trying to protect us both. What we're doing, dangerous as it is—it's the right thing to do. You know it is. Don't mess it up just because you're having a bad night."

A painful knot formed in my throat, and I swallowed hard. It was an argument we'd been having for the past month, ever since I had agreed to continue to impersonate Lila. Originally it hadn't been my choice; after Prime Minister Daxton Hart had bought me at a gentlemen's club, he'd knocked me out, and I'd woken up two weeks later to discover he'd had my body surgically altered—Masked, he'd called it—to be an exact copy of his niece, Lila Hart, whom he'd secretly had assassinated for leading a rebellion against him. I was supposed to take her place and stop it.

Instead, thanks to Knox, Lila was still alive and hidden underground. And as for me—turned out I wasn't okay with standing by and letting the government slaughter the people I love.

That was the only reason I'd agreed to stay when Knox had asked me three weeks ago. It had been after an exhausting night and day, when Augusta Hart, Daxton's mother and the real iron fist around the country, had tried to not only kill me and Lila, but Benjy, too. Instead, I'd put six bullets in her. Now, with Lila seriously injured, it was up to me to pretend to be her until someone took the Prime Minister out of the picture.

That was easier said than done. I'd tried once before and failed—and as a result, Daxton had been in a coma long enough to miss the worst of the fight. When he'd woken up, he'd pretended not to know I wasn't Lila, but we both knew who I really was. I was nobody to these people. I had been raised as far away from the life of a VII as you could get, in a group home full of Extras born to parents who were only allowed one child. It hadn't been the most luxurious upbringing ever, but at least I could have had a cheeseburger without having to beg. And at least I'd known exactly who I was. The more time I spent as Lila, the less certain I became that I knew myself anymore at all.

"Think you can handle another hour?" said Knox, crossing his arms over his broad chest.

"One more hour," I muttered, trying to shove aside my frustration. Knox was right; I'd known exactly what I'd agreed to, and playing nice with the Ministers was part of it. "But Benjy gets to stay with me tonight after the meeting."

He raised an eyebrow. "You know the risks."

"I'll pretend I'm staying in your suite. You can tell everyone we had the best sex of your life—"

"It would probably be the worst."

I kicked his shin with my heel. "You're a jerk tonight."

He swore and rubbed his leg. "And you're going to get you and your boyfriend killed if you don't—"

The doorknob rattled, and without warning, Knox pinned me to the wall. His fingers tangled in my straw-colored hair, and his lips found mine as he kissed me with burning hunger I couldn't escape. I didn't fight him. Better to be forced to kiss him every once in a while than to have someone catch us talking about my real identity—or worse, the rebellion against the government that we were leading together.

The door opened, and I broke away from Knox, trying my best to look embarrassed. "If you don't mind, we're sort of busy—"

I stopped, and all the air left my lungs. Even after two months of coming face-to-face with him on nearly a daily basis, Prime Minister Daxton Hart never failed to make my heart skip a beat. And not in a good way.

He loomed in the doorway, his bushy eyebrows raised in surprise. They were slowly going salt-and-pepper, matching his dark hair that was graying at the temples. "I apologize. I didn't mean to interrupt," he said in a smooth voice. "Lila, darling, your guests are anxiously awaiting your return."

I held his stare. His dark eyes met mine, and for several seconds, neither of us blinked. Knox had no idea that the Prime Minister knew who I was. Daxton had kept his own secret masterfully, only tipping his hand at Augusta's funeral in order to scare me into compliance. It hadn't worked. This was our own private game of chicken, and I wasn't going to be the first to blink.

"We'll be along in a minute, sir," said Knox. For a moment, I almost felt bad for him. He was the only one in the room who didn't know what was really going on. I should've told him Daxton remembered everything—that should've been my first conversation after the funeral. But no matter how much I trusted him more than the others, I didn't trust him completely, and I'd hesitated, focusing on rallying the people for the Blackcoats instead. Eventually time had passed, and I knew the fallout would be bad—the kind we would never recover from. So instead I'd selfishly held on to the truth as a trump card, to play when I needed it most. Or to never play at all.

Knox did know one thing, though: the secret that I had given up at the funeral, when I had brushed my fingertips against the VII on the back of Daxton's neck and felt the V underneath. I wasn't the only Hart who had been Masked. The only difference between us was that I still had my handler breathing down my neck. Now that Augusta was dead, the man pretending to be Prime Minister Daxton Hart had no one to stop him from doing whatever he wanted—including killing anyone who dared to step in his way. When everyone I cared about happened to be doing exactly that, it made things personal.

"One minute." Daxton raised a finger in emphasis. "I would hate for you to miss your birthday surprise, Lila."

I shuddered to think what he might have cooked up for me, but I forced a smile. "One minute."

As soon as he shut the door, I leaned in to Knox's ear and whispered, "How are we getting away for the meeting? He's not going to let me out of his sight."

"Leave that to me," whispered Knox, and he winked. Backing away, he ran his fingers through his hair and smoothed his black shirt and trousers. I tugged on my short purple dress. Three months ago, I would have never believed I'd be allowed to touch silk, let alone wear silk dress after silk dress custom made for me. As nice as the wardrobe was—and the shoes, and the food, and the luxuries I could have never dreamed of as a III—it wasn't worth risking my life pretending to be Lila, and it definitely wasn't worth risking Benjy's by dragging him along.

I swore. He was still waiting for me. "I'm supposed to meet Benjy for a minute—"

"You'll see him after the meeting." Knox tucked a stray lock of hair behind my ear. "No matter how bad tonight is shaping up to be, don't do anything stupid, Kitty. I mean it. Whatever brief flash of joy you get out of it won't be worth being sent Elsewhere, and you know it."

Yes, I did. "Benjy and I. All night in your suite."

"All night, as long as I don't have to hear you." Knox smirked and opened the door. A round of applause met us as we walked arm in arm back into the throng of VIs, and several people I didn't recognize descended upon us, drinks in hand. I steeled myself for another round of pointless small talk. I'd long since stopped trying to remember names. Lila wouldn't have bothered, and I wasn't about to make the effort when all they wanted out of me was the power behind my VII. If only they knew what lay underneath it.

"Do you want another drink?" said Knox, even though I still held my full champagne flute. I shook my head.

"But if you can get me one of those puff pastry things—"

Bang.

A shot rang out, and in an instant, my mind went blank. All I could see was crimson against white, a stark contrast that wouldn't go away no matter how much I tried to block it out.

Bang.

The sight of Augusta's body going limp, and blood pooling around her on the carpet.

Bang.

The cold metal of a gun in my hands as I squeezed the trigger again and again, knowing that if I didn't, Augusta would kill Benjy.

Bang.

"Lila—*Lila.*"

Knox's voice filtered through the haze toward me. I cracked open my eyes. Even though he hovered only a few inches away from me, he seemed far off, and his face was blurry. I sensed others lurking nearby, but the dull roar in my ears made it impossible for me to hear what they were saying.

"They're just fireworks," said Knox, his breath warm against my cheek as his hands gripped my shoulders. Cold seeped through my dress from the marble underneath me, and it took me a moment to realize I was on the floor. "See? Look over there."

I twisted around as another bang went off. Reflexively I ducked again, but Knox's hands remained steady. Bright bursts of color filled the grand ballroom, and I had to blink several times before my vision cleared enough for me to make out each one through the floor-to-ceiling windows.

Fireworks. Just fireworks. Not gunshots. No one was in any danger, except for Knox if he didn't get his hands off me.

"I'm fine," I mumbled, shoving him away. He took a step back, and it was then that I noticed the group of people who had formed a tight circle around us. Each of them stared openly, ignoring the display and instead paying attention to me. Terrific. Not only had I broken down, but I'd done so in front of the country's highest and mightiest. "I—" I began, wracking my muddled mind for an excuse, but a familiar voice rang through the crowd, cutting me off.

"Lila!"

Benjy burst out from between Minister Bradley and his slack-jawed daughter, and he slid across the floor, kneeling beside me. As soon as I felt his warmth, the knot in my chest began to loosen.

"Are you all right? You were screaming." His blue eyes were wide and anxious, and his short red hair was disheveled. He reached out to touch my face the same way Knox had, but his hand stopped an inch away. Too many people were staring at us, and no matter how concerned he was, he couldn't give me away. He couldn't give *us* away.

"I'm fine, I promise," I said again. My cheeks burned, and I pushed myself to my feet, ignoring the way my knees shook. Birthday party or not, I had to get out of here. "I just—I just forgot to eat, that's all."

"Back up," said Knox to the crowd, and he began to corral them away. "Give her some air. Benjy, take her to my suite. I'll be there in a moment."

Benjy tucked his arm around me, and I shot Knox a grateful look. Aware of everyone staring at us, I allowed Benjy to lead me to the exit as the bang of fireworks echoed from the garden. Each one sent a shiver down my spine.

This wasn't normal. I'd never reacted this way before, and it'd been weeks since I'd killed Augusta. It wasn't as if I'd done it in cold blood. She'd had it coming, after what she'd done to me and Benjy—after what she'd done to her own *family,* trying to kill her daughter and granddaughter—but apparently my conscience wasn't interested in listening to reason.

Nor did I have any ends to justify my means. Killing Augusta hadn't done me any favors—it had only removed Daxton's leash completely, leaving all of us in grave danger. And that, I thought, was the worst part of all. I'd saved Benjy's life in the short term by pulling that trigger, but in the long term, we were both one whim away from death.

Daxton stood waiting for us by the double doors, his arms crossed as he regarded me with a look of mock concern. "I'm so very sorry, my dear," he said, reaching out to take my free hand. I made a point of wiping my sweaty palm against his. "I wasn't thinking. After all you've been through…"

"I'm fine," I said for a third time. "I just need to sit down."

"I'm sure your…friend will be willing to help you with that." He eyed Benjy up and down, and red-hot anger shot through me. Augusta may have been the power behind the throne, but Daxton was still the snake who sat on it.

Benjy cleared his throat. "Knox asked me to help her," he said. "I'll be down after."

"Take your time, boy," said Daxton, and he shifted his gaze to me. "The most important thing is that dear Lila's all right."

His slimy voice followed me even after Benjy and I walked away. I could feel his stare lingering on us, and though my knees still shook, I forced myself to walk faster toward the elevator. As soon as we were inside and the door closed, I let out a breath and turned into Benjy, hugging him tightly and burying my face in his chest.

"I'm sorry," I said, my voice muffled by his shirt. "I don't know what happened."

He wrapped his arms around me protectively, rubbing circles on my back, and the heat of his body warmed me from the inside out. If I could have stayed like this for the rest of my life, I would have. "You have nothing to be sorry for. Those fireworks scared me, too."

"Leave it to Daxton to figure out a way to terrorize me at my own birthday party," I grumbled. "How long do you think we'll have before Knox comes looking for us?"

"Not long enough," he said, and I sighed. It was never long enough.

The doors slid open, and together Benjy and I headed into the fourth floor wing. My suite was down the hall from Knox's, and I would have given anything to drag Benjy inside and disappear for the rest of the night. But the party wasn't the only thing happening tonight, and I wouldn't have missed another Blackcoat meeting for anything. I was already behind enough—immediately after Augusta had died, Knox and the Blackcoats had seized the opportunity and sent me around to several cities across the country to rally supporters while Daxton was still too busy recovering to pay close attention. Denver, New York, Seattle, Los Angeles—I'd traveled for over a week, and by the time I'd returned, everything within the Blackcoats had shifted. Lila and her mother—Daxton's sister, Celia—had gone underground to hide, leaving Knox in control. Even now, weeks later, I was still catching up on the plans they'd come up with while I'd been away. I couldn't miss anything else.

The lights in Knox's suite turned on automatically as we stepped into the sitting room. Even though my knees had stopped shaking by now, I let Benjy help me to the couch, eager for as much contact as we could get before Knox returned. It had been days since I'd been able to steal as much as a simple hug from Benjy, who, as a legitimate VI, had earned his place as Knox's assistant. But with Knox constantly hovering over us, raising an eyebrow each time I so much as dared to smile at Benjy, it was next to impossible to find any time to just *be* with him. And that, above all else, was what I missed about my old life.

"I'm sorry I didn't find you earlier," I said, tucking my legs underneath me on the sofa. The navy leather was cool against my skin, and after spending hours in the sweltering ballroom, I welcomed it.

"Don't be. It isn't your fault." Benjy sat beside me and draped his arm over my shoulder, and I wasted no time curling up against him. "I nearly punched Minister Bradley for the way he was looking at you, though."

I grinned. "That would have made the whole thing infinitely more interesting."

"Until I was sent Elsewhere," he said. "Then it wouldn't have been as funny."

My smile vanished. I touched his cheek, turning his head until he was facing me. "You know I won't let that happen, right? No one's going to hurt you, not while I have something to say about it."

"I'm not the one you should be worried about." His gaze met mine, and he leaned in slowly until his breath was warm against my skin. "Promise me you won't take any more chances, Kitty. What happened tonight—"

"I couldn't help it," I said. "I didn't even know what was happening until it was over."

"That isn't what I meant," he said softly. "I overheard what you said to Knox. You're doing this for the right reasons, all right? I know it's hard sometimes—"

"You have no idea." My face grew hot, and frustration boiled inside me, threatening to burst the last ounce of self-control I had left. "Having to be someone else all the time—never getting to be me anymore, having my every move watched... I'm losing myself, Benjy. Sometimes I look in the mirror and forget this isn't my real face. And sometimes—sometimes I feel like Kitty Doe died, and even if Knox lets me walk away from this tomorrow, I'll never find her again."

Heavy silence settled over us, and Benjy's gaze bore into mine as he traced my lower lip. Lila's lower lip. "She didn't die," he whispered. "I see her every time I look at you. You are vivacious, and no one—not even Lila Hart—will ever drown you out. I don't care what you look like. The real you will never fade."

He had no idea how badly I needed to hear that right now—or maybe he did, and that was exactly why he'd said it. I slowly gravitated toward him, my entire body aching to be as close to him as possible. But before I could kiss him, he shifted and slipped his hand into his suit pocket.

"I almost forgot—I made you a birthday present," he said, and I sat back, disappointment washing over me.

"It isn't my birthday," I said. "It's Lila's."

"Then consider this a belated birthday present. Or an early one. Whichever you'd like." From his pocket he pulled a white cloth napkin, the sort that had been folded into peacocks around the buffet. He'd refolded it into a simple square, and I raised an eyebrow.

"It's...lovely," I said. "Thanks?"

He laughed, a deep, throaty sound I would never get tired of hearing. "Open it."

I unfolded the napkin, and my eyes widened. On the inside was a simple ink drawing of a house on a lake. Sitting in a field beside the lake were two stick figures—one with long hair, and one with Benjy's freckles. They cuddled together as the sun shone down on them, and a lump formed in my throat.

"I can't make this better right now," said Benjy, "but I can promise that it will be one day. We'll have our cottage in the woods, or our cabin on the beach—whatever you want. I'll go anywhere as long as you promise you'll be there with me. I'm going to spend my life with you, Kitty, and I don't care if the entire country tries to stop us. You're my future. It's always been you for me, and it always will be."

Finally he closed the distance between us and kissed me—a sweet, gentle kiss that held within it every single one of the thousand days I'd loved him as my everything, long after I'd begun to love him as a friend. I shifted into his lap, not caring whether or not someone could walk in at any moment and see us. I needed this. And after all we'd been through together, Benjy and I both deserved this.

He wrapped his arm around me again, safe and secure as I ran my fingers through his hair. He tasted like home. Like everything I missed about my old life, where we would spend the evening curled up together as he read to me. We would never have those moments again, but as soon as we were free of this place, we could make new ones. I'd spent so much of my time worrying about the present, worrying about being Lila, that I'd never let myself stop and think about what my future might hold. It seemed almost like asking too much— like I was challenging the universe by thinking about a life with Benjy as far away from the Harts as possible.

But Benjy had always been an optimist. He'd always seen good in the world where I wasn't so sure it existed. And this kernel of hope, this ink on cloth, was exactly the future I wanted. I knew in that moment, as I deepened the kiss between us, that I would do whatever it took to get it.

"Kitty," he whispered, breaking away long enough to glance anxiously at the door. "We shouldn't be—"

"I am so sick of being told what I should and shouldn't do," I murmured. "Everything will be fine. Trust me. Knox agreed to let me stay in here tonight. He's pretending I'm sleeping in his room, but he's going to let us have the night together."

Benjy's gaze snapped back to me. "You mean—?"

I nodded. "I think it's about time, don't you?"

Even though we'd been together for years, finding a moment alone in a group home with thirty-eight other kids hadn't exactly been easy, and neither of us had wanted it to be rushed. Now that we were both seventeen, I was Lila Hart, and Benjy was my fiancé's assistant. It *was* dangerous, but behind closed doors, with Knox willing to cover for us—we would finally have that freedom. I wasn't wasting it.

"The wedding's less than a month away," I said. "We might not have another chance before then, not like this. And I'll be damned if I'm marrying Knox without showing you exactly how much I love you."

Benjy blinked, looking torn between eagerness and confusion. "Is that why you want to do this? So Knox isn't—"

"If he thinks I'm ever letting him touch me no matter how married we are, he's going to lose his hand," I said. "I want to do this, Benjy. More than anything. If you don't, we can wait, but—"

"I want to." He sounded breathless, and he pressed his lips together, his eyes locked on mine. "Like you said, more than anything. I love you. I just don't want Knox to be the reason you're doing this."

"He's not, and he never will be." I brushed my lips against his again. "You're the only reason I need."

"Ahem."

I sprang apart from Benjy, my heart racing. Knox stood framed in the doorway, his arms crossed and his brow furrowed. "Ever heard of knocking?" I said, glaring at him.

"Considering it's my suite, no." He pushed off the wall and closed the door. "If you keep this up, it'll only be a matter of time before someone catches you. I won't be able to protect you then."

"So I'll tell them the truth—sometimes a girl just needs to be kissed instead of slobbered on." I tucked Benjy's drawing into the pocket of my dress. "Is the party over already?"

"No, but I couldn't very well stay down there while my fiancée was ill upstairs. Speaking of, how do you feel?"

"Better," I said, doing my best to look like nothing was bothering me at all. "When are we going?"

"*We* are not going anywhere." Knox moved to his desk and bent down to touch the screen. "*I* am leaving now."

"What? But—"

"Do you really think I'm going to let you come, after what just happened down there?" said Knox. "You need your rest."

"That wasn't my fault."

He straightened. "Fainting aside, you're having a bad day, and the last thing you need is a long night. The last thing *I* need is to worry about whether or not you're holding up all right."

"I'm fine," I insisted. "Knox, please. We're in this together. You said so yourself—"

"And right now that means I have to look out for you and

your health. You're exhausted. Your temper's shorter than it's ever been. Look at you—you're practically shaking. You're a liability, Kitty, and tonight is too important for me to take that kind of risk. I'll fill you in when I get back, but right now, I need to go."

I gaped at him. "You can't just cut me out like this—"

"I'm not cutting you out," he said steadily, but there was an edge of impatience to his voice. "It's one meeting."

"I've already missed three because of the speeches."

"There will be plenty of others," said Knox. "And look on the bright side—you'll have even more time to spend with Benjy."

Tempting as it was, staying behind meant missing the entire reason I had agreed to put up with this and people like Minister Bradley in the first place. I would have the rest of the night to be alone with Benjy—right now, I wanted to be a Blackcoat. I wanted to do what I was here to do: be the voice of a rebellion that, if successful, would mean Benjy and I would one day have that cottage by the lake. It would mean never looking over our shoulders again, worried someone might see us and catch on to who I really was. It would mean being Kitty Doe again instead of Lila Hart. It would mean finding myself and being the person Benjy saw when he looked at me. The more meetings I missed, the more excuses Knox would have to dismiss my opinions and push me aside. I was here to fight. Not to be his prop or his mouthpiece. And no matter how much he insisted I wasn't, everything he had done that evening had said otherwise.

I cast a frustrated look at Benjy, and he slipped his hand into mine, giving it a reassuring squeeze.

"It's probably better if you relax tonight," he said. "I think you'll like this new book I bought the other day. I'll read some of it to you, if you'd like."

"Enjoy some time with your boyfriend, Kitty," said Knox. "I'll be back soon enough. If anyone checks on us, tell them I'm in the shower."

"Yeah, taking a cold one," I grumbled. He didn't rise to the bait, and instead he disappeared into his closet and up through the secret passageway that lay behind it. He'd shown it to me one of my first nights in Somerset, and it was the only safe way we had of leaving the property undetected.

As soon as he shut the door, I stood. "I'm going after him," I said, tugging down the hem of my dress. Not the outfit I would have chosen, but I didn't have time to change. "Cover for me."

Benjy stood as well, reaching out as if to stop me. "Kitty, you heard him—"

I twisted away from his grip. "If it wasn't for him, we'd have this by now." I gestured to the napkin sticking out of my dress pocket. "We wouldn't have to worry about the Harts or the wedding or fireworks driving me crazy. We'd be happy, and we'd never have to think about this nightmare again. Instead, Knox asked me to stay, and I did. Not for him, not for Lila, not for the parties or the jewelry or the private planes, but because of *this*." I jabbed my finger toward the closet. "If I'm not there, then what's the point of doing any of this anymore? I'm not his property, and he doesn't control me. I'm not letting him leave me behind."

Benjy sighed, but at least he didn't argue. "Then I'll go with you."

"Someone has to stay behind and make sure no one finds

out we're gone," I said. He opened his mouth to protest, but I cut him off. "Please, Benjy. It'll be safer if it's just me anyway."

He gritted his teeth, and a muscle in his jaw twitched. "Okay. Just—be careful. And here, take this."

He shrugged off his suit jacket and draped it over my shoulders. I slipped my arms inside the sleeves, the fabric warm from his body. "Thanks," I said, softening. "Make sure no one discovers we're gone, all right?"

"I'm sure I'll figure something out," said Benjy, scowling. I stood on my tiptoes and kissed him.

"I love you. When I get back, I'm yours for the rest of the night. Okay?"

He nodded, and without giving him another chance to talk me out of it, I stepped inside the closet. Knox may have thought he owned Lila, but I wasn't her. Tonight, I was Kitty Doe again, and I wasn't going down without a fight.

II

MIDNIGHT MEETING

The passageway above the fourth floor was as dusty and dirty as ever. Without a flashlight, I was plunged into darkness, and even after my eyes adjusted to what little moonlight filtered in, I couldn't see more than a few inches in front of me. Cobwebs caught my hair and cheeks, and once I thought I felt a spider running down the back of my dress, but I forced myself to stay calm and move forward. I'd taken this route a dozen times before. I could do this.

At last I found the staircase that led downward, and from then on out, it was only a matter of not tripping. The heels I wore made that more difficult than it should have been, and twice I had to catch myself on the wooden bannister. By the time the creaky steps turned into the dirt tunnel underneath the grounds of Somerset, I'd collected two splinters in my palm, and I was fervently wishing I'd stopped long enough to grab a pair of boots.

The tunnel was pitch-black. I ran a hand across the dirt wall to guide me, keeping my ears peeled for any sign of Knox. But I would have seen the light from his flashlight if he was still in the tunnel, and satisfied that I was alone, I picked up the pace. I had no guarantee I'd be able to slip into the bunker undetected. By now the guards knew me, but I didn't have the codes, and I'd have to catch up to Knox if I wanted access. Even then, it was entirely possible he'd tell me to go home, though if he thought I would listen after his little speech in the suite—

"What the hell do you think you're doing?"

A hand clamped over my wrist, tugging me away from the wall, and I swore loudly enough that they probably heard it back in Somerset. Yanking my arm away, I thrashed wildly in the darkness. "Let—me—*go!*"

Light flooded the tunnel, and Knox stood with his free hand still wrapped bruisingly around my wrist. "Not until you answer my question."

"I *will* kick you again," I said, squinting against the brightness.

"Still not an answer."

I scowled. "What do you think I'm doing? I'm coming with you."

"No, you're not."

"Yes, I am."

His eyes narrowed, and for a long moment, we stood face-to-face, both waiting for the other to back down. Neither of us did.

"Do you understand how delicate this situation is?" said Knox. "If you and your aversion to obedience say the wrong word to the wrong person—"

"Maybe if you stopped acting like I'm an untrained dog and started treating me like a person who's as much a part of this as you are, I'd stop pulling against your invisible leash," I said. "I have every right to be there, and you know it. If you keep acting like I'm a liability—"

"I wouldn't if you stopped *being* a liability."

"—then I'll leave," I finished, ignoring him. "If I can't work with the Blackcoats, then I don't have any reason to be here anymore."

"Oh?" Knox arched an eyebrow. "And where would you go?"

"It doesn't matter. I'm here because you asked me to be part of this, and I agreed, because it *is* the right thing to do. But this—leaving me behind, treating me like I'm incapable of making a right move without you—this isn't what I signed up for. If you don't let me go to that meeting, then I'll disappear. I don't care how many Shields you have searching for me. Scour the entire country. You will never find me."

His brow furrowed, and a muscle in his jaw twitched. "I asked you to stay because I thought you'd cooperate and help us. The more time I spend chasing after you and cleaning up your messes, the less time I have to focus on the rebellion. Do you understand?"

"The more you treat me like a child, the more likely I'll be to act like one," I said calmly, keeping a tight rein on the anger boiling inside me. I wasn't about to give him any reason to dismiss me. "Do *you* understand?"

He narrowed his eyes. "Fine. You start behaving, and I'll start trusting you."

"Good. Now let go of me."

Knox released my wrist, and I rubbed it, hoping it didn't bruise. Purple would be hard to hide against Lila's porcelain skin.

"Come on, we're going to be late," he said, and he led me down the dirt tunnel, the beam of light swinging with each hurried step. "Celia and Lila are supposed to be there tonight, which means you have to watch what you say, all right?"

"Watch what I say about what?" I said, concentrating on putting one foot in front of the other without stumbling.

"They still don't know Daxton's an impostor," he said. "No one does."

I blinked. "Wait—you mean you haven't told any of the Blackcoats?"

"Of course not. One of them will inevitably leak the information to Celia, and as soon as she finds out, she'll storm Somerset and throw our entire plan into jeopardy."

I frowned. Celia, Lila's mother and Daxton's sister, was the reason so much of this had happened in the first place. After Daxton had brutally executed her husband, she'd created the Blackcoats, an underground army bent on seeing the Harts stripped of their power and the ranking system abolished for good in favor of the democracy on which America had been built. In the process, she'd used her only daughter, Lila, to captivate the crowds and ensure even more support from the higher ranks for her rebellion. Lila had been reluctant, though, and as the target on her back grew and word of her impending assassination reached their ears, she and Knox had formed a plan: fake her death and hide her underground, where Daxton would never find her. No one else, not even Celia, had known.

The only thing they hadn't counted on was Daxton having someone else Masked to take Lila's place—me. And as soon as they discovered what had happened, my education about the real horrors of the country had begun. They'd involved me in the Blackcoats' plans ever since, and like hell was I giving up my chance to make a difference just because Knox said so.

But Knox had kept Celia in the dark about nearly everything. Even she hadn't known about her daughter still being alive until she had kidnapped Greyson, Daxton's son, in an attempt at retribution. She'd never wanted to harm him, but the Harts hadn't known that, and in the process of rescuing him, they thought they'd killed Celia—and me, for that matter. Luckily for both of us, we'd survived.

While I had agreed to take Lila's place on a more permanent basis, however, Celia had been forced underground. Not that I thought she minded, but Knox was right: if she found out Daxton wasn't really Daxton after all and she—or Greyson—should have been ruling the country instead, she would have unleashed the Blackcoats on Somerset without a second thought. Or a cohesive plan in place.

"We have to tell Sampson and the others eventually," I said. "If they know, maybe they can strategize—"

"It won't matter," said Knox as we reached the metal door that opened up to an abandoned alleyway. "They could try to out him, but the media is in Daxton's pocket. Anyone who went to press with the news would be labeled a traitor and executed before sundown. No one should have to make that sacrifice for nothing."

The cold December night made me shiver, even with Benjy's jacket. But it wasn't far to the bunker, and I hugged myself and toughed out the chill. "The Blackcoats don't have contacts in the media?"

"Of course we do," he said. "That doesn't change the fact that it won't make any difference. There are a million ways Daxton could spin it, and he'll never let anyone close enough to prove it."

"What about Greyson?" Daxton's eighteen-year-old son was less than enthusiastic about following in his father's footsteps, but even inexperienced, he would be infinitely better than Daxton.

Knox's mouth formed a thin line, and he wrapped his arm around my shoulders. Normally it would have been a sweet gesture, but tonight it felt more like a threat. "Do you want to see the masses go after him once the rebellion begins?"

"You mean it hasn't already?" I said, but he didn't answer. I bit my lip. Greyson was one of my only friends, and the last thing I wanted was for him to get caught in the cross fire.

We were meters from the bunker when Knox stopped and faced me, his dark eyes bearing into mine. "Listen to me, Kitty," he said in a low, hurried voice. "Telling the others about Daxton doesn't outweigh the risks of Celia finding out—and if the other Blackcoat leaders know, she *will* find out sooner rather than later. And what happens after that is anyone's guess. Do you understand me?"

"But maybe one of them could think of a way to get the word out and turn Daxton's supporters against him," I said. "Too many people have already died—"

"Those people were willing to risk it," said Knox. "We're all willing to risk it."

"I'm not willing to risk Benjy's life," I said. "He didn't agree to any of this, and if there's a war on Somerset, he'll get caught in the middle."

"I've already promised to protect you both—"

"You're not a god, Knox," I said. "You can't guarantee we'll both get out of this alive, and you know it. If we tell them, we could find a way to replace Daxton and have a revolution without anyone else dying—"

"There's no such thing as a bloodless revolution."

Knox's voice cracked like a whip through the alleyway. He glanced around quickly, as if to reassure himself we were alone, and then leaned in close enough for me to smell the champagne on his breath. Not strong enough to knock me over, but it was a stark reminder of the evening we'd had.

"I've made you a lot of promises, Kitty, and I intend on keeping them. But I can't do that if you second-guess every move I make and insist on being in the middle of everything. Do you want a rebellion, or do you want to keep things as they are? Because this isn't a problem that a single bullet will solve. Even if we cut Daxton out of the picture, we still have the entire government to worry about—including all twelve Ministers of the Union, who will see a chance to seize power for themselves and do everything they can to make it happen. Daxton *will* be removed from his position one way or the other, but there are countless other steps we have to take in the meantime before we even consider putting that plan into action. People are going to die no matter what we do. Right now, all we can do is try our best to minimize the casualties."

Furrowing my brow as I digested everything he said, I crossed my arms to stop myself from shivering more than I already was. "I'm just saying there might be another way to do this."

"If there was, we would have figured it out already." Knox straightened. "Promise me you won't bring up Daxton."

"Promise me you'll at least consider trying it my way."

He scowled. "Fine."

"Fine."

He punched a nine-digit code into a small metal box, and a moment later, the door to the bunker opened. We stepped inside. A long concrete hallway stretched out in front of us, and the darkness obscured the high ceiling. I swallowed hard and tried not to think about what was up there, just out of sight: two dozen guards, each with a rifle pointed directly at us.

Guilty until proven innocent. That was how it was for the government, and that was how it was for the Blackcoats. Knox could talk about a rebellion and change until he was blue in the face, but as I followed him through the corridor, my head down and Benjy's jacket clutched around my shoulders, I began to wonder whether or not anything would really change if the Blackcoats succeeded. I believed in freedom and democracy with everything I was, but if Celia and Knox won the rebellion, the people would still be under the rule of the Hart family. In the end, how many lives would really change for the better?

I pressed my lips together. The Blackcoats weren't perfect, but they were fighting for the rights of the people—the same rights Daxton Hart and the twelve Ministers of the Union took pleasure in denying them. As I watched Knox punch in another code at the end of the dark corridor, the day of my testing flashed through my mind, and cold fear prickled down my spine, a ghost of a life that was slowly slipping away from me with each day that passed. I knew what it was like to be one of them. I knew what it was like to wake up every morning wondering if today would be the day I ran across a Shield in a bad mood, and he would drag me into the street and shoot me in the head just because he had a gun and I didn't. I knew what it was like to watch it happen to others and worry I was next. And I knew what it was like to consider the possibility that maybe it wouldn't be the worst thing in the world after all.

It was preferable to the alternative: being sent Elsewhere, a place that, until two months ago, I had deluded myself into thinking was some kind of summer camp for criminals, the elderly, and those deemed unfit for society. Daxton had cleared that up for me my first day as Lila, when he'd taken me hunting in a lush forest. We hadn't been hunting deer or quail, though. We'd been hunting humans.

That was why I was doing this. Not for the people who wanted to keep their heads down and live as happily as their ranks allowed, but for the people whose lives didn't belong to them anymore. For the people who saw what this world was really like and had no way of escaping it.

Knox led me through a twisting hallway full of armories and colorless bunks, where refugees and members of the Blackcoats stayed. The heart of the bunker was set in the center, where roughly a dozen people had gathered on ratty and worn chairs and couches, each poring over papers I knew would be burned once the meeting ended. Several heads raised when Knox and I joined them, and a few of them even waved. Knox didn't wave back.

I watched them closely. Most were decades older than me, their faces lined by age and stress. A handful looked to be in their twenties, but even they seemed weighed down. My heart sank. Whatever was going on, it wasn't good.

In the center of the ragtag group sat an officer wearing a black-and-silver uniform. Sampson, a high-ranking member of the Shields, and one of the leaders of the Blackcoats. I'd only met him a few times, but as I found a place at the edge of the group, he offered me a warm smile. I smiled back.

"Well?" said Knox impatiently. "What happened?"

Sampson's smile faded. "The raid failed."

Knox swore loudly. "How? We had everything planned down to the last detail—"

"Celia found out right before it happened," said Sampson. "She changed the plan."

Silence. Slowly Knox's face went from pink to red to purple. Not once in the past few months, not even when I'd been at my worst, had I ever seen him turn those colors.

It was then that I noticed Celia and Lila were missing, despite Knox's assumptions that they'd be there tonight. Was this why? Was Celia avoiding him? Or had she been uninvited from her own rebellion?

"You know not to listen to Celia without going through me first," said Knox in a low, dangerous voice. "No matter what she says—"

"Her ideas weren't bad," said Sampson. Even he seemed to shrink under Knox's glare. "And what was I supposed to do? Say you'd taken over her own army?"

"You should have protected our people." Knox slammed his fist into a worn wooden coffee table, and half the group jumped. I dug my nails into my palms. "Days—that's how long we have. Days, Sampson. We *needed* those supplies. Celia doesn't have the military knowledge or experience—"

"And you do?" snapped Sampson.

"I'm not some spoiled VII who's never had to work for anything a day in her entire life," said Knox.

Before I could stop myself, I snorted.

All eyes turned toward me. My face grew warm, but it was Knox's stare that made me feel as if I were about to spontaneously combust.

"Did you have something to say, Kitty?" he said. His voice slithered through me, turning my blood to ice.

I should have kept my mouth shut. After everything that had happened that evening, the last thing I should've done was add fuel to the fire that was Knox's temper, but something inside me broke. "If you're going to rag on Celia for inheriting her VII, then at least acknowledge you had your VI handed to you, too. We all know your father's title will pass to you one day, and it wouldn't do to have the next Minister of Ranking with a IV or a V, would it?"

As I repeated the very words he'd said to me when he'd first told me he'd never taken the test, Knox's face drained of all color, and the silence around us turned deafening. "If you have a problem with any of this, then there's the door," he said in a deceptively even voice. But the dark look in his eyes offered me a single promise: if I walked out of there, I would never be allowed back.

"I'm sorry, I didn't mean—" I sucked in a deep breath. I didn't owe him an apology for defending Celia, not when he was acting like this. "I'm just saying, we're here because none of us believes in the rank system in the first place. You have every right to be upset with her, but don't drag Celia down based on her rank. It only makes you look like a hypocrite when your VI is as good as my VII."

"Perhaps so," said Knox coldly, "but between us, I'm the one who could earn my VI if I had to, while you're the one who earned a III."

My mouth dropped open, and his words twisted in my chest like a knife. No matter how bad a mood he was in, no matter how rebellious I was feeling, he had never used my III against me before.

Guilt flashed across his face. He knew what he'd said, but

he made no move to apologize. We stared at one another as the seconds passed. My hands tightened into fists, and the edges of my vision went dark as I tried to figure out what to say. He was right, of course—I'd earned my lowly III, but not because I wasn't smart. I couldn't read anything more than my name, and I'd had to take the test orally, which had resulted in me never getting the chance to finish it. If I had—maybe I'd be a VI, like Benjy. Maybe Daxton would have never hunted me down, and maybe my life would be completely different.

But I couldn't live off of maybes, and neither could Knox. He might have thought he was the smartest person in the room, but that didn't mean the rest of us were worthless. That didn't mean my opinion didn't matter at all. And if this was what he really thought of me, then no matter what I said, no matter how many good ideas I had, he would never really listen to them. Why would he, when his VI was so superior to my III?

With my chin raised, I turned to face the others, pointedly ignoring Knox. Bad day or not, if this was how he was going to be, then screw him. "Daxton died last year, in the explosion that killed his wife and son."

"Kitty—"

"He's been Masked," I added as if Knox hadn't said a word. "The impostor is actually a V. I don't know who he is or where he came from, but the real Daxton's dead."

Sampson looked back and forth between me and Knox, disbelief coloring his sharp features. "Is this true?"

Reluctantly Knox nodded, his jaw tight and his fists clenched. "Yes. I found out shortly after it happened. No one else knows, and it needs to stay that way. If Celia finds out—"

"We would all be marching on Somerset before the night

was out," said Sampson gravely. "But even if we cannot tell her, this changes everything, Knox."

"We can't go to the media. You know we can't," said Knox. "We'd be throwing away our contacts' lives—"

"I'm not suggesting we do," said Sampson. "I am, however, suggesting we discover who this man truly is. If we can find proof, we'll have leverage against him. He knows the Shields won't follow an impostor. The Ministers of the Union would revolt. We would have the ability to effectively strip him of his power completely and give the country something to unite against, all in one fell swoop."

"Why don't you just kill him?" I said. "Wouldn't that solve everything?"

"We already tried that, remember?" said Sampson, eyebrow raised. I scowled.

"Don't look at me like that," I grumbled.

"Like what, Kitty?" said Knox. "Like if it wasn't for you, this mess would've been over with months ago?"

I bit the inside of my cheek hard enough to draw blood. I'd been the reason the assassination attempt hadn't worked. I'd stupidly let Celia talk me into helping her out, and instead of giving Daxton the full dose, I'd chickened out and given him half. "Give me another syringe. I'll kill him this time."

Sampson shook his head. "We never approved an assassination in the first place. That was Celia's idea."

I glanced at Knox, but he wouldn't meet my eye. Sanctioned by the Blackcoats or not, he'd been the one to supply Celia with the poison.

"There must be *something* we can do to get rid of this guy," I said. "He's one man. He's not invincible."

"You're right, he is one man," said Sampson. "And if by some miracle we managed to get around his heightened security and succeed, the government would live on without him. No one would ever know he was Masked. Right now, he's more valuable to us alive as someone for the people to rally against. Dead, he's a martyr, and we cannot instigate real change within order. We must take advantage of the chaos revealing his true identity would provide. Besides," he added, leaning in closer to me, "Greyson is next in line, and he's an unknown. A weak, inexperienced unknown at that. He would crumble under the pressure from the Ministers within days. Celia is far too unstable to take control of the country by herself right now, not to mention everyone thinks she's dead. That leaves you, Kitty. Do you want to be Prime Minister?"

I frowned. "I'd rather go back to being a III."

"Then, while I thank you for this additional insight, why don't you let us try things our way for a while?"

I stared at my hands, fighting the instinct to keep arguing. Unlike Knox, Sampson wasn't in a piss-poor mood, and I had to trust one of us knew what we were doing.

"So, what now?" said a woman with a scar running down the side of her face. "How are we going to figure out who the Daxton impostor is?"

"We get boots on the ground and dig," said Sampson. "There must be a paper trail. Augusta wouldn't have allowed a stranger into a position of power without having some leverage over him."

"*If* it ever existed in the first place, Daxton would have made sure it was destroyed by now," said Knox, his expression stormy.

"That would be the logical thing to do," agreed Sampson. "We still have to look."

"But the chances of any evidence still existing—"

"Kitty," said Sampson, interrupting him. I snapped my head up. "If you had something to tie you back to your old life, would you keep it or destroy it?"

I blinked. It was a stupid question, but he had no way of knowing that. I clung to the things that made me feel like Kitty Doe as if my life depended on it. "I'd hold on to it," I said. "I'd keep it secret, but I wouldn't destroy it if it was the only evidence I'd ever existed in the first place."

He gave me a small smile. "Exactly. If the impostor has found it, there's a good chance he kept it. Knox, that's where you come in. Do you think you can get close enough to find it?"

"I'll try," he said, lacing his fingers together so tightly that his knuckles turned white.

"You'll do more than try. If we know who he is, that could give us enough power to make all the difference in this war. An armory isn't always made up of guns and knives. Sometimes information is the most powerful weapon of all."

Knox scowled deeply, but at last he said to Sampson, "If this gets me killed, I'm blaming you."

But as he said it, his eyes met mine, and we both knew the truth: he would blame me instead.

III

IMPOSTOR

The meeting dragged on for nearly an hour. They discussed plans for missions I didn't understand, people whose names I didn't recognize, and endless back and forth about whatever was due to go down in a few days. No one mentioned specifics; it was clear they had discussed the details at the meetings I'd missed, and I couldn't decide whether to be offended they wouldn't tell me now or to agree that they were making the right move not letting me know.

As badly as I wanted to be allowed in on things, Sampson and Knox were right. I didn't know anything they didn't. My role was to impersonate Lila and give their speeches to audiences around the country, as I'd done in the weeks after Augusta's death. I wasn't a soldier. I wasn't a strategist. I wasn't a politician. I was nothing more than the face I wore, a face that wasn't even mine. As the minutes dragged on, I felt more and more like the little kid hanging around the group home with the big kids all over again, pretending to know what they were talking about as they sniggered into their hands and whispered behind my back. I was nothing but a hanger-on. And if there was one thing I hated, it was being useless.

After the meeting was over, Knox led me back into the dirt tunnel under Somerset without saying a word. I hadn't tried to speak to him on the way out of the bunker, but now that we were alone without dozens of weapons pointed directly at us, the silence grew too loud to bear. It was my fault he had to risk his life now, all to find evidence we didn't even know existed, and no matter how upset we both were with each other, I couldn't shake the guilt that ate away at me.

"I'm sorry it turned out this way," I said. "But they had a right to know."

Knox said nothing. Instead he quickened his pace, and I had to all but jog to keep up.

"Knox—stop. Come on. They know how dangerous it is to tell Celia. They'll keep it quiet."

"If *you* had kept it quiet like we'd agreed, I wouldn't be in this situation in the first place," he snapped. They were the first words he'd said to me in an hour.

I gaped at the back of his head. "Maybe if you hadn't been such a jerk, I wouldn't have blurted it out. I'm more than just a III, and you know it."

"Are you?" He stopped suddenly, and I nearly ran into him. "Because sometimes I'm not so sure, Kitty."

I straightened to my full height, despite the blisters that had formed on my feet. "I don't know what crawled up your ass and died, but whatever it is, stop taking it out on me. I'm sorry the raid failed, and I'm sorry for being a mess at the party, but I am *not* your punching bag."

"Then what are you, Kitty?" He took a step nearer to me, swallowing up every last inch of distance between us. The heat from his body radiated to mine, and with him this close,

I could barely breathe. "What the hell have you done to help? Every chance you get, you sabotage not only yourself, but me, too. Do you realize that if you fail, so do I? We're supposed to get married in less than a month. Is this your plan? To have me killed just because you can't keep yourself under control?"

"That won't happen," I said as evenly as I could. "Daxton wouldn't hurt you to prove a point to me."

"Oh? Why the hell do you think Celia's husband was executed?"

I faltered. I had never heard many details about what had happened to Lila's father, only that he had been publicly executed by firing squad in front of her and her mother. It had been why Lila had joined the Blackcoats and agreed to give her mother's speeches, but other than that, her father and his death were mysteries to me.

"If you keep spiraling like this, then it's only a matter of time before I can't protect you and Benjy anymore," said Knox. "Is that what you want?"

"I'm sorry," I muttered. "It's been a rough night, all right?"

"It's always going to be a rough night, Kitty. This is nothing compared to what's coming. So stop acting like none of us deserves your cooperation, and start proving you're more than that III on the back of your neck."

"How? By blindly obeying you?" The words were out before I could stop them.

He surveyed me, his dark eyes bearing into mine. Leaning in close enough for me to feel his warm breath on my lips, he whispered, "Yes. It'll be the smartest thing you've done in months."

Fury ripped through me, tearing my guilt to shreds. "If I'm so useless to you, then why don't you marry the real Lila instead?"

"Believe me, if Lila was willing, I would have never asked you to stay in the first place," he said shortly. "At least she knows how to play the game."

"Then do it," I said coldly. "Because I'm done."

I stepped around him and stormed ahead through the tunnel. He didn't try to stop me, and that only spurred me on. I wouldn't stay where I wasn't wanted. I had a life to live that had nothing to do with him or the Harts, and if he was so convinced he would be better off without me, then I wasn't going to sacrifice myself for him any longer.

Even from a distance, his flashlight was enough to help me see where I was going, and I reached the door into Somerset in record time. I dashed up the creaky wooden staircase and scampered across the ceiling, dropping back down into Knox's closet with a thump. I didn't care if anyone heard me. Let them. I'd be gone before they knew it.

"Benjy." I burst into the living room and headed toward the door. "Pack a bag. We're leaving."

"What?" He sat up from his spot sprawled out across the couch, his red hair a mess and his eyes bleary. Apparently he'd been napping. "Where are we going?"

"Anywhere, as long as it isn't here."

"Kitty—wait." He jumped up and crossed the room, catching up with me in only a few long strides. "What's going on? I thought—"

"Knox doesn't want me here, so I'm not wasting our time and risking our lives."

He glanced uneasily at the open closet door. Knox would show up at any moment, but if he had a problem with this, too bad. If I wasn't good enough for him, then he could find another Lila. "We don't have anywhere to go," said Benjy. "I know it's dangerous here, but out there, with Shields hunting us down, we won't last ten minutes."

"Yes, we will," I said firmly. "Sampson and the Blackcoats will help us."

"Sampson and the Blackcoats will want you to go back so you can keep being Lila." He touched my cheek. "Kitty, listen, I know it's been a tough night—"

"It isn't just tonight," I said, keeping my voice as steady as possible despite the bubble of urgency rising inside me. "I need to get out of here, Benjy, and I'd rather be running from Shields than imprisoned by Blackcoats."

"If we stay here, Knox can help us," he said. "But if we leave—"

"Knox doesn't want me here. You should've heard the things he just said to me, Benjy. He can't stand me. He'd rather have the real Lila here than me. He thinks I'm a liability and that I can't be trusted, and maybe—maybe he's right." The cold, hard truth of it settled over me until I felt as if I couldn't breathe. I wasn't just doing this for myself and Benjy. If I was gone, that was one less thing for Knox to worry about, too. "Please, Benjy. I know it isn't the smartest thing I've ever suggested, but I can't do this anymore. I want my own life. I want to be me again—I want to be *us*. And the longer we stay here, the more afraid I am that we'll never both make it out of here alive."

Benjy was silent for a long moment, running his fingers through my hair and staring at me without so much as blinking. At last he took a deep breath, exhaling slowly. "Okay," he said. "We're in this together, even if that means making a monumental mistake."

I let out a sigh of relief. "Thank you, Benjy. It won't be a mistake." I hoped. "Get your stuff. I'll be back in a minute."

I stood on my tiptoes to give him a quick kiss, and I could feel him watching me as I hurried out the door. It wasn't fair for me to pull him from his life as a VI, one he'd earned on his own, but I'd meant what I'd said. The longer we stayed here, the better the chances were that one or both of us would wind up dead, and that, above all else, spurred me down the hallway toward my suite.

I opened the door and burst inside, only to stop short. My living room was an exact replica of Knox's, except instead of navy and wood, mine was made entirely of white. The carpet had been replaced since Augusta had died in front of the fireplace, but I still couldn't stomach looking at that spot. Unfortunately, right now, someone else was standing only inches away, staring directly at it.

"Greyson," I said, surprised. I closed the door. "What's going on?"

Greyson, Daxton's son and Lila's cousin, stood on the shag carpet in front of the fireplace, his hands tucked loosely in his pockets. He was tall, but the way he slouched made him look several inches shorter than he was, and his shaggy blond hair fell into his eyes. They were dark, like his father's, and even though he was almost nineteen, he looked younger than me. If he hadn't been my almost cousin, I would have thought he was cute, but I was too entrenched in Lila's head to even think about that now.

"Sorry for intruding," he said. "I tried knocking, but you weren't here, so I thought I'd leave it, but then I got distracted, and..."

He trailed off. He didn't have to say anything else. Other than Celia and Lila, who were now safely hidden in the Blackcoat bunker, Augusta had been the only real family Greyson had left. And I'd been the one to kill her.

"You got me something?" I said. The last time he'd brought me a gift, he'd done so thinking I was Lila. She had been his best friend, and it had taken him all of ten seconds to realize I wasn't really her. His quiet acceptance, as if her supposed death had been inevitable, had nearly broken my heart. Worse, the perpetual haunted look in Greyson's eyes never let me forget that I was one more constant reminder of his string of painful losses.

I touched the silver disk hanging from a chain around my neck, the same one he'd still given me even after figuring out I wasn't Lila. It looked like nothing more than a pretty charm, but when pulled apart the right way, it was a lock pick that could open virtually any lock—including an electronic one. I should have given it to Lila when I found out she was still alive, but selfishly I'd hung on to it.

Greyson nodded, and from behind his back, he produced a small box wrapped in silver paper. "Happy Birthday."

"You know it's not really my birthday, right?" I said with a small smile. He shrugged, and my smile faded. Gift or not, he still hadn't forgiven me for killing Augusta. I crossed the carpet and accepted the present. Unwrapping it carefully, mindful of the beautiful swirling paper, I cracked open the black box underneath, and my eyes widened.

Inside the box lay a gold picture frame with a labyrinth pattern carved into the edges. It wasn't the frame that surprised me, though—it was the picture of Lila and Greyson inside. They sat together in the library buried in the heart of Somerset, and though Greyson held a book, he watched Lila out of the corner of his eye, a secret smile playing on his lips as he tried to see what she was drawing on her sketch pad.

No, not Lila's sketch pad, I realized with a jolt. Mine. That girl wasn't Lila—she was me.

I studied the look on Greyson's face in the picture. He looked relaxed and happy—the kind of happy you couldn't fake. "When...?"

"While Daxton was unconscious," said Greyson. He cleared his throat, and his cheeks flushed. "Right before you saved my life."

"I didn't save your life," I said. "It was never in any danger in the first place."

He shrugged again. "I was going to tell Grandmother I didn't want to be Prime Minister. I think she knew, but if I outright refused..." His Adam's apple bobbed, and his eyes turned red. "Do you think she would have replaced me, too?"

Forgetting for a moment all that had happened and every reason he had for not wanting me anywhere near him, I closed the distance between us and wrapped my arms around him. "I don't know," I said honestly. "I do know she loved you more than anything, though."

At first he didn't move, but after several seconds, he finally returned my embrace, hugging me tight enough to bruise. "Because of who I am," he managed, his voice breaking, "or because of who I was supposed to be once she decided to get rid of the impostor and make me Prime Minister instead?"

I couldn't answer that. Maybe that was all Augusta had ever been—the kind of person who had no problem saying goodbye to the people she loved if it brought her more power. Or maybe that had been the armor she'd worn to protect her deepest vulnerabilities. I'd only ever seen the bad in her; it was Greyson who had seen the good, if there'd been any to begin with. "It doesn't matter now," I said. "Remember her the way you want, and try to forget the rest."

His shoulders shook, and he clung to me the way I clung to Benjy in my worst moments. He had no one. His parents and older brother were dead; the man pretending to be his father was really a Masked stranger; Lila had disappeared underground; and Knox was so busy trying to change the world that half the time he didn't have a second to spare for me, let alone Greyson. I was it, and whether or not he'd forgiven me for what I'd done to the last family he had left, his face in the picture had said it all. And I was going to walk away from him to save my own skin.

No, he would have Lila once the rebellion was over. She and Celia would return, and Greyson would have his family again. He wouldn't have to be Prime Minister if he didn't want to be, and in the end, everything would work out for him. If I wasn't there to make sure of it, Knox would.

"Sorry," he mumbled, pulling away after nearly a minute had passed. I started to tell him he had nothing to be sorry for, but he took the picture frame from me and fiddled with something on the back. "Here. This is what I wanted to show you."

I took the frame back and blinked. Instead of Greyson and I sitting together in the library, it now held a picture of Benjy with his arms around a girl with a round face, dirty blond hair, and bright blue eyes.

My mouth dropped open. Once again, that girl was me—*actually* me, Kitty Doe, before I'd been Masked as Lila. Benjy's shock of red hair was as vivid as ever, and he bent his head to kiss my cheek as I grinned ear to ear. Unlike the picture with Greyson, I remembered the moment this had been taken, almost a year ago. The brand-new sweater I wore gave it away. It had been our last Christmas together in the group home—the last one our matron, Nina, had seen before Daxton had hunted and killed her in the vast forests of Elsewhere.

I traced my old face over the glass. Everything about it was different now, and I would never look in the mirror and see Kitty Doe again. I almost hadn't recognized myself, and seeing this picture now—the only one I had from before I'd been Masked as Lila—made my insides knot together. I'd had nothing then, only Benjy and the hope of a better future. That better future had turned into a III and a job cleaning sewers, and only the strange color of my eyes had saved me from a short, brutal life underground. If I forgot my own face so quickly, then what hope did I have of anyone else remembering it? I had been a nobody. I still was a nobody, but at least now I was a nobody who might be able to make a difference in the lives of the IIs and IIIs who hadn't been lucky enough to have the same eye color as Lila Hart.

And here I was, about to run away from the only thing that made my life worth anything at all.

More than my guilt over leaving Greyson, more than my trepidation over dragging Benjy underground, that was what cracked my resolve. I would still leave—I had to, to save Benjy's life, to save my own, and to give Knox a chance at seeing his plans through without me getting in the way. But I'd be damned if I wasted this chance to make the difference I'd risked my life for in the first place.

"How did you find this?" I said, still staring at the photograph. It had been less than a year since that moment, but it felt like another lifetime. Nothing was the same anymore, and nothing would be ever again.

Greyson shrugged. "I found it in Grandmother's things with the others."

"Others?" An idea began to form in my mind. If Greyson could find a picture of me, one I hadn't even known existed, then Sampson must have been right—there had to be one of the real Daxton.

"She had an entire file on you," he said. "Pictures, test results, your birth certificate—"

My head snapped up. "Birth certificate? Why would she have all of that?"

"I don't know." Greyson frowned. "I didn't read everything, but there were reports on you, too—yearly ones, like she'd been keeping tabs on you. I thought you knew."

I blinked. I'd had no idea. "Do you know where the file is now?"

"I don't know. Daxton cleared everything out after she died." His face fell. "I'm sorry, I should have saved it. I wasn't thinking—"

"It's okay," I said hastily, my mind whirling as I clutched the picture frame. "Thank you—for this, for the frame, for everything."

"'Course," he mumbled. "There's a switch on the back—here, like this." He took it gingerly and pointed to a barely visible button. "Hold it down for five seconds, and it'll change into you and Benjy. Press it again, just once, and it'll change back to us."

"Thanks." I took the frame back and tried it. My face dissolved into Lila's once more. Instead of being sorry to see me go, I was relieved. This was my life now. As much as I wanted to go back in time to last Christmas, all I could do was go forward. It was the only option any of us ever had.

Greyson shuffled his feet and shoved his hands into his pockets again. "You were really pretty before."

"Thanks," I said quietly. It didn't matter, not anymore. I was stuck as Lila Hart for the rest of my life, however long or short it might be.

He cleared his throat. "I'm sorry for—for being distant. You don't deserve that."

I did, though. "I get it. I'd be distant, too."

Greyson jerked forward, as if he wanted to move toward me but had stopped himself at the last instant. "Grandmother—she deserved what she got. I'm not mad at you. I'm mad at her for everything she did. She didn't have to, but she did and...I'm sorry."

For a second time, I hugged him tightly. "You don't have anything to be sorry about, okay? You're my friend. You'll always be my friend, no matter where we are or what's going on."

"You, too," he mumbled. "When this is all over and I'm—I'm Prime Minister, I'll make sure you get to be that girl again, okay?"

A lump formed in my throat. "Okay."

He let me go, and the smile on his face nearly made me forget how impossible his promise really was. I could never be Kitty Doe again, and if he ever had to be Prime Minister, it would mean only one thing: I had let him and the entire country down, and the Blackcoats had lost.

The way Greyson's gaze lingered on me as we said our good-nights made it seem almost as if he knew tonight would be the last time we saw each other. I watched him leave, part of me aching to give him one last hug, and another part of me wishing I didn't have to say goodbye at all. But I had no choice—I had to get Benjy out of there, and there was no more reason for me to stay. I wanted the future he had drawn on that napkin. I wanted the lake, the cottage, the sunshine, the happiness, and the only way I would ever have it was to get out of the line of fire before the war began.

I couldn't leave yet, though—not until I found proof that Daxton was an impostor. I wasn't useless. I wasn't just a stupid III who was only good for cleaning sewers. I wasn't going to make Knox put his neck on the chopping block because of me, and I wasn't going to let the entire world come crashing down around Greyson, trapping him in a life he didn't want the way Daxton and Knox had trapped me. He deserved better. We both did.

After I changed into the most durable outfit Lila owned—jeans, a thick sweater, a leather jacket, and a pair of boots I could actually walk in—I stuffed a duffel bag full of clothes, jewelry, small electronics, and anything we might be able to pawn for food and shelter until we found someplace more permanent. A single one of Lila's bracelets was worth more than most IIs and IIIs made in a decade, and she had several jewelry boxes full of them. I would've felt guilty if I hadn't known the Harts could replace them without batting an eye, but it was a fair price for stealing my life.

A knock on the door made me jump and drop a pearl earring into the bag. "Who is it?" I called, my heart racing. I shoved the duffel bag underneath the bathroom sink.

"It's me."

Knox. I scowled. "I'm busy."

"I don't care how busy you are—I need to talk to you."

Damn. Knox must have caught Benjy packing, which meant he was here to stop me. I couldn't let him try, not yet. Not when I didn't know what he'd do to keep me here, and not when the Blackcoats needed that file. Knox wouldn't stand a chance sneaking around Daxton's office, but I did. "Fine," I called. "I'm changing. Give me a minute."

I looked around the living room frantically. How was I supposed to get past him when he was right outside the door?

Stupid question. My eyes fell on the ceiling in the corner of the room, where a grate led into a maze of metal tunnels that made up the ventilation system throughout the entire fourth level of Somerset. I'd used them to sneak around undetected before Augusta's death, but I'd been forced to show my hand to Knox and Benjy, rendering my secret useless. Until now.

As quietly as I could, I pushed the end table underneath the vent. Using the shelves on the bookcase, I climbed up and pushed the grate out of place. It had been weeks since I'd done this, but before becoming Lila, I'd been an expert at sneaking in and out of tight spaces—namely the maze of sewers underneath the Heights, the poorest corner of the city. Somerset was less than twenty miles away, but they couldn't have been more different.

I crawled through the metal vent, making sure to nudge the grate back into place. It wouldn't take long for Knox to figure out what I'd done once he grew tired of waiting for me, but he was too big to follow, and he'd have no way of guessing where I was going. For now, all I could do was move as quickly as possible and hope to hell Daxton was asleep.

Fifteen minutes later, I peered down through the metal slats and into Daxton's office. The lights were dim, and I could hear the distant trickling of water from the fountain near his doorway. The screen on his desk was dark, but I wouldn't need it. If Greyson had dug up a photograph, there must have been more to find than a few computer files I wouldn't be able to read anyway.

I dropped down into his office, wincing as my heavy combat boots thudded against the wooden floor. I stood still for the space of several heartbeats, waiting for a sign someone had heard me.

Silence.

Gliding across the floor, careful not to make another sound, I searched for anything that might have held a file Daxton wanted to keep hidden. His desk was the most obvious place, but when I tried to open the drawers, they were locked. Unclasping my necklace, I unfolded the lock pick and had each open within seconds; however, they held nothing more than official-looking papers I couldn't read, all bearing the Hart family crest. In one, a half-empty bottle of what looked like whiskey sat hidden underneath a false bottom—the same kind I'd used to hide my few possessions at my group home—but no matter how hard I searched, I couldn't find anything that looked like it might have hidden the secrets to Daxton's real identity.

I straightened and looked around. The walls of his large office were covered ceiling to floor in bookshelves, each one fuller than the last. The ones closest to the door looked neat and organized, as if they hadn't been touched in years. The closer they got to the desk, however, the more disorganized and cluttered they became. Was it possible he'd hidden something in a book?

No—I wasn't thinking about this the right way. Daxton would never leave something like that out where anyone could accidentally run across it. He would put it someplace hidden, but secure. Someplace no one would dare to look. Someplace only he would have access to.

Which meant it *had* to be in this office. After my little stunt trying to kill him, he was the only one with access, even though he pretended he'd lost the memory of that incident. No one else had been allowed in his office without his personal guards present, not even Greyson. This was his most private room in Somerset. If the evidence still existed, it was in here.

I began to touch everything. The chairs, the couches, the fireplace, the lamps, the end tables—nothing in the office got past my hands. But the harder I looked, the less confident

I became. Just because I would have kept some sentimental token of my past didn't mean he would. What if he really had destroyed it? Then what chance would the Blackcoats have of gaining the support of the Shields and the Ministers of the—

Click.

I stilled. My hand rested on the gold frame of the Hart family portrait painted a year earlier, before the deaths of the real Daxton, along with his wife and elder son. On the very edge, where the portrait met the wall, there was a sliver of space that hadn't been there before. Underneath my thumb, I spotted a tiny button that blended in perfectly with the frame.

My heart sped up as I nudged the frame open. Surely enough, the massive portrait concealed a steel safe—or at least I thought it was a safe. For all intents and purposes, it looked like a square sheet of metal imbedded into the wall. There was no dial, no number pad, nothing.

I searched for any sign of how to open it, but once again, nothing. That made things difficult. Frowning, I brushed my fingertips against the metal, feeling for any slight indents that might give me a clue.

Instantly blue light appeared, forming a square in the center of the safe. I waited for something else to happen, but the blue square didn't change. Did it want a handprint? No symbols had appeared, and a handprint was the only thing that would reasonably fit in that square.

It didn't matter what it wanted. My handprint was Lila's now, and somehow I doubted Daxton would have granted her access to whatever was inside the safe. I clasped my necklace so hard that it left indents in my palm. Time to see how good Greyson really was.

I passed the silver disk in front of the sensor and held my breath. If it didn't work, would the sensor just ignore my attempt to break in, or would half of Somerset be alerted? I glanced at the opening in the ceiling. It would take me several precious seconds to scale the bookshelves and make it up there. If there were guards outside waiting, or if Daxton was anywhere nearby—

The light changed from blue to white, and to my astonishment, the safe popped open. Apparently Greyson *was* that good after all. I opened the door and, with trembling fingers, removed the collection of a dozen files inside.

Several of them were nothing but papers I couldn't read and maps of places I had never been. Another was what looked like a report detailing the car explosion that had killed the real Daxton and his family, leaving Greyson alone. But as interesting as they might have been, it was the thickest folder that I cared about.

I flipped it open, and my real face greeted me with a smile. It was my school picture, clipped to a report card I couldn't read. I must have been seven or eight—I still had freckles from staying out in the sun too long, and I was missing my front tooth.

Tearing my eyes away, I flipped through the other pictures. There were more than I could have ever imagined, detailing every important moment of my life, including what looked like the day I was born. I squinted at the typed pages that filled the folder to bursting, hoping in vain that the words would make sense for the first time in my life. But they remained a mystery, and the only clues I had were those pictures.

Some of them were noticeably older than the others, yellowing around the edges and slightly discolored. This wasn't a file Augusta had compiled after I'd been Masked as Lila—she'd been keeping tabs on me throughout my entire life. But why?

I frowned. As badly as I wanted to know, I had another

more important question right now, and I was holding the answer in my hands. There was only one file left I hadn't looked through, and I opened the pages, careful not to touch whatever was inside.

It was slimmer than mine, but still full of the same things—papers I couldn't read, what looked like a copy of the test everyone in the country had to take on their seventeenth birthday, and certificates I didn't recognize. And at the bottom of the pile was a single photograph.

Two young men with light hair and dark eyes stood side by side, sporting carefree smiles I envied. They both wore black uniforms, and insignias on their lapels announced their high ranks. One of the men looked strangely familiar, but they both resembled one another in a way that only family could. Brothers? They had to be. They had the same nose, the same eyes, and the same dimpled chin, and the way they slung their arms around one another made it obvious they were more than comrades or patrol partners.

Which one had been Masked as Daxton? I glanced back and forth between them. Did I recognize the man on the left because I subconsciously associated him with Daxton, or had I seen him before? And the man on the right—he shared Daxton's eyes, the only part of the human body doctors couldn't modify to resemble someone else's. Then again, they both did.

The soft sound of footsteps outside the door pulled me from my trance, and I snapped the folder shut and gathered the rest. As silently as I could, I tucked the unnecessary folders back into the safe and closed the portrait before climbing up the bookshelves toward the grate, my file and Daxton's tucked securely in my arm.

Once I settled back in the ventilation system, I took a deep breath, my mind spinning. Benjy would tell me what was in my file. He would read it to me, and I would know within the hour what secrets Augusta had kept from me.

But if I went to Knox instead, it was the other file that would give me leverage. It could buy me a way to keep Benjy safe outside of Somerset. Something this valuable to the Blackcoats—it could be the ticket to everything we both wanted. I couldn't change my past, but my future was wide-open. And I wanted it to be as far from D.C. as possible.

My mind made up, I crawled through the vent, pushing the files along in front of me. If Knox wanted to know who Daxton really was, then I hoped he was in the mood to bargain.

IV

CURIOSITY KILLED THE CAT

By the time I dropped back into my suite, I held only my thick folder. It had taken me another twenty minutes to hide the fake Daxton's file where no one would ever find it, not without my help, and the only way Knox was going to get it was if he helped me first.

Now that that was done, I turned to unlock the door that led out into the hallway, wondering if Knox was still standing there or if he'd given up and returned to his suite by now. Either way, we had to talk before I left, and I wasn't going to wait until morning.

"You know you're not supposed to crawl around the vents anymore."

I jumped and whirled around, the folder nearly slipping from my grip. Knox sat in front of my fireplace, his dark eyes gleaming with annoyance and a glass of something I wasn't so sure was water in his hand.

"Have you really been waiting this whole time?" I said casually as if this wasn't weird at all. I crossed the room to Lila's desk and set the file down.

Knox rose. "Where have you been, Kitty?" he said, a note of warning in his voice. "It's been an hour."

"Saving your cowardly ass, that's where."

"My ass is anything but cowardly," he said as he approached, glass still in hand. I wrinkled my nose. Definitely not water. "What's that?"

"This?" I opened the file and began to flip through it. "Oh, you know, nothing too much. Just my entire past." I held up a picture of me at five years old. "Care to explain why Augusta had this?"

Knox furrowed his brow and snatched the file from the desk. A handful of pictures fluttered to the floor. "Where did you get this?"

"The same place I found Daxton's file," I said, bending down to pick up the photos. "Along with evidence of who he really is. You're welcome."

"I'm not thanking you." A second later, the weight of what I'd said seemed to settle over him, and he stilled in the middle of rifling through the pages. "You have a file like this on the fake Daxton?"

I nodded. "There's only one picture, but it has other documents that must have his name on them somewhere."

"Where is it?"

"I'll make you a deal," I said. "Help Benjy and me get to the bunker safely, guarantee us the Blackcoats' protection, and I'll tell you where it is. After you tell me why Augusta has been watching me my whole life, of course."

He moved closer, towering over me. "The Blackcoats need that file, Kitty."

"And I need to get out of here before you decide I'm not worth the trouble and have me and Benjy killed," I said. Shock flickered across his face, and his eyes widened as if he couldn't believe I would ever think that poorly of him.

Good. Now he knew what it was like.

Knox's expression quickly returned to a smooth mask of neutrality, and he stared at me. "You know I would never do that."

"Do I? Because lately I'm not so sure. I'm a liability, remember?"

Silence settled over us for the better part of half a minute. Without responding, he flipped through the file, his gaze lingering on a picture of Benjy and me on his sixteenth birthday. I'd scooped a glob of green frosting from my piece of cake and wiped it onto the tip of his nose, and in retaliation, he'd kissed me, smearing some of it on my cheek. It was one of the most recent photographs in the collection.

"It's a win-win situation for you," I said. "Tell me what it says, and I'll not only tell you where Daxton's file is, but I'll also be out of your hair permanently. You'll never have to deal with me again."

He sighed. "If this is because of what I said before—"

"This is because I have a right to make my own choices and know what's going on in my own life, and I don't trust you to tell me without incentive," I said coolly.

"That's not what I meant," he said. "Why are you leaving, Kitty? You're not only going to hurt yourself, but the rebellion, too. You're no good to us locked in a bunker."

"Apparently I'm no good to you anyway," I said. "You don't have to make this difficult, Knox. Just help me, and you'll get your information. If you don't want to, then I'll have Benjy read the file to me instead, and the Blackcoats will never find Daxton's folder without my help. I guarantee it. But one way or the other, I *am* leaving."

He had no way of knowing that I had every intention of handing Daxton's folder over to Sampson if he wouldn't help me, but after all we'd been through, part of me desperately wanted to see a flicker of the old Knox again. The one who had believed I could be Lila when no one else would. The one who had treated me like I mattered.

His foot tapped impatiently, but at last he muttered, "Fine. All that's in here are old report cards and progress reports from your matron."

I exhaled. "Keep looking. There has to be something."

Knox frowned, and his gaze shifted back to the pages inside the file. He flipped through them, reading the words I couldn't. Page after page after page, with no flicker in his expression to give anything away. Slowly doubts began to creep into my mind. Maybe it *was* useless. Despite the obvious aging in several of the pictures and papers, maybe Augusta had found them after the fact and collected them inside the file.

Knox turned another page, and his foot stopped tapping. He stilled, and his eyes scanned the same document over and over. My heart leaped.

"What is it?" I said, craning my neck to try to see what he was looking at. A certificate of some sort—one with the official Hart seal on it. He pulled the file away before I could get a good look, but it wouldn't have helped anyway. As always, the letters on the page looked like gibberish.

"Did anyone see you?" he said. The edge to his voice made me square my shoulders.

"Of course not. What does it say?"

He ignored my question. "Good. Now for the last time— where did you get this?"

"I'm not playing this game with you, Knox. *What does that say?*"

He slapped the folder down on the end table. "It's the sad story of a girl who was born an Extra, got terrible grades in school, received a III after failing to complete her test, and then blew the opportunity of a lifetime to help not only herself, but the entire country just because she was too stubborn to cooperate. I don't know how it ends, but at this point, I can virtually guarantee you that her sad life is going to be a short one if she keeps acting like this."

"My sad life was always going to be a short one," I said. "If you ever want Daxton's file, you're going to cut the bullshit and tell me what you read. *Now.*"

His eyes flickered to the left before locking on mine again. "A report on the operations they put you through to turn you into Lila. It took longer than I thought, that's all. There's nothing in there about why Augusta was watching you or why they chose you—just report cards and pictures."

I set my jaw. He was lying. I'd never said anything about wanting to know why they'd chosen me to be Lila. I already knew the answer: our eyes were the same rare shade of blue. But with one slip of the tongue, Knox had told me there was more to it. And he had also told me I couldn't trust him anymore.

We stood only inches apart, and he ducked his head, his lips brushing my ear. "Tell me where you got this, Kitty, before Daxton discovers it's missing."

"I'll put it back," I said.

"No, you won't." We both reached for the folder at the same time, but Knox, with his lightning-fast reflexes, snatched it up first. I glowered at him. "We both know you're going to go straight to Benjy and make him read every page to you."

"And what's wrong with that?" I said. "If you're telling the truth, then you don't have anything to worry about."

"I have plenty to worry about, especially if you found this where I think you did," he said. "Is the other file there, too?"

I considered him for a long moment. "Yes," I lied. "And if you let me put mine back, I'll bring you Daxton's."

"Not a chance," he said. "It's only a matter of time before Daxton notices it's missing, and I won't have someone killed for your curiosity. You're lucky Daxton doesn't—"

He stopped suddenly, and his face went from red to pale to ashen in seconds as he flipped through the file again. I frowned. "What?" I said.

His Adam's apple bobbed. "He knows you're Masked," said Knox. "If he hid this file after Augusta died, then he knows."

"Oh." I exhaled. "Right. He remembers everything that happened—that I was Masked, that I tried to kill him, that Celia was probably in on it...everything. He's been lying the whole time."

Knox clutched the file and closed it again, slower this time. "He remembers everything? All of it? How—" He clenched his jaw, and I could see the muscles shifting underneath his skin. "How can you be so sure?"

"Because—because after Augusta's funeral, he touched the ridges on the back of my neck and made it obvious he knows everything. And—" I swallowed hard. "I might've touched his, too."

The ridges below our tattoos were the only things that set us apart from the real Harts. My VII hid a III—my real rank. The fake Daxton's VII hid a V, the rank he'd been before being Masked as the Prime Minister. They were the only evidence anyone had to prove we'd been Masked, and as Harts, we were lucky enough that no one would ever question our VIIs. Except each other.

Knox exhaled sharply and turned away from me. From the

way his shoulders rose and fell, it was obvious he was trying to collect himself. At last he faced me again, his neutral expression barely hiding the rage lurking underneath.

"You didn't think it would be a good idea to tell me this sooner?" he said, and I shrugged.

"What difference would it make?"

"It makes all the difference in the world." His voice broke. "You have no idea—"

"So tell me," I said. "Instead of treating me like a child and keeping secrets from me, why don't you try trusting me instead?"

"Like you trusted me with this?" His expression grew dark. "Where did you find this file, Kitty?"

"I—"

"*Where did you find it?*"

I scowled. "Daxton's office, behind the portrait. But you can't just waltz in there in the middle of the night and—"

Before I could finish, Knox was already halfway out the door. Despite the heavy boots he wore, the plush carpet absorbed the sound of his footsteps, and I ran after him.

"Knox—wait. *Wait.*" I caught up to him and grabbed his elbow. "The other file, it—"

"You *will* stay here," said Knox dangerously. "And you will *never* mention this to anyone, do you understand me?"

My mouth opened and shut. "What's the big deal? It's just a file."

"And you stole it," he said. "There was a reason I was the one assigned to this job and not you. I can read and gather all the relevant information without Daxton ever knowing we have it—and without ever knowing the Blackcoats have support in Somerset. Now, thanks to you, all of that's in jeopardy.

If he discovers you're behind this, then he will figure out I'm helping you. Do you understand?"

"But—it doesn't have to be you," I said. "It could be anyone—"

"Who else? Benjy?"

All the air left my lungs, and I could feel the blood drain from my face, leaving my skin cold and clammy. "No. He doesn't have anything to do with this, and you will *not* frame him—"

"If you get caught, then it's either him or me," said Knox. "Sometimes you have to sacrifice a pawn to win the game."

"You won't," I said, rage surging through me. "If you try, I'll tell Daxton everything. I don't care if he kills me."

"Then let's both try to make it out of this alive," said Knox coldly. "Stay here and let me fix this. I won't tell you again."

He walked away, his strides long and purposeful, and for a moment I considered not following him. All I had to do was grab the duffel bag I'd hidden and walk straight into Knox's suite, and Benjy and I would be halfway across the city before Knox realized what we'd done. We'd be free.

I was two steps from the door before I stopped myself. We wouldn't be free. We would never be free, not until Daxton was dead and Greyson—or Knox, or Celia, or whoever was in charge—gave me my life back. The Shields would hunt us until they found us, and if we were lucky, they'd kill us before Daxton had the chance to send us Elsewhere. There was no such thing as freedom, not in this country, and if Knox was serious about framing Benjy for his crimes, then there was no telling what Daxton might do to him for treason.

I had to know what Knox was doing. He'd kept me in the dark long enough—I couldn't let him run the show, not this time.

My mind made up, I took off down the hallway, avoiding the corners where the guards were positioned. I ducked through the atrium and past the elevator, making sure I was below the railing so the guards couldn't see me. My footsteps were as silent as Knox's, and before long, I crouched a few rooms down from the entrance to Daxton's suite. Two guards stood outside, both alert with their eyes straight forward. I swore inwardly.

I slipped through the nearest open door, into a dark sitting room meant for guests of the Prime Minister. Squinting, I peered into the corners, and relief washed over me when I spotted a vent.

Within seconds, I climbed onto an end table and pulled myself up. I had memorized the ventilation system when I'd first moved into Somerset, and it was only two quick turns to Daxton's private living quarters.

I stilled, listening for any signs of life. In the distance, I picked up a soft murmur, but it was too far away for me to make out. Fear prickled in the base of my spine. If Daxton had caught Knox trying to replace my file...

Crawling as quickly as I dared, I made my way from room to room, searching for the source of the conversation. His bedroom and sitting rooms were empty; the same with his multiple guest rooms. At last I came to his office, and with a sinking heart, I situated myself over the vent. Two voices rose up to meet me: Daxton's and Knox's.

"...don't care," said Daxton, his tone clipped with annoyance. "I've given you far more chances than you deserve."

"I'm not asking for another chance," said Knox. His voice cracked, and he sounded like a cornered animal. "I'm asking you to look at the facts."

"I am," said Daxton, "and what I see is a long list of reasons why I should stop putting up with this foolishness. The files are only the beginning. My patience is wearing thin, Lennox, and though I am a peace-loving man, there are some things not even I can tolerate."

Silence. I held my breath, waiting for Knox to respond, but instead something shifted through the grates. Daxton stood directly below me, his hands clasped behind his back. He was fully dressed, even though it had to be well into the small hours of the morning by now.

"This is my final offer. Take it or leave it, Lennox. I am no longer interested in babysitting, and she must be detained."

She. My blood ran cold. They weren't talking about Knox—they were talking about me.

"And what happens if I don't take it?" said Knox. I began to slide backward. Detained meant one of two things: it meant Elsewhere, or it meant death. And Knox had promised me months ago that he would kill me before he would let Daxton send me to be hunted by the very VIs who would have happily watched Lila burn.

"You know what happens then," said Daxton, his voice fading. I didn't care. I had to get back to Benjy before they found me, and we had to leave. Free or not, I had every intention of waking up the next morning as alive as I was today.

Once I'd cleared the office, I didn't bother trying to keep quiet. I crawled as fast as I could back to the sitting room, where I dropped to the floor and raced into the hallway. I took the corners half blind and oblivious, but once I was clear of Daxton's wing, the guards were at a minimum.

I reached my suite in record time. Bursting inside, I grabbed the duffel bag from underneath the sink and ran back into the hallway. I tried the knob to Knox's suite, but it was locked. Swearing, I fumbled with my necklace, yanking the chain over my head. My fingers trembled, but I managed to unfold the lock pick and make quick work of it.

I nudged open the door and tugged the necklace back around my neck. Benjy had to be packed by now. If he'd stuffed his bag full of books instead of clothes—

I stopped cold. Benjy stood in the middle of the room, but he wasn't alone. Knox stood beside him, and at first glance, it looked completely innocent. Benjy was pale and his shoulders hunched defensively, however, and his expression silently begged me to turn around and run. I opened my mouth to say something, but instead I spotted the glint of steel pressed against Benjy's spine, and my stomach nearly turned inside out.

"Knox—what—" I began, but a cold hand settled on my shoulder, and I froze.

"Hello, my dear," said Daxton, and my throat swelled. Shit. Shit shit *shit*.

"What's going on?" I managed to force out. "Is everything okay?"

"You know it isn't, Lila," he said, tracing the three ridges on the back of my neck. "Tell me where you put the file."

"What—what file?" I locked eyes with Benjy, and my heart raced. It would be okay. It had to be okay. This was *not* going to be the end.

"You know exactly what file I'm talking about," said Daxton. "Guards—check her bag and search her suite."

Half a dozen guards appeared from the fringes of the room, and while five of them marched out into the hallway, the last one ripped through my bag. Jewelry glittering with diamonds spilled from the pockets, along with the clothes I'd stuffed inside. My airway threatened to close up. That alone was worth an arrest.

"Knox, tell him it wasn't me," I said, but he didn't move. *"Knox."*

"He won't lie for you," said Daxton. "Tell me the truth, Lila."

I searched Knox's expression for any sign he had a plan, but instead he held my stare blankly, as much of a challenge as it was a surrender. There wasn't a plan. This was it. We were the pawns, and Knox was making the necessary sacrifices to win the game.

Screw the game. If he wanted to play, then I'd play. "Knox stole that file, not me," I spat. "He's hiding the one on you, too. How do you think he got the first one? Do you really think I'd willingly hand it over to him?"

"Yes," said Daxton smoothly, "because that is exactly what you did. Will you be honest with me, Lila, or do I have to bleed it out of you?"

"I *am* being honest. Knox is trying to frame me. He's the leader of the Blackcoats—him and Celia. All this time, they've been working together to destroy you."

A strange sound emanated from deep within Daxton, and it took me several confused seconds before I realized what I was hearing. He was laughing. "Wrong again, my dear. You're on quite the roll tonight, aren't you? Knox has been working for me—reporting back on Blackcoat activity, telling me their next moves. How do you think we've been ahead of them the whole time?"

"I—" I faltered. Knox didn't meet my eye, and his grip on Benjy's shoulder tightened.

No. Not possible. After all this time and everything he'd done to help me—*not possible.*

"He's lying," I said, the words tumbling out of me in a rush as I tried to convince Daxton as well as myself. "He might be feeding you tidbits to make it look like he's on your side, but he's really telling the Blackcoats everything he knows about you and—"

"Everything I tell him to say," said Daxton. "Why do you think the Blackcoats haven't gotten any closer to their goal? Why do you think tonight's raid failed? Why do you think they're cut off at every turn before they can find their footing? No one, not even my sister, is that incompetent."

I was going to throw up right there on Daxton's leather shoes. "Knox?" I said, my voice shaking. "Is he telling the truth?"

"He seems to be the only one in the room who is," said Knox coolly.

"It's not here," said the guard. He'd ripped apart my duffel bag, and it hung in pieces from the handles. In the room over, I could hear the sounds of furniture breaking and glass shattering.

Daxton's fingers dug into my neck until the edges of my vision began to darken. "You have two choices," he said with remarkable calm. "You can tell me where you hid it, or I can kill you right here and now."

I forced myself to breathe steadily. In and out, in and out, slowly and deeply. "All right—okay," I said. "Just—don't hurt me, okay? The file..."

Daxton's grip tightened. "Yes?"

I locked eyes with Benjy, my gaze unwavering. He knew how much I loved him. He knew I would do anything to save his life. But I couldn't do this to save mine, not when it meant giving Knox and Daxton exactly what they wanted.

I'm sorry, I mouthed to him, before I said out loud, "The file's exactly where it should be. Stuck so far up your ass that it'll never see the light of day again."

An enraged roar ripped through the room, and a burst of white-hot pain shot through me as Daxton forced me to the ground by my neck, pressing my cheek against the wooden floor.

"Last chance, little girl," he whispered. "Five...four...three...two..."

"Sir!" A guard burst into the room, and Daxton's grip relaxed enough for me to breathe. "It isn't in her suite."

"You're sure?" said Daxton. "You looked through everything?"

"Yes, sir. If it's in there, it's in a place no one will ever find it."

"Good." I could hear the smile in Daxton's voice, and he released me. As I began to stand, however, he stomped down on my back, digging his shoe into the middle of my shoulders. I bit back a cry. "Had you cooperated, we might have been able to avoid this sideshow of unpleasantries," he said. "It does make for a bad taste in my mouth. But as it stands, you have left me with no choice."

Even with half my face pressed against the floor, I spotted Daxton stroking his pistol lovingly. My eyes widened, but I kept my mouth shut. I refused to give him the satisfaction of making me beg.

"You have been nothing but a thorn in my side, dear niece, and the time has come to weed the garden," he said smoothly. "I can't say I'll miss you."

"Daxton." Knox's voice cut through the room, sharp and as much a warning as it was a reminder. The man who was supposed to be my uncle sighed dramatically.

"Oh, very well." He gestured toward Knox with the gun. "Only because I like you, mind. Let's get it over with."

Knox grimaced, and my mind raced. What were they talking about, getting it over—

Bang.

A shot rang out, and my entire body turned cold with dread. An excruciatingly slow second passed, but pain didn't blossom like I thought it would. Instead, the only agony I felt came from the pressure of Daxton's shoe and the throbbing in my neck where he'd grabbed me.

But I wasn't their only prisoner. Across the room, Benjy went rigid, and his eyes grew wide. He seemed to fall in slow motion, his knees hitting the floor first, making a resounding *crack* against the hard wood. One moment our eyes were locked, and I saw the fear and pain and trepidation on his face—and the next, he slumped lifelessly to the ground.

My world went silent. I couldn't breathe. I couldn't blink. I couldn't move. As had happened when I'd killed Augusta, I was vaguely aware someone was screaming, and soon enough I realized it was me. My mind detached from my body, separating itself so completely that I felt as if I were looking down on myself, fighting underneath Daxton's foot as he uncapped a syringe. Ten feet away, Knox knelt beside Benjy's body and touched his throat as if he were feeling for a pulse. But even as he did so, I couldn't look away from Benjy's stare—his cold, empty stare void of any life or love or warmth, and I didn't have to see Knox's satisfied nod to know.

Benjy was dead.

Benjy was dead, and Knox had killed him.

"Now, my dear, this could have been so much simpler if only you'd listened," murmured Daxton above me. His knee replaced his foot between my shoulder blades, and the needle stung as it slid into my neck. "Whatever the rest of your short life brings you, I do hope this was worth it."

Unbearable pain rushed through me, setting my body on fire. But the heat of whatever it was Daxton had injected into my veins was nothing compared to the agony of losing Benjy, and as it burned me up from the inside out, I stared at his lifeless face, tears flooding my eyes.

"I'm sorry," I whispered in vain hope that my voice would be the last thing he heard. But it was pointless—he was gone.

Everything went black.

V

SECTION X

Somewhere nearby, someone was singing.

I shielded my eyes from the morning light and groaned. My head pounded, and my throat was dry and scratchy, as if I hadn't had anything to drink in days. I reached blindly for the glass of water I kept at my bedside, but my hand rammed into a rough wall, scraping my knuckles.

I opened my eyes and sat up, my heart pounding. I was in a cold concrete cell barely long enough to fit the cot beneath me, and it wasn't much wider than I was tall. Wedged beside the bed was a metal nightstand with an empty bucket underneath, and the tiny window was high up in the corner of the room, far too small for me to fit through even if I climbed up to reach it. The air smelled like damp mold, and the metal door had a thin slit for peering out, but there was no way I could slip my hand through and undo the lock. Wherever this place was, it was as far from Somerset as I could possibly get.

Suddenly the memory of what had happened in Knox's suite hit me, forcing all the air from my lungs. Pain sliced straight through me, and if my heart could have broken in half, I was sure it would have.

Benjy couldn't be gone. He'd been alive hours ago, laughing and teasing and drawing our future on a napkin. It couldn't just end like this. Maybe I was wrong—maybe I'd misunderstood what I'd seen.

But deep inside, I knew I'd understood just fine.

Benjy was dead.

I would never see him again. I would never touch him, never hug him, never kiss him—our future, the future we'd both dreamed of for so long, would never happen. We would never sit in the grass by a pond and have a picnic in the sunshine. I would never again be able to tell him how much I loved him. And he would never know how sorry I was for not giving up that file when I had the chance.

He was gone.

Grief overtook me like quicksand, so solid that it felt as if I were drowning in it. I sank back onto the cot as the tears began, hot and bitter as they carved out their paths running down my face. He would still be alive if I had just done what Daxton had told me to do. If I hadn't trusted Knox—if I had run away with Benjy while I still could—

Infinite *what ifs* buzzed around me, smothering me until I couldn't think. I should have made Daxton kill me. I should have killed myself instead. I should have never valued the Blackcoats' useless revolution over Benjy's life—they stood no chance, and I'd known it all along. I should have listened to my gut. I should have never let Knox convince me to stay as Lila in the first place. I should have done anything else, and Benjy would still be alive.

My fault. This was all my fault.

Agonizing sobs tore through me, ripped from depths I

couldn't imagine. Every single one felt like a knife to the heart, and in that moment, I wanted nothing more than to die right then and there. I'd read stories about prisoners who had done it—who had somehow willed themselves into death through the sheer power of their mind. But no matter how badly I wanted it to end, it couldn't. Not yet. Daxton would never let me die that easily, not when he still had the opportunity to inflict as much pain as he could.

"It's about time you woke up," said a voice on the other side of the metal door. "Much longer, and you'd be eligible for a coma."

I swallowed my sobs, causing a hard knot to form in my throat. "Who's there?" Even to my own ears, I didn't sound right, and for a second I wondered if they'd turned me back into my old self. The last time I'd been knocked out and brought to a strange place, I'd woken up looking exactly like Lila Hart—would they do the same in reverse?

No. I would never be that lucky. The only time I would ever be me again would be in death.

The screech of metal against metal filled my tiny cell, and the door swung open, revealing a woman with blue eyes and a long blond braid hanging over her shoulder. She wore a white uniform with silver trim, and she held a medical kit loosely in one hand. In the other, she balanced a tray of eggs, bacon, and toast, along with a porcelain bowl full of colorful fruit and a tall glass of orange juice.

"Breakfast was hours ago, but I thought you'd appreciate this more than a stale sandwich," she said, setting the tray on the nightstand with impeccable balance. Despite the wry smile tugging at her lips, her tone wasn't cheerful. If anything, it was strained, as if someone had told her to be nice even though she had no intention of doing so. "How do you feel?"

I blinked. "Where am I?"

"Answer me first." There—now I could hear the edge in her voice she'd been trying to hide. "How do you feel? Is your mouth dry? Do you have a headache? Are you in pain?"

"What do you think?" I said dully. "Best day of my life, right here."

"If you're not careful, it'll be the last," she warned.

My gaze flickered to the gun holstered to her hip. One bullet. That was all it would take, and this would be over. "Why don't I give you a free shot this time?" I said. "I won't even fight you. You'll get to tell all your friends you killed Lila Hart."

"Tempting." She offered me a strip of bacon. "Eat."

Reluctantly I took it from her and nibbled. In another life, I would have fought a dozen Shields for a chance to taste something this good. Today, it might as well have been made of chalk.

Still, it seemed to placate her, and she pulled a thermometer out of her medical kit and ran it across my forehead. It beeped, and she set it aside, seemingly satisfied. "Now, are you going to tell me how you feel, or am I going to have to resort to drastic measures?" she said. I shrugged.

"Headache. Sore throat. Dry mouth." *Empty hole where my heart used to be.* "Who are you?"

The corners of her mouth twitched with annoyance, as if she expected me to know exactly who she was. "Hannah Mercer. Head of Section X."

"Section X of what?"

Her thin eyebrow rose, and she looked at me as if I'd asked what one plus one was. "Section X of Elsewhere."

Elsewhere.

Elsewhere.

CAPTIVE

For a fraction of a second, the grief inside me gave way to a new emotion: pure, unadulterated panic. Daxton was going to hunt me down, just like he'd hunted Nina. I would die screaming and terrified in the woods like a wild animal, without dignity or any hope of escape.

But I would be with Benjy again. That single fact alone made the tightness in my chest ease, and I managed a strangled exhale. There was no dignity in death, only in life. Benjy had lived with dignity. I would, too.

Before I could ask how long it would be before I was dumped in the woods, the metal door opened again, this time revealing a tall man who looked eerily familiar. I blinked, my mind racing to place him. He was dressed in a white uniform nearly identical to Hannah's, though he wore a hat with his, the military style similar to the one that was part of the Shields' uniform. His dark hair was cropped short, and his face was long, with a strong jaw that reminded me of the IIs who sat on their stoops in the hot D.C. summers, chewing jerky and grumbling about their work on the docks.

One look at this man, though, and it was obvious he'd never done a day of hard labor in his life. I was sure I'd seen him before, but my mind was too muddled with shock to place him. Until—

Our eyes met, and a chill shot down my spine.

The picture in Daxton's file. He was the man on the left, the one who'd looked familiar then, too.

Mercer. The name rattled around my head until an image of an airstrip in the middle of the woods appeared in my mind. He was the official who had met Daxton and me the day I'd visited Elsewhere.

What the hell was he doing in my cell?

"Miss Hart," he said, his voice laced with admiration I

didn't expect. "It's a pleasure to see you again, though I do wish it were under different circumstances. I don't believe we've ever been formally introduced—I'm Captain Jonathan Mercer. I'm the one in charge here."

He paused, as if he was waiting for me to say something, but I stayed silent. I had nothing to say to him. I wasn't going to beg and plead for my life—I wasn't going to ask for his mercy. Neither would work, and with Benjy dead, I didn't want them to, either. Growing up in the Heights, the roughest part of D.C., had taught me how to survive, but seeing the deadened eyes of the IIs who were days away from working themselves to death and the smiles on the faces of the corpses who already had—that had only proven to me that sometimes, death was a relief.

I would be another smiling corpse. Whether that day would be today, tomorrow, a week from now—I didn't care, as long as it was soon.

Once it became clear I wasn't going to say anything, Mercer cleared his throat. "Right, then. Before we begin, I wanted to extend an invitation for you to stay with us at Mercer Manor once you're moved from the holding cell. I think you'll find it a far sight better than your other accommodations would be."

"I'm not staying here?" I said before I could stop myself.

Mercer looked down his blunted nose at me, and the corner of his lips twitched upward, as if he were pleased he'd made me talk. "No, no, this is just a holding and prep area. You'll be released once we're through."

"Through with what?" I said, but as I spoke, I noticed Hannah digging through the medical supplies bag she'd brought. "I'm fine," I added hastily. "I don't need anything."

"This isn't for your benefit," she said coolly, and when she straightened, she held a syringe and a strange tool that looked like the tip of a knife attached to a pen. "Stay still."

Her gloved hand ran over the back of my neck, and I jumped to my feet, scrambling into the corner of my cell. "Don't touch me," I said in a strangled voice, but it was already too late. Her blue eyes had widened a fraction of an inch, and though she quickly wiped her expression of any trace of surprise, I knew she'd felt the three ridges on the back of my neck, unlike the VII Lila should have had.

She knew I was Masked. She knew I wasn't a real Hart. I braced myself for her to blurt it out to her husband, but instead, as if nothing had happened, she rose smoothly and crossed the cell to join me.

"It won't hurt, I assure you," she said, setting her hand in the tender spot between my shoulder blades, exactly where Daxton's boot had nearly crushed my spine. Underneath my hair, her fingertips brushed against the back of my neck again, slower this time. Our eyes locked, and for several infinite seconds, she searched mine. I stared back, silently daring her to speak. She said nothing.

At last she guided me back to the cot and gathered my hair in a clip. Fighting would do me no good—she was close enough that I could grab her gun and shoot, but the memory of what had happened with Augusta was too fresh in my mind, and I couldn't bring myself to do it again, even if it meant the quick death I was hoping for. If I couldn't do that—the one thing that might save me from dying alone in the woods, hunted by the madman who ran the country— then in that moment, I decided I would do one last thing with the time I had left: figure out why she was keeping my secret from Mercer.

The pinprick in the center of my tattoo was nothing compared to the way Daxton had stabbed me with his needle, and I closed my eyes as the liquid she injected burned underneath my skin until the back of my neck was numb.

"What are you—" I began, but before I could finish, Hannah unclasped my necklace and handed it to Mercer. "Hey! That's mine."

"Wearing something like that here could get you killed," she said as he pocketed my lock pick. "I'm doing you a favor. Stop moving."

I gritted my teeth. "You *will* give that back to me," I said, but both Mercer and Hannah ignored me. I opened my mouth to protest again, but something pressed against the numbed skin, and my words caught in my throat as a warm trickle ran down my neck.

Blood.

Instinctively I reached behind me, but Hannah caught my hand in an iron grip. "I'm not done yet."

I yanked my hand away. "What are you doing to me?"

"Removing your rank," she said. A sickening burning smell filled the air, and at last Hannah rose from the cot. "There."

My fingers trembled as I brushed them against the back of my numb neck. The three ridges were still there, but two diagonal slashes of puckered skin cut through them now, forming a scarred X over the spot where my tattooed VII was.

I swallowed the lump that formed in my throat. It didn't matter what rank I was now—death wouldn't care if I was a III or a VII. Or an X. But the loss of that VII felt more real than this cell or the rough cot I sat on, or even the cold concrete beneath my feet. That VII had given me a chance to be someone—to matter in the world more than I ever would as a III. It had given me a purpose, and now all I had to show for it was a scarred X and a life that dwindled with every passing second.

The despair I'd been struggling to hold at bay crept through me, and I rapidly blinked back tears. I wouldn't let the Mercers see me cry, not over something this stupid. But it wasn't stupid, not to me—it was the death of any hope I'd ever had. And it was the crushing pain of reality setting in. This time, there would be no Benjy or Celia or Knox there to save me. This was it, and I'd never been more alone in my life.

"Change into this, and I'll take you to the manor," said Hannah, tossing a plastic-wrapped bundle of clothing into my lap. A shirt, underwear, bra, and jumpsuit—all the same stomach-churning shade of blood-red.

"I'm not going to the manor," I mumbled, slowly unwrapping it. Red had never been my color.

Hannah started to reply, but Mercer cut her off. "You will," he said, his kind voice taking on a note of authority. "Believe me, with your name and former rank, the last thing you want is to mingle with the general population."

"I don't care," I said. I'd been nothing special for nearly all of my life. With my VII gone, there was no point in pretending to be Lila anymore. "I'm not staying with you."

Mercer's forehead furrowed, causing a well-worn crease to form between his eyebrows. "You don't understand. The people out there, they aren't civilized like you and me. They're—"

"If she wants to stay with the other criminals, then we'll let her," said Hannah. "If she survives the night, she'll be knocking on our door by sunup."

Mercer's lips thinned, and he eyed me with concern, but I couldn't muster up the energy to care. "Very well. Bring her to Scotia—she'll keep an eye on her."

Hannah's expression darkened, but she nodded shortly. "Change," she ordered. "I'll be back in five minutes."

The foreboding edge to her voice almost made me change my mind. No matter how much I loathed them already, maybe staying with the Mercers was the smart thing to do.

They aren't civilized like you and me. Mercer's voice cut through my thoughts, and my resolve hardened. *They* were human. *They* were no less than the Mercers or the Harts or the Ministers of the Union. *They* probably wound up in this place doing nothing more than trying to survive a world that had cast them aside the moment they'd earned less than a IV. Not everyone here would be a III and below, but what laws would a IV or above ever need to break? The system was designed to cater to their every want and need, while IIs and IIIs had to fight just to stay alive.

Hannah and Mercer slipped out of the room, closing the metal door behind them. I took a shaky breath and touched the X scarred into my skin. No matter what rank the others in Section X had been before, we were all equal now.

The napkin Benjy had drawn for me was still in my pocket. That discovery nearly pushed me over the edge all over again, and it was only through a supreme act of willpower that I managed to change my clothes with dry eyes. I tucked the napkin in my pocket, careful to fold it along the same lines, and the slight padding was enough to make me feel I wasn't completely alone.

As promised, Hannah came to fetch me five minutes later, and she led me out the door and into the area beyond it. My cell wasn't located in the maze of concrete I'd expected. Instead, the short hallway outside my door opened up into a much wider and brighter corridor. I trudged after Hannah, my head down as I memorized the path she was taking.

"This building is the holding area," she said as we turned a sharp corner. "All citizens of Elsewhere are processed here, and if you decide you don't want to play by the rules, this is where you'll end up for however long I deem fit."

"What are the rules?" I said as we passed through the short hallway filled with nondescript doors. There were no frills or flourishes in this place—it was exactly what it needed to be, nothing more. Even my bare-bones group home in the Heights had had more soul.

"Do whatever I tell you," said Hannah shortly. "Don't piss the guards off. And whatever you do, don't try to escape. No one ever has, and no one ever will. Be respectful, be obedient, and you might just live longer than you think you will."

"And if I'm not interested in a long life expectancy?" I said before I could stop myself. Hannah eyed me, and her hand crept toward the weapon holstered to her hip.

"Then I'm sure you'll find a way to get what you want soon enough. Through here."

She passed her wrist over a sensor on the wall, and a heavy metal door slid open, revealing a flood of sunshine. I squinted, but I didn't dare shield my eyes. We stood in a snow-covered yard with two guards on either side of the metal door, holding rifles and standing at attention. As soon as my eyes adjusted, I looked around, taking in Section X of Elsewhere.

It also wasn't the destitute collection of cramped jails and cells I'd thought it would be. Instead it looked almost like a small town, with a main road that ran farther than I could see. The gray buildings were shoved together, but unlike the cluttered feeling of the Heights, every inch of this place seemed to have a purpose. In the distance, an impossibly high chain-link fence rose above the slanted roofs, and I spotted more uniformed guards on a raised walkway surrounding the perimeter, guns in hand.

Every half block or so, a smaller street crossed the main road, and I spotted several men in orange jumpsuits walking down the road carrying metal crates. Beyond them, a collection of women in red jumpsuits like mine lined up at the door of a building, each wearing a bulky khaki jacket that didn't look like anything that would have ever graced Lila Hart's wardrobe. None of them were shivering, though.

Guards stood stationed at the entrance to many of the gray buildings, but none so much as glanced at us as Hannah led me down the street. Despite the foot of snow on the ground, someone had cleared the road, and chunks of salt crunched underneath my boots. The men in orange headed toward us, but instead of passing by, they crossed to the other side of the road, giving Hannah and me more space than we needed.

"Are those people prisoners?" I said.

"We prefer the term *citizen*," said Hannah, her hand still lingering on her gun. "But, yes, they were either born in Elsewhere or arrested and sent to us. Everyone has a role to play here, and should you choose to cooperate, you can live a decent life. It isn't as hopeless as you think."

My only experience with Elsewhere had been a forest where Daxton had hunted down people for sport—not a village where people lived and worked like they did in society. "So, if you get in trouble here, that's when the VIs and VIIs get to hunt you?"

Hannah arched an eyebrow so high that it disappeared beneath her hat. "Some prove to be unfit for any society, even one as regimented as ours. However, we make every effort to give each of our citizens a chance at rehabilitation. No matter what you think of us, Lila, we're not barbarians."

I bit back a sharp retort. As far as I saw it, anyone who allowed another human being to be hunted like a wild animal lost any opportunity they had to be considered civilized.

She led me through the snow and salt at a brisk pace, and I had to nearly trot to keep up. The streets formed a grid—easy to remember and impossible to tell apart with the same gray buildings again and again. Only two stood out: a looming three-story building toward the center of the section, only a few places down from the holding area we'd left, and a pristine white manor in the distance, near one of the corners.

"Mercer Manor," said Hannah, nodding to the property. "Should you change your mind about living among the general population, my husband insists you're welcome to stay with us instead."

"But you'd rather I not."

"I don't care what you do, as long as you behave."

I itched to ask why she hadn't immediately told her husband I'd been Masked, but the words turned to sawdust on my tongue. I didn't know the value of my secret here, and the thought of trusting her with it made my insides churn. I had no choice, though, and in the meantime, I wouldn't give her a reason to use it against me.

She led me down another street, and at last she stopped in front of a two-story building with a *23* stenciled and spray-painted near the door. There were no windows, only endless gray stone, and Hannah opened the door delicately, as if she were afraid it was infected with some flesh-eating bacteria.

"Your new home," she said with a sniff. "The other girls will help you find a bunk. Once you're settled, ask for Isabel Scotia. She'll find you a welcome kit, which will have your basic necessities. If you want anything more, you're going to have to earn it."

I didn't want to know what the Mercers did and didn't consider to be basic necessities. At this rate, I'd be lucky if I got a toothbrush.

"If you change your mind, you know where the manor is," she said, but once again, her tone made it perfectly clear that if I were smart, I'd stay as far away from her home as possible.

I stepped inside the bunkhouse, certain that whatever waited for me inside was infinitely better than standing there in increasingly uncomfortable silence with Hannah. She let the door spring closed behind me, and the sharp rap of wood against rock made me jump.

It took a moment for my eyes to adjust to the dim light. Like the streets of Section X, everything in here was gray. Two rows of bunk beds covered in gray blankets were packed tightly together, leaving a narrow aisle running down the center of the room. At first glance, it looked as if there was no space between the beds at all, but as I moved closer, I noticed the few inches that separated them. If I wanted to get into one of the beds, I'd have to climb into it from the end.

On the other side of the door was a tiny room barely bigger than the holding cells, but it had some semblance of privacy. Beyond that was another door, and though it was only cracked open, I spotted gray tile. A bathroom. At least I wouldn't have to trudge into the cold to pee.

Daylight flooded the bunkhouse again, and behind me, a voice drawled, "Look what we have here."

I whirled around. Standing in the doorway and blocking my only exit was a pack of four girls, each wearing the same red jumpsuit. They seemed like they were around my age—seventeen, eighteen at the most, but they looked rough in a way that only the older IIs in the hardest parts of D.C. did. Their skin was already showing signs of aging from being underneath the sun all day, and their eyes were hardened and devoid of hope. Instead, all I saw was malicious glee, and the dark-haired girl at the front of the pack—the one who'd spoken—stepped forward.

"Mercer told us to expect a very *special* guest," she said in an accent I didn't recognize. "He never said you were a Hart."

The girls shifted toward me, effectively surrounding me in the doorway. I'd dealt with plenty of territorial girls growing up in a group home, but with all four of them eyeing me like I was their ticket home, this would be anything but a fair fight.

"*Was* a Hart," I corrected calmly. "Not anymore."

The leader smirked, showing off her chipped front tooth. "No, not anymore," she agreed, and without warning, her fist flew out, connecting squarely with my jaw. "Welcome to Elsewhere, bitch."

VI

SCOTIA

All four girls descended on me, punching and scratching and pinching every square inch of me they could find. On my way down, my head hit the doorway with a resounding *crack,* and for a split second, everything went white.

I lay there motionless as the leader pummeled the air out of my lungs, leaving me wheezing. I didn't fight back. It wouldn't help, and besides, maybe these girls would do what Daxton and Knox and the Mercers refused to—maybe they would kill me, and this all would end. Despite the pain, relief flooded through me. It wasn't the easiest way to go, but at least I'd be going.

Suddenly a shout echoed through the bunk, and the leader cried out. She flew backward, and with quick succession, the other three joined her on the other side of the door, each cursing in protest. One girl held the left side of her face, and even with my blurred vision, I could see a red mark the shape of a boot print forming on her cheek.

"How many times do I have to tell you not to fight in my bunk?" growled a new voice. I squinted upward. Looming over me was a tall, thin woman with dark skin and sleek hair pulled back into a ponytail. She glowered at the girls, and the look on her face would've made Daxton piss himself. "You're already on probation, Maya. You want the cage, too?"

"I don't want another snitch wandering around," the leader—Maya—spat, though there was a quiver of fear in her voice. "We've got enough to worry about without a Hart lording over us."

"Doesn't look like she'll be lording over anyone anytime soon." The woman bent over me. Our eyes met, and I saw a spark of fury that made me wish Maya and her friends had knocked me out. "Get up."

My head pounded, and my lungs still struggled to suck in oxygen, but I shakily sat up. The bunk spun around me, and I gritted my teeth, hating myself for showing any sign of weakness. But what was the worst they could do? Kill me?

"You listen up, bitch," said Maya, and she took a menacing step closer. "You're dead. Your heart might think it's still beating, but it'll find out soon enough what we do to snitches in this place."

"And you're about to find out what I do to bitches who don't listen to me," said the woman behind me in a dangerously quiet voice. "Get out of here, Maya, before I change my mind about letting you."

I expected Maya to protest or challenge her—anything other than walk away. But that was exactly what she did, cursing and sputtering to herself while her friends followed. Once they were gone, I closed my eyes and let my pounding head lull forward.

"Should've let them kill me," I muttered.

"Don't worry, you'll be dead soon enough." She grabbed my arms, hoisting me to my feet with impossible strength. I stumbled, but she didn't let go until I was steady. "You always so good at making friends?"

"I don't think they like my face," I said, eyeing her. She was nearly half a foot taller than me, and the sleeves of her red jumpsuit were tied around her waist, showing off a black tank top underneath. Tattoos decorated her bare arms, which were sinewy and more muscular than most Shields', and the look in her eyes alone could've reduced a grown man to tears. No wonder those girls had taken off.

"You'll find most people around here have a problem with the Harts," she said, eyeing me right back. "Don't accept any supposed 'special privileges.' Don't eat anything anyone gives you. If someone tells you to do something that doesn't sound right, check with me first. Everyone here's interested in one thing and one thing only, and that's protecting their own necks, which almost always means throwing someone else into the line of fire. I'm the only real friend you'll ever have in this place, so do yourself a favor and don't piss me off. Got it?"

I nodded numbly, and the edges of my vision started to darken. "I need to sit down."

"Your bunk's here." She pointed to the bottom bunk closest to the door. At least I wouldn't have to climb through the foot of the bed like everyone else. "I'm in this room right here. Anyone gives you shit, you come find me, got it?"

I eased down onto the thin mattress. It squeaked underneath me, and when I tugged the blanket aside, I spotted a strange brown stain that looked like someone had only half bothered to scrub it. Perfect. "I'm not a snitch."

"You're a Hart. That's infinitely worse." She crossed her arms. "Get some rest. If anything feels broken, I'll take you to the infirmary later."

She spoke drily, without a hint of any real concern for me.

Not that I expected her to care. The only person who ever had was dead. "I'm fine. Are you Isabel Scotia?"

"Just Scotia," she said. "Call me Isabel, and I'll give you another black eye. Dinner's in a couple hours, and I don't care how sick you feel. The last thing you want to do here is voluntarily miss a meal."

With that, she turned on her heel and disappeared into the tiny bedroom across from my bunk, pulling the curtain shut behind her. I took a deep breath, wincing as my ribs protested, and I let it out slowly. So this was it, then. This was the rest of my life. Sleeping on a stained mattress across from a woman who looked like she'd enjoy ripping me to shreds, while every person I met wanted to see my head on a stake. I swallowed the lump in my throat and closed my eyes. It wouldn't be any better when I woke up, but maybe I'd get lucky and Maya would return, and I wouldn't have to wake up at all.

As I rested, my head filled with dreams of Benjy. I could see his smile, feel his fingers laced through mine, and the scent of his soap drifted toward me, bringing me back to the happiest moments of my life. Ones I would never see again. With his name on my lips, I opened my eyes, and a pair of brown ones stared back at me.

"She's awake," whispered a girl with dark hair and freckles, and behind her, several others whispered excitedly. I blinked and sat up, rubbing the sleep from my eyes.

More than a dozen girls surrounded my bunk, each one staring directly at me. Some looked like they were my age; others looked several years older, but none was more than twenty-five. Most had a hardened look to them, the same one Maya and her friends wore—all of whom were conspicuously absent. But the girls surrounding the bed stared at me curiously instead of maliciously, as if I were some zoo animal on display rather than a member of the family that was likely responsible for where they were now.

It was better than trying to rip my throat out. Probably. But it was still unnerving.

The moment I sat up, several of them scattered, but a few brave ones stuck around, each vying for a better position. The girl closest to me, the one with wide brown eyes, leaned in until I could see the green that ringed her irises.

"You're Lila Hart," she said. "I'm Noelle. Did you just get here?"

I nodded, eyeing the others suspiciously. No matter how friendly anyone seemed, I couldn't forget that this was all a game of survival, and I was in last place. "Are you going to kill me?"

"Kill you?" said Noelle. "Why would we want to kill you? You can help us."

I frowned. "Help you?"

All at once, the remaining girls started to speak, their words and voices jumbling together in my muddled mind until I couldn't tell one from the other.

"—pardon—"

"—of course I was framed, how would I possibly—"

"—want to go home—"

"Enough," snapped a sharp voice that rose above the rest. Scotia stood behind them in her doorway, her arms crossed and her expression stony. "You see her suit? What color is it?"

"Red?" said one of the girls.

"Very good, Chelsea. And what does that tell you?"

Noelle piped up, her brown eyes still locked on mine. "She's one of us now. She can't get any of us pardoned, else she'd get herself pardoned, and she wouldn't be here at all."

"Look at that," said Scotia. "One of you still has a brain."

With the sudden revelation that I wasn't their golden ticket out of there, the girls grumbled and dispersed, leaving me alone. Except Noelle.

Now that she didn't have any competition, she perched on the edge of my mattress, her gaze never wavering from mine. "Why are you here?"

"Don't you have somewhere to be, Noelle?" said Scotia, who was still framed in the doorway. Noelle shrugged.

"Probably, but I'm happy here."

Scotia looked at me, a question in her stare, and I shrugged, too. Noelle seemed harmless, even if the way she looked at me made me feel like I was being tested. I'd had more than my fair share of tests throughout my life, thank you very much. I didn't need another one at the end of it.

"Fine," said Scotia. "Make sure she gets dinner. And no wandering off."

She disappeared into her separate room, and Noelle inched closer to me. "So why are you here?" she repeated in a hushed voice as if she were afraid someone would overhear. Everyone around us seemed to be doing their own thing, but with how close the bunks were, there was no privacy in this place. And the girls close enough to listen had their heads tilted toward us as they remained strangely silent.

"I pissed off the wrong people," I said shortly. "I take it you did, too."

"Me?" Noelle's eyes widened. "Oh—no, I was an Extra. My parents already had one baby, and they couldn't pay the fines for me, so here I am. That's what happens to most of us, you know."

"I know what happens to Extras," I said, but in truth, I'd never let myself think too much about what my life would've been like if my parents hadn't been able to pay the fines to keep me out of Elsewhere. Before, when I'd thought this place was some kind of paradise where those in overcrowded cities were sent, there was nothing malicious about it, just mysterious. But now that I knew what Elsewhere was—did the Harts really care so little for their own people?

Before she'd died, Augusta had lectured me on why things were the way they were. Overpopulation, a lack of resources to feed and shelter everyone—but now that I was here, now that I knew what Elsewhere was, it didn't seem like justification. It seemed like an excuse.

"So—what, you've never been outside Elsewhere?" I said, wincing as I shifted. My ribs were definitely bruised, but nothing felt broken. Noelle helped me up, and I mumbled my thanks.

"Never," she said. "I've always wanted to, you know—I've heard about things like cities and beaches from the other girls, and it all seems so *magical*. I don't know why anyone would misbehave and risk winding up here in the first place."

I opened my mouth to tell her how the government starved the IIs, barely giving them enough to eat—how the Shields patrolled the streets, looking for even the most innocent violations. How they were paid per violation they reported, and sometimes, if it were a particularly bad day, they'd shoot us or arrest us just because they didn't like the way we looked at them. But the wistful gaze on Noelle's face made the words die on my tongue. Let her have her fantasy. I wouldn't gain anything by ruining it.

Besides, compared to this place, maybe the real world *was* a magical fantasy land full of hopes and dreams and possibilities. At least to people like Noelle, who had never known anything more than the gray walls of Elsewhere.

"They're stupid," I said in agreement, gently brushing my

fingertips against my left eye. It was puffy and tender to the touch, and I didn't want to know what it looked like. It was a minor miracle I was even recognizable as human right now, let alone as Lila Hart.

"Oh, your eye—stay here," said Noelle, and she jumped up and darted into the dingy bathroom. While the sounds of running water filtered into the bunk, I glanced at the other girls uneasily. Most of them stared at me, not even pretending to do anything else anymore.

"If anyone wants to finish the job, be my guest," I said. Nearly all of the two dozen girls looked away, and several of them formed smaller groups and hurried out into the cold, not daring to look at me as they passed my bunk. I frowned. What had I said?

It didn't matter. In a place like Elsewhere, there were a million ways to die. I would find one eventually.

By the time Noelle returned a minute later, the room had all but cleared out. She giggled and gently pressed an ice-cold rag against my swollen eye. "It's not you, you know. Well, it might be, but you seem really nice. I don't think they're scared of you."

"Then who are they scared of?" I said, wincing and taking the rag from her. The cold felt good, even if the pressure made my temple ache.

Noelle glanced toward Scotia's room and licked her lips nervously. "You have to be careful what you say around here and who you upset. Some people don't really care anymore, but others—" She hesitated and lowered her voice, even though we were practically alone. "If you can get on the Mercers' good side, it's a really nice gig. But usually it takes ratting other people out and showing the guards you're more loyal to them than the other citizens."

"You mean snitching," I said, eyeing Scotia's doorway. It didn't take a genius to put two and two together. Why else did Scotia have her own room and Mercer's admiration?

Noelle nodded, her eyes widening. "Anytime we do something wrong, the Mercers find out right away. So you have to be careful. There are lots of people who want to be a guard one day—"

"You can do that?" I said.

"Of course." Noelle blinked at me as if I'd just asked if snow was cold. "How do you think we get guards? Most of them were born Extras or arrested, and they snitched their way to the top. There are rumors—"

She stopped herself, but while she focused on her hands, the way she didn't change the subject made it obvious she wanted me to ask. So, with an inward sigh, I said, "Rumors about what?"

She immediately brightened and leaned in closer. "There are rumors even Hannah Mercer was one of us," she whispered, touching the back of her neck and turning around enough for me to get a good view.

A scarred X ran through her otherwise unmarred skin. So she hadn't been lying—as an Extra, she'd never taken the test that determined what a citizen was worth, and she had never been anything but an X of Elsewhere.

"But if Hannah was a prisoner, then how did she work her way up to the top?" I said, baffled. I could buy someone snitching their way toward being a guard. But the head of an entire section?

"How do you think?" Noelle gave me a meaningful look.

"Being a snitch isn't the only way to get treated nice here. It's against the rules to have any kind of relationship with the guards, but if someone important enough likes you…"

She trailed off, and I didn't need her to paint me a picture. Hannah had gotten *close* with someone important.

"Who?" I said, lowering my voice. "Mercer?"

Noelle shook her head. "That's what everyone thinks, and maybe it's true, but Mercer was only promoted to the Head of Elsewhere when he married Hannah last year." She glanced over her shoulder toward Scotia's room again, then leaned in so close that I could feel her warm breath against my ear. "No one talks about it anymore, but back when I was little, everyone used to say that Hannah had an affair with the Prime Minister himself."

I blinked. "Daxton? You mean Hannah—"

"Don't you two have somewhere to be?" Scotia's voice cracked through the air, and even though I couldn't see her behind the curtain, I knew she'd been listening to every word.

Noelle turned red. "We were just leaving." She grabbed my arm and pulled me out of bed, seemingly unconcerned about the fact that just sitting up was enough to make me groan, let alone standing. "Come on. Are you hungry? It's cheeseburger night."

"Cheeseburgers?" My stomach growled, but the thought of red meat only made me remember Lila's birthday party the night before. And with that flood of memories came the image of Benjy's smiling face and the picture he'd drawn for me of our future together—a future we'd never have now.

Nausea replaced the hollow feeling in my stomach, and I swayed on my feet. "I'm not hungry."

Noelle looped her arm in mine. "I know it's hard here, especially at first, but you'll get used to it. If you don't want to eat, that's okay, but at least let me show you around."

I started to say Hannah had already done that, but Noelle dragged me out of the bunk before I could form the words. It was strange—when Benjy's life had been in danger, used by Augusta as a bargaining chip to ensure my behavior, I'd imagined what it would be like to lose him. Not by choice, but it had been impossible to ignore that ocean of fear and darkness lingering in front of me, stripped of all happiness and hope. I'd thought it would be quicksand, the way it had been when his death had first hit me. I'd thought I would go under, and there would never be anything more than that all-encompassing grief.

But I hadn't drowned. I was still breathing. I was still moving, and no matter how badly I wanted it all to end, life didn't work that way. Not without a bullet or a broken neck. I was floating over that grief, skimming it with the tips of my toes, always aware of it beneath me and always in danger of falling. As Noelle led me down the snowy street, chattering on about what each day was like in this place, I focused on each breath I took. In and out, in and out, until only the crunch underneath my boots felt real anymore.

I'd never imagined it, but there was life after Benjy. And in a way, it was fitting that it was entirely new and foreign—at least now I wouldn't have to look at anything familiar and pretend it was still the same.

Noelle didn't seem to notice that I'd tuned her out, or maybe she didn't care. We reached a large dingy building a few blocks from the bunker and a quarter mile from the fence. The only difference between the dining hall and the rest of the makeshift town was the smell wafting from the kitchens. It reminded me sharply of the market Benjy and I used to frequent—sizzling meats, baked bread, even the rich aroma of coffee. My stomach flip-flopped, torn between hunger and that sick knot of despair.

We stood in a winding line with dozens of others, and when it was our turn to order, Noelle pointed to a pair of cheeseburgers wrapped in foil. The cook—also dressed in red, and clearly another citizen—tossed them onto our trays, and we continued down the serving line, Noelle mindlessly piling my plate with limp, gray vegetables, something yellow that might have been fruit once upon a time, and a brownie that looked hard enough to break a window. Before becoming a Hart, I'd never been picky about food, but apparently they'd stolen that from me, too.

"Why does it smell so good and look so awful?" I said as Noelle led me through the rows of tables, most already taken by others wearing red and orange jumpsuits.

"They make the guards' food here, too," she said brightly, seemingly not at all bothered by this. "Sometimes, if they make too much of it, we get it for the next meal. The corn bread's really good. You just have to be careful when you're biting into it, else it could break your teeth."

She sat down at an empty table in the corner of the room. Nearby, a handful of old men and women ate together quietly. Their hair was gray, their skin turned to leather in the sun, and their bodies curled in on themselves as if they'd spent their entire lives leaning over. I stared. Other than Augusta Hart, they were the oldest people I'd ever seen in my life.

"You should eat before it gets cold," said Noelle. She had already taken three massive bites of her burger. Reluctantly I unwrapped mine and stared at the first cheeseburger I'd been allowed in months.

So this was what it took to have red meat, or whatever

passed for it in Elsewhere. Would last night have turned out differently if I hadn't argued with Knox over those stupid puff pastries? Would he have still turned on Benjy when he found out about the file? Would I have gone after them at all?

I took a bite. It tasted nothing like real meat, and only months of eating food I hated prevented me from spitting it out. Chewing slowly, I forced myself to swallow it, then set the rest of the cheeseburger down. I could put starving to death back on the list after all.

Noelle patted my hand sympathetically, and she pushed her stale brownie toward me. "Here, you can have mine."

"Thanks," I mumbled, and I broke off a corner. It was crunchy, but still edible, and though my stomach protested, I managed to keep it down without gagging. The smell of freshly baked bread and seasoned steak attacked my senses, and I began to breathe through my mouth. Of course they cooked the better meals where the prisoners could smell it. Why waste such a perfect opportunity to torture them?

Us, I reminded myself silently. I was one of them now.

My eyes watered, and my breaths came in short gasps. Benjy was dead. I was Elsewhere. Nothing would ever be the same again, and I was griping about the food. I bit my lip, fighting the urge to cry, but my cheeks grew hot. Hastily I rubbed my eyes. I wouldn't break down in front of everyone like this. I couldn't let them think I was weak. One wrong move, and—

"Hey," said Noelle softly, and she set her hand over mine again. Her kindness only made a fresh wave of hopelessness wash over me, and I laced my fingers through hers and squeezed.

"I—I'm sorry—" I began, but I hiccupped before I could say anything more. Noelle handed me a rough napkin, and I dabbed my cheeks, flinching. They were still sore from Maya and her friends.

"No, I'm the one who's sorry," said Noelle. "I shouldn't have dragged you to dinner if you weren't hungry. I just thought..." She hesitated. "I just thought if you saw that it isn't so bad here, you wouldn't be so afraid. It isn't all hopeless."

"Isn't it?" I said, unable to keep the bitterness from my cracking voice. "What's the point to all this? You sleep. You eat shit. You work and do whatever they tell you, and then what? You get to do it all over again the next day? You get to live as long as they feel like?" I shook my head. Tears flowed freely down my cheeks now, and I caught several people staring at us, but I didn't care anymore. "You don't understand. This is all you've ever known. This isn't a real life. You don't get to—to have hobbies or fall in love or have a family or—or any of that. We're slaves. We don't matter to anyone anymore."

Noelle stared at me, her eyes wide and her face drained of all color. "I matter," she squeaked. "You matter, too. We're all a family here—you just arrived, so you can't see it yet, but you will. We love each other. We look out for each other. And—and I like to read," she added. "We have a whole library, and they let you check books out if you're good. And—and some people like to build things, or draw, or cook. Don't you like to do any of those things?"

I couldn't answer her even if I'd wanted to. My throat closed up, and I fought to breathe as my vision went blurry from the tears. It was over. It was all over. I hadn't just lost Benjy—I'd lost everything.

Noelle stood and took my hand. "Come on," she said again, and she pulled me to my feet and dragged me out of the dining hall. I stumbled after her, struggling to pull myself together, but the quicksand had me now, and I didn't know how to find the surface.

The cold air hit my lungs like a fist to my gut, and I gasped, bending over in the middle of the street and dry heaving. Only that half-digested bite of burger and brownie came up, but my stomach tried, again and again and again, until I was a sobbing mess.

Noelle rubbed circles between my shoulders and pulled my hair back expertly, as if she'd done this a thousand times before. I couldn't stand to think about how many girls had come before me—how many had relied upon her expertise of this place before they adjusted to their new lives. If they adjusted at all.

"I have an idea," she said once I'd straightened. My knees felt weak, and suddenly the cold cut through my jumpsuit, making me painfully aware of the fact that I'd forgotten my coat. "I can trust you, Lila, can't I?"

There was a strange tone in her voice—a question underneath her words I didn't completely understand. Trust seemed like such a foreign concept in this place that for a long moment, I stared at her, wondering if I was as much of a question mark to her as she was to me.

Or maybe, despite growing up in Elsewhere, she knew my face. Maybe she, like so many others, thought they knew Lila Hart because they'd spent their lives reading stories of her exploits and hearing her name attached to rumors they took as fact. Even here, in hell, I couldn't escape Lila. Hannah knew I'd been Masked, and because of that, the truth was bound to come out eventually. But until it did, if being Lila still gave me an edge—if it made Scotia want to protect me, Mercer want to shield me from the worst this place had to offer, and if it made Noelle trust me with her secrets—then I was an idiot not to play along.

"You can trust me," I said, my voice rough.

Noelle beamed and took my shaking hand. "Then come on," she said. "We don't have much time."

VII

FIGHT

Noelle led me through a maze of streets and alleys, around gray buildings that blended together and seemed to turn into one as dusk began to fall. Her grip on my wrist was bruising, but I didn't protest, and she didn't bother letting go.

We neared a spot in the wire fence between two guard towers, and my heart began to race. On the other side was another set of gray buildings identical to ours, with only the fence to mark the boundary between them. Before we reached it, however, she pulled me against a wall, hidden in the shadows of the setting sun. We crouched down, and she took my freezing hands between hers, rubbing them to warm them up.

"I was raised on that side of the fence," she said, nodding beyond the border. "I thought I was going to live there forever. That's what usually happens—once you're assigned a section, it never changes. That's Section J," she added. "Most Sections are separated by what you're there for. There are a few of them—M and P are the worst—that are for violent criminals. Section J is designed for Extras. There's a nursery for babies, and there's even a school we get to go to for a few years before we start work."

She smiled as she spoke, her expression lighting up as if she were talking about some kind of fairy tale. But the happiest moments of her life had been spent inside that chain-link fence, among gray buildings and people who never knew what the real world was like. Maybe for Extras raised here, it *was* a fairy tale. Maybe their ignorance of the possibilities that lay beyond Elsewhere gave them a chance to be happy.

"What's Section X for?" I said thickly, forcing my heavy tongue to form the words.

"The special cases handpicked by the Mercers," said Noelle. "The ones they want to keep a close eye on. It could be for any reason—some of us become guards, and some of us…" She hesitated. "The turnover's really fast. Most people aren't here for more than a few years."

"What happens to—" I began, but before I could finish, Noelle held up her hand, and I fell silent.

Near the edge of the fence, a silhouette of a man appeared. I ducked down, making myself as small as possible in the darkness. Something long and thin rested over his shoulder, and when he passed over a light, I could make out the barrel of a rifle.

Instead of shrinking into the shadows with me, Noelle stood, a gleeful smile on her face. She headed toward the fence, all but skipping, and when I tried to make a last-ditch effort to grab her ankle, all I caught was air.

"Noelle!" I whispered. "He's a guard!"

She either didn't hear me or didn't care. She paused a few feet from the fence, glancing around to make sure no one was watching, and then stepped up to greet him.

I expected the guard to warn her off—or worse, point his

rifle at her and take a shot—but instead, his own stiff posture relaxed, and even from several yards away, I could see a goofy grin spread across his face.

Their fingers snaked through the wire, intertwining with one another, and despite the fence that stood between them, he ducked his head to kiss her between the wires. I held my breath. Only an hour before, Noelle had told me how a relationship between a prisoner and a guard was against the rules—and breaking the rules in a place like Elsewhere meant death. Yet here she was, kissing him in front of me, in plain sight of anyone who happened to be looking their way.

At last they broke apart, and Noelle waved me over. I stood cautiously and looked around, joining them only when I was sure no one was watching.

"Are you crazy?" I whispered. "Anyone can see you out here."

"The guards change shifts right now," said Noelle, still beaming. "No one's in the towers."

"And they won't be for another ten minutes," said the man. He was only a few inches taller than me, and up close, it was obvious he was only a couple years older, too. He still had a baby face, and his wavy brown hair flopped in his eyes despite the hat he wore, but he eyed me warily. "Noelle, are you sure...?"

"I'm not going to snitch on you," I said before he could finish that sentence. Seeing them standing there, as close as they could with the fence between them—it tugged at something inside me, and my eyes threatened to well up all over again. That was exactly what life with Benjy had been like for the past three months, ever since I'd been Masked as Lila. Close enough to touch. Close enough to kiss. But never truly together. "I'm Lila Hart."

"I know you are," he said, a hint of protectiveness in his voice. His fingers tightened around Noelle's. "I'm Elliott."

"He's my boyfriend," said Noelle, apparently oblivious to the fact that he didn't trust me nearly as much as she did. "We've been together for our whole lives."

Elliott glanced at me nervously. "You swear you're not a snitch?"

"I'm not stupid," I said. "You're the one holding the gun, not me."

"She's my friend," added Noelle as if that settled it. He pursed his lips, stroking her knuckles with his thumb.

"Not our *whole* lives," he said at last, his shoulders slumping. "Just since we were ten."

I saw this for what it was—as much of a seal of approval as I was going to get from him, at least for now. I smiled slightly. "That's a long time," I managed, my throat threatening to close up again. Was this what my life with Benjy would have been if we'd both been sent here instead?

"We grew up together in Section J before he was promoted," said Noelle, her eyes shining as she gazed up at him. "He's my best friend."

I turned away briefly, swallowing hard and struggling to keep it together. "Yeah?" I said, my voice breaking. "And now..."

"And now we're waiting for Noelle's placement to be approved." There was an edge to Elliott's words, as if he were daring me to challenge him. "She's been in Section X for months. It should be coming through any day now."

"Any day," said Noelle blissfully. "And then we'll get to be together."

They kissed again, and everything I'd been struggling to hold back threatened to rear up once more. "I'll just be..."

I trailed off, not bothering to finish. Instead I trudged back into the dark alleyway, turning away as they spoke in hushed tones. Hot tears streamed down my cheeks, and I gulped in the cold air, fighting to keep my head above the quicksand. Not here. Not like this.

For one horrible moment, I considered blackmailing Elliott into using his gun. It would be easy—threaten to tell the Mercers about him and Noelle if he didn't do it. If he shot me in the back of the head, it would be quick and painless for both of us. I wouldn't have to watch him pull the trigger, and he wouldn't have to look me in the eyes while he did it. No one would ever have to know why.

But when I glanced over my shoulder and saw him murmuring into Noelle's ear, the idea died within me. I couldn't do that to him, not when he and Noelle were so close to their own happiness. I would find another way to die.

In the meantime, I couldn't watch them. Shoving my numb hands into the pockets of my jumpsuit, I began to trudge back toward the center of the compound, hoping against hope I'd spot someone or someplace I recognized.

I didn't make it more than a few dozen feet before an air horn went off, echoing throughout the entire section.

"Lila!" cried Noelle, and I turned around. Elliott had disappeared, and she ran toward me, her footsteps echoing between the buildings. "Come on, we can't be late."

"Late for what?" I said. She looped her arm in mine and once again dragged me down another street, toward the center of the gray buildings.

"When the warning goes off, we have to go," she said. A handful of men and women emerged from nearby buildings, and we followed them.

"Go where?" I said, but she shook her head and didn't respond. Even more citizens appeared, joining us until a crowd formed. We all seemed to be heading in the same direction, but no one said a word about what was happening. Even Noelle was strangely silent, her face pale and her nails digging into my arm.

Another horn went off two minutes later, and Noelle quickened her pace. I had to all but trot to keep up with her as we wove in between the others. A handful of women toward the front of our group chattered, and their voices carried as we neared them.

"—couldn't be Darcy. They only took her this morning," said one woman, her arm wrapped around the shoulders of another.

"You know damn well that doesn't matter," said the second woman in a cracked voice. Her eyes were red and puffy. "Last month, when they took Monica, she was in the cage hours later."

"The cage?" I said to Noelle. "What are they talking about?"

Her mouth formed a thin line. "That," she said, nodding toward a domed structure on a raised platform a few hundred feet in front of us.

In the middle of Washington D.C., it could've sat on the side of the street and been considered art. But in a place as gray and utilitarian as Elsewhere, everything had a purpose. As we moved closer and I got a better look, a sick feeling settled in the pit of my stomach, and suddenly I understood what everyone was talking about.

It was a human-sized cage. Guards surrounded the base of the platform, each holding a rifle identical to Elliott's, and their frowns seemed set in stone. Noelle grabbed my hand and pushed our way to the front of the crowd, and we leaned against the cold metal barricade that kept us a good ten feet from the cage itself. I searched for any sign of a door either on the base or the cage that rose above our heads, giving everyone in the surrounding crowd a view, but I couldn't spot anything.

"What's happening?" I said. Noelle found my hand and clutched it, smashing my cold fingers together. I squeezed back.

"Detention," she said, her voice breaking. I shut my mouth. Somehow I doubted the word meant the same thing here as it did back in the D.C. educational system.

A third and final horn went off from the top of the cage, and I winced. The crowd went silent, and everyone around me seemed to be holding their breath.

The screech of metal against rusted metal echoed through the square, and two figures rose from either end of the cage. The girl nearest me had dark hair that hung in a messy braid, and it was only when she glanced around that I saw her face.

"Maya?" I said, stunned. The girl who had attacked me—the one directly responsible for my swollen eye. And once I placed her, I recognized the other girl in the cage, too: one of her friends who had also jumped me. "But—I don't understand. What's happening?"

"No one fights on my turf and gets away with it," said a voice beside me, and I jumped. Scotia stood at my elbow, and without looking at me, she draped a heavy jacket over my shoulders. "You forgot something."

I let go of Noelle's hand, trembling as I pulled my arms through the sleeves. The rough fabric was cold, but it was better than the thin jumpsuit alone. "What do you mean? What are they doing up there?"

"It's our punishment when we're caught breaking the rules," said Noelle softly, her eyes rimmed with red as she looked up at Maya and her friend, who now stared at each other as if they were waiting for something. "Only one comes out alive."

My head snapped up. "What?"

"You heard her," said Scotia. "Maya knew the rules, and she thought she could get away with it. Now she has a choice—kill Poppy, or let Poppy kill her."

Horror filled me from the inside out, and what little I'd eaten churned in my stomach. "You have to stop this," I said, my voice rising as I looked at Scotia. "Tell the guards to let them go."

Scotia snorted. "You're dumber than you look, aren't you? Even if I had that kind of power, those girls tried to kill you. Mercer was never going to let them off with a warning."

She nodded at a rooftop on the other side of the cage. Through the bars I noticed Mercer, his hands set on a railing as he gazed down at the girls in the cage. Behind him, I spotted Hannah's blond braid as she leaned over to speak to someone I couldn't see.

"You have ten seconds to begin," boomed Mercer. All traces of friendliness were gone from his voice, and he nodded to the guards below.

They each raised their rifles, but instead of pointing them into the silent crowd, they aimed inside the cage.

"Ten," began Mercer. "Nine. Eight. Seven…"

Maya began to advance, looking like a cat eyeing an injured bird, while Poppy cowered against the cage. "Please," she begged. "Maya, please, don't—"

Her pleas were cut off as Maya pounced and grabbed her hair. I expected the pair to fall to the ground and pummel each other, but instead, with one quick twist, Maya broke Poppy's neck.

Poppy's body fell to the ground, her eyes still open and staring directly at me. I swallowed hard, my nails digging into my palms as my chest tightened, making it impossible to breathe. I'd seen death more times than I could count—on the streets of the Heights, the hunting grounds of Elsewhere, the white carpet stained red by Augusta's blood. But the sickening crack of Poppy's neck echoed in my head, and all I could see was her empty gaze, the same one that had been in Benjy's eyes as he'd fallen lifelessly to the floor.

Noelle wrapped her warm arms around me, and at first I thought it was because she needed the comfort. But it wasn't until I felt the tears freeze on my cheeks that I realized I was the one who was crying.

The crowd was silent as a guard climbed into the cage through a trapdoor and dragged Poppy's body away. Maya remained in the cage, and as another woman entered—older this time, and a cry of anguish nearby told me that this must have been Darcy—I buried my face in Noelle's shoulder, refusing to watch.

Maya won all three fights, killing her opponents within seconds of Mercer's countdown beginning. After the third match, Scotia grunted her approval. "She gave them a painless death," she said. "Good. Thought she'd play with her food."

It was only through an act of supreme willpower that I managed to keep the contents of my stomach where they belonged, and finally I raised my head. "Is that it?"

Scotia nodded. "Should be. There's never more than three."

"What's going to happen to Maya now?" I said, chancing a glance up into the cage. Maya stood in the center, her shoulders hunched as she breathed heavily, looking like she, too, was about to be sick.

"She's earned another chance in the general population,"

said Scotia. "Might be sent to a different section, considering she went after you, but—"

She stopped suddenly, and beside me, Noelle squeaked. "What's he doing?"

Mercer stood against the railing at the edge of the rooftop, holding a gun with a scope mounted on top. Hannah stood beside him, her mouth tugged down in a frown, and instantly I understood. But before I could look away, Mercer squeezed the trigger, and a shot rang out.

Hot, wet droplets of red splattered my face and the front of my coat. Noelle's scream pierced my eardrums, and my brain caught up with what I was seeing just in time to register the hole in the center of Maya's chest as she collapsed like a puppet whose strings had been cut. On the rooftop, Mercer lowered his weapon, and a dark figure appeared at his side.

"Back to your bunks," ordered Mercer over the sounds of shrieks and sobs. "Curfew begins in ten minutes. Anyone caught outside will be shot on sight."

"Come on, you two, before he gets trigger-happy," muttered Scotia, tugging at my elbow. But I didn't budge. I didn't breathe. I didn't so much as blink.

Instead I stared up at the man who stood on the other side of Mercer. In the dying light, his features were nearly impossible to make out, but the way he held himself was unmistakable, and I would have recognized his cold gaze anywhere.

Knox.

VIII

SPY

Knox was here.

Knox was Elsewhere.

After all he'd done to me—after talking me into giving up my freedom, after betraying me to Daxton, after killing Benjy and the last hope I had left for a happy life, he had the nerve to show up here and not even bother to face me.

Rage burned me up from the inside out, leaving nothing but blind hatred in its wake, and the hollowness Benjy's death had left in my chest filled with a single need:

Make Knox pay.

Without thinking, I pulled myself over the railing separating us from the cage. *"Knox!"* I screamed, my voice echoing through the crowd. I was going to kill him. I was going to rip him apart with my bare hands until he resembled nothing more than meat at the butcher's, and then I was going to feed him to the dogs. I'd show him the same mercy he showed Benjy, and for the rest of his pathetically short life, he would regret everything he'd done to him—to us.

Knox looked down from his spot on the rooftop, and he

searched the crowd before his eyes locked on mine. A strange expression flickered over his face—surprise I was still alive? Relief there were hundreds of people between us? I couldn't tell and didn't care. I would crawl over them if I had to and climb up to that rooftop brick by painted brick. One way or the other, no matter what it cost me, I was going to kill him.

Before I could swing my legs over to the other side of the railing, however, two pairs of hands grabbed my arms and pulled me down. "Are you crazy or just incredibly stupid?" hissed Scotia. "Get yourself killed on your own time, but don't you dare give Mercer a reason to point that gun at all of us."

At last I tore my eyes away from Knox. Scotia gripped my arm so tightly that I would have a handprint-shaped bruise in the morning, and Noelle huddled beside her, looking every bit as pale as before. "Knox—that's Knox," I said, struggling to get the words out. My tongue had turned to lead, and my lips were numb, making every word a trial. "He—he killed—"

"I don't care who he killed," snapped Scotia. "The only thing I care about is Mercer not killing you."

"Let him," I choked out, looking back up at the rooftop. Knox had disappeared, but Mercer remained, his eyes fixed on us. A shiver ran down my spine, and I tried to push Scotia's hand away. Let Mercer kill me.

A bullet to the brain. It would be a relief.

No matter where I was or whose face I wore, my life would always be in the hands of someone else.

"You can't kill Knox if you're dead," said Scotia, her grip tightening. "Play out your little soap opera somewhere else, princess. I'm not interested in being in the line of fire, and neither is Noelle. Now come on, before I have to drag you by the hair."

With a hard shove, Scotia pushed both of us away from

the cage and back toward the bunk, muttering curses under her breath. I stumbled forward, my mind on mute as I stared at the snow beneath my feet. One step after the other, white stained red, and a bullet to the brain. That was all I could think about. But somewhere in the back of my mind, in a portion that was still alive—that was still rational—Scotia's words settled, taking root.

You can't kill Knox if you're dead.

No, I couldn't. And if I had to stay alive long enough to see it happen, then I would. For Benjy.

I only came to when she shoved us through the door and warmth hit my numb cheeks, causing them to burn. With my bunk nearest the door, the freezing air invaded my space, but I tugged off my coat and threw it down on the stained mattress.

A plan. I needed a plan.

"Who was that man?" said Noelle. Her bunk was only a few down from mine, and while the other girls huddled together at the other end of the room either for warmth or to avoid me, Noelle returned to my side once she'd stripped her own coat off.

"Lennox Creed. Lila's fiancé," said Scotia from the doorway to her private room. The curtain must have kept some warmth inside, but she didn't invite us in even though the icy wind continued to blast through to my bunk as more girls spilled through the doorway.

Noelle gasped. "Your fiancé? He's here?"

"Former fiancé," I managed, my teeth chattering now that feeling was returning to my extremities. "He—he was on the roof with Mercer."

Her eyes widened. "But why do you want to kill him?"

"He killed my b—my best friend," I said as the quicksand tried to swallow me again. I fought to stay above it. No one else would hold Knox accountable for killing Benjy, but I would make him pay. I had to stay whole and alive until then.

"If he loved you, why would he do that?" said Noelle, her brow furrowing.

"To teach me a lesson." My throat tightened painfully, threatening to close completely, but I swallowed hard. "I refused to do exactly what he told me to do, so he killed Benjy." I looked at Noelle, my eyes burning with unshed tears, and I whispered, "He was my Elliott."

"Oh!" Noelle's lower lip trembled, and she pulled me into a hug. "I'm so sorry, Lila. That's..." Her arms tightened around me. "I'm so sorry."

In the doorway, Scotia remained stoic. "Dying's a condition of living," she said. "Everyone does it eventually. There's no point trying to fight it."

"If you really believed that, then you wouldn't still be alive," I said thickly. "I'm fine dying. I never expected to live this long anyway. But Benjy—he was pure good. He didn't deserve to die, and if Knox thinks he can get away with it—"

"What are you going to do?" said Scotia, staring down at me. "March up to him and snap his neck?"

"If that's what it takes," I said, glaring at her in return, silently daring her to report me. "At least I have the guts to finish him off myself."

The entire bunkhouse went silent. Noelle stiffened, and she pulled away from me, shooting Scotia a nervous look. Before Noelle could say anything, however, Scotia stepped toward me, a dangerous mask of calm settling over her features.

"And what is that supposed to mean?" she said.

"Those girls—Maya and Poppy and the others—they didn't have to die," I said. "You knew what would happen the minute you turned them in."

"And they knew exactly what would happen if they were ever caught fighting on my turf," said Scotia. "Just like I bet you knew exactly what would happen to your friend if you betrayed Knox."

My blood turned to lava, and fury erupted inside me. Before I knew what was happening, I flew across the aisle, my fingers curled into claws as I tackled Scotia to the ground. Part of me was vaguely aware I was screaming obscenities as I tried to rip her to shreds, but in one fluid motion, Scotia flipped me onto my back and pinned my legs and arms, knocking the wind out of me.

"You might be used to people kissing your ass and telling you what you want to hear back home, but you're not a Hart anymore, princess," she growled. "You're no better than the rest of us."

She hovered over me, close enough for me to smell the chocolate on her breath and see flecks of gold in her irises. I didn't turn away. Instead, with anger still raging within me, I spit in her face.

Scotia didn't so much as flinch. "Consider this your warning," she said. "And be thankful I'm being so generous, you ungrateful bitch."

She climbed to her feet and wiped my spit off her cheek. Several of the girls began to whisper, but with a single look, she silenced them and stalked back into her room.

With effort, I sat up, my side aching from the way her knee had dug into me. Noelle knelt beside me, even though I belatedly realized I'd managed to land in a puddle of melted snow someone had tracked in from outside.

"You really shouldn't push her," she said softly, rubbing circles between my shoulder blades. "It won't do you any good."

"Like she said, I'm no better than the rest of you," I said, glaring at the curtain that now separated Scotia from us. "And neither is she. She had no right to talk about Benjy like that."

"I'm sure she already feels bad about it," said Noelle. "Scotia's a really good person, I promise. But if you give her a reason to turn you in—"

Suddenly the door to the bunkhouse burst open, revealing a burly guard clutching a rifle. His massive frame took up nearly the entire doorway, and he lumbered into the room, his boot missing my toes by inches. "Inspection! Stand by your bunks, hands on your head, all of you."

Noelle scrambled to her feet, pausing only long enough to help me to mine before she hurried over to the foot of her bunk. The other girls stood by theirs, all with their hands placed behind their heads. My heart pounded, and I stumbled the few steps it took to reach mine, leaning against the ladder while gingerly lifting my arms high enough to mimic their poses. The guard met my eyes, and a shiver ran through me. Was he staring because of who he thought I was, or had he been sent here to plant something on me, finally giving Knox an excuse to kill me?

Half a dozen guards stormed into the room and began to tear the place apart. Mattresses were pounded, pillows were ripped open, and though I didn't have any personal belongings, the guards rummaged through the others'. More than once I heard paper ripping, and Noelle winced as a guard tore through the pages of a book she had under her pillow.

At last, three quarters of the way down the aisle, a weedy guard straightened. "Sir," he called, holding up what looked like a candy bar. The girl whose bunk he was searching started to turn around, but one look from the guard and she straightened again, her face pale.

The first guard lumbered up to her. Chelsea, I remembered.

Her name was Chelsea. "You're aware that the possession of contraband substances is strictly prohibited by Article 18, Section B of the penal code?" said the first burly guard.

"It—it was a present from a guard," she said in a trembling voice. "I thought—because he gave it to me—"

The guard snapped his fingers, and the one who had found it pocketed the candy bar and twisted her arm behind her back. "Out you go," he said in a shrill, excited voice that made my stomach turn. Chelsea stumbled forward, her face red and eyes full of tears. Our gazes met, and suddenly all I could see was the hole in Maya's chest.

Even though it was stupid, even though Scotia had just given me my first and final warning, I stepped into the aisle between bunks to block their way.

"It's a *candy bar*," I said. "You're really going to throw her into the cage for that?"

Behind the guard, Noelle shook her head furiously, silently begging me to stop. I ignored her. Better not to get her involved in this, too.

"It's an item from outside the zone," said the first guard, the burly one who looked like he could challenge a bear and win. "You break the rules, you get arrested. Plain and simple."

So Elsewhere was exactly like D.C., except the Shields had been replaced by the prisoners themselves, and instead of going Elsewhere, you were sent to the cage. For a candy bar, for an orange—it was all the same thing. "It's a stupid rule," I said.

The guard stepped up beside me, towering over me the same way he'd towered over Chelsea. "Would you prefer we not arrest her?"

"I'd prefer you have a little decency and realize a candy bar is just a candy bar," I shot at him. "You heard her. A guard gave it to her. For all we know, it could've been you, for the sole reason of coming in here to arrest her for your barbaric entertainment tomorrow night."

He narrowed his eyes and bent down until our noses were nearly touching. "I'll tell you what, Miss Hart. I'm gonna do you a favor. Just for you, just because you think it's unfair, I'm not going to arrest her."

I exhaled, my tense muscles relaxing slightly. "Thank you. That wasn't so hard, was it?"

"Not at all," he said, and he straightened. "Take her to the street."

Several girls gasped, and the weedy guard shoved Chelsea down the aisle and out the door. The blast of cold air hit my face, and forgetting the other guards still searching through the bunks, I hurried after them.

The weedy guard forced Chelsea to her knees under a pool of yellow light in the middle of the street. She trembled, and a choked sob escaped her. "Please," she begged. "Please, I'll tell you where I got it—I'll tell you anything you want. I'll do anything you want. Just don't—"

"Shut up," said the weedy guard, and he kicked her in the spine. I started forward, but someone grabbed my collar and held me back.

"Don't even think about it," said Scotia, her voice dripping with venom. The burly guard chuckled as he stepped around me.

"You should listen to Scotia," he said, giving her an enormous wink. "She knows how to handle herself, don't you, sweetheart?"

"I'm not your sweetheart, Williams," she said coolly, but he merely chuckled and descended the steps into the snowy street.

"Someday I'll change your mind. But this one here..." He

drew his weapon and looked straight at me. "Maybe this will help you change yours, Miss Hart."

Before I could move, before I could think, before I could react at all, he pressed the barrel of his rifle to the back of Chelsea's head. A gunshot cut off her strangled scream, leaving dead silence in its wake.

Her blood stained the snow red, mixing with the yellow light and appearing an eerie shade of brown. With cold efficiency, the weedy guard dragged her body to the side of the street and spoke into a device clipped to his shoulder. "Cleanup requested, Street 8, Block B."

"All clear, sir," called another guard from inside the bunkhouse, as if nothing had happened. Their boots squeaked against the wet floor as they headed out the door, each one brushing me as they passed.

"Get inside," hissed Scotia in my ear, and she tugged me backward and into the building. I was too numb to fight. I was too numb to do anything but stare blankly at the bunk bed that, seconds before, had belonged to a girl who was now dead.

Every single pair of eyes turned toward me. Some were red; some stared at me accusingly. But for the first time, none of them looked away.

"At least in the cage, she would've stood a chance," said Scotia, pushing me back to my bed. I sat down heavily, and the springs squeaked from my weight. "Get it now?"

I nodded wordlessly, and she turned her glare from me to the others.

"Chelsea was a good person," she said. "You're all good people. I don't care if Mercer himself hands you contraband—do *not* give them an excuse to kill you, because I promise you they will take it."

With that, she turned on her heel and headed back behind

her curtain. A few quiet sobs echoed from the other end of the bunk, and the low murmur of voices filled my ears as I curled up on my bed, my back to them as I stared at the entrance to Scotia's room.

It was the only place the guards had left untouched.

Scotia was the snitch.

By the time lights out came two hours later, I was certain. She had turned Maya and her friends in without a second thought; and after smelling the chocolate on her breath, I would have bet every heartbeat I had left that she was the one who had tipped off Williams about Chelsea's candy bar and told him to search the bunk.

While the others fell asleep, their whispered conversations fading one by one until the entire room was filled with the sound of two dozen girls breathing evenly, I continued to watch the curtain separating Scotia from the rest of us. It might as well have been a steel door, the way the other girls treated it, but all I could think about was what she'd done to deserve that privacy in the first place.

Snitch out her bunk mates, clearly. Keep us all so afraid of her that no one stepped a toe out of line in fear of being sent to the cage. But why the others didn't gang up on her and take care of the problem, I didn't know.

Even if I'd wanted to sleep, I couldn't. My mind flipped between the horrors of the past twenty-four hours like some nightmarish slide show. Six people—that was how many had died in front of me since Knox had betrayed me. Benjy. Maya. Poppy. Darcy. Chelsea. And another whose name I'd never known.

Guilt and despair burrowed inside me, nestling up against the need for vengeance that fueled every breath I took. The true horror of Elsewhere wasn't the hunt Daxton enjoyed so much; it lay in the twisted hope Mercer and the others offered the prisoners. Betray your friends, betray the only family you have in this place, and we might let you become one of us. We might let you pull the trigger next time.

I wouldn't just kill Knox, I decided. I would take out the Mercers, too—and Scotia, and Williams and the weedy guard, and everyone else who dared to build up their authority on the deaths of others. I would burn Elsewhere to the ground if that's what it took to help these people. I might have still looked like Lila Hart on the outside, but it was time to be Kitty Doe on the inside. It was time to remember who I was and once again find the courage it took to face this kind of brutality day in and day out, and somehow still make it out alive.

But never, not even on the Shields' worst days, had I ever seen anything like this on the streets of D.C. No matter how hard I tried to prepare myself for whatever tomorrow had in store for me, I knew nothing in my experience could even begin to compare. And facing that bleak unknown was more terrifying than any disgruntled guard with a gun could ever be.

Over an hour after everyone else had fallen asleep, the curtain rustled. I squinted, and cloaked by darkness, Scotia slipped out of her room, her boots silent against the stone floor.

With stealth I would have found impressive if I hadn't hated her so much, she opened the door and exited the bunkhouse, leaving a swirl of icy air and snow in her wake. Without hesitating, I sat up and shoved my feet into my boots, remembering to grab my coat this time. I wasn't nearly as quiet as she was, but with everyone asleep, I had no reason to care.

By the time I slipped outside, she was halfway down the

block, her head bent and hands shoved into her pockets. She walked as if she knew she had nothing to worry about, not bothering to keep to the shadows or mute the crunch of snow and ice with every step she took. And why would she, when she was so favored that not even the guards dared to disturb her privacy?

I made sure to fall into the rhythm of her gait, in case she could hear my footsteps as well as I could hear hers. Unlike Scotia, I stuck to the shadows, wishing I were wearing anything but red so I could blend in easier. But we passed no guards, and Scotia never looked over her shoulder, not even when she stopped beside a metal gate that blocked the winding drive leading up to Mercer Manor.

I crouched behind the corner of a building as Scotia waited, in plain sight of anyone who happened to pass by. Mercer Manor loomed only a few hundred feet away, a stark contrast to the other buildings around it even in the darkness. Scotia tapped her foot impatiently, and half a minute later, she huffed with indignation. Whoever she was supposed to meet was late.

Another set of footsteps echoed through the quiet street, and a tall figure approached, walking down the drive. When he stepped underneath the lamp secured on top of the gate, the light illuminated his features, and I raised an eyebrow. Mercer.

"You're late," said Scotia, annoyed. "You know it's freezing out here."

"I'm sure I could figure out some way to keep you warm," he said, sliding his arms around her waist. "How are you, my dear?"

"Your goons killed another one of my girls tonight." Despite the anger in her tone, she looped her arms around his neck, pressing her body against his. "I'd appreciate it if you told them to leave us alone."

"I'm afraid I can't do that, darling," said Mercer, and he nuzzled her cheek. I made a face. "If someone breaks a rule, my hands are tied."

"That's bullshit and you know it," she said, and he chuckled.

"Yes, I suppose. But I also suspect she did something to deserve it, did she not?"

Scotia grumbled. "Williams caught her with contraband. The Hart girl opened her big mouth and tried to stop her arrest, and since Williams couldn't take it out on her, he took it out on Chelsea instead."

Mercer clucked his tongue disapprovingly. "She'll settle in quickly enough."

"In the meantime, I'm not her babysitter," said Scotia. "Give her to someone else."

"I'm afraid I can't do that, my dear," he said, brushing snow from her cheek with one gloved hand. "No one else could protect her the way you do. I heard what you did this afternoon."

Scotia stamped her feet. "It was nothing. Just pulled a few girls off her. You didn't have to kill that girl in the cage tonight. She earned her freedom."

"My dear, no one earns their freedom here." He tried to kiss her, but she turned her head. "Isabel, darling, don't be like that. I had no choice, and you know it."

"You could've sent her to another zone," said Scotia, an edge to her voice that hadn't been there before. "You didn't have to murder her in cold blood."

"I have my orders, as you very well know," he said. "I had to make an example of her. I'll have to do the same to anyone else who attacks Lila, so if you'd rather I not have any more blood on my hands, then I would suggest doing your job and watching her back."

She muttered something I couldn't hear, and Mercer sighed.

"If I told you I brought you a present, would that make it any better?" he said, releasing her. Instead of storming off, Scotia stayed where she was, crossing her arms.

Mercer pulled off his gloves and slid his hand into his pocket, retrieving something I couldn't make out. I leaned forward and squinted. Light from the lamp reflected off a small silver disk that dangled from a chain, and my mouth dropped open. My necklace. Mercer was giving her my necklace.

"Here you go," he said, and he fastened it around her neck. "Something for you to remember me on those cold, lonely nights."

The edges of my vision turned red, and I dug my nails into my palms. That was mine. But there was nothing I could do that wouldn't announce my presence to them both, so I sat back on my heels and seethed. If I'd had any doubts whether or not she was the spy, seeing Scotia touch my necklace and kiss Mercer in thanks was enough to dissolve them completely.

"Come inside where it's warm," said Mercer. "Hannah's asleep."

Scotia shook her head. "Not tonight, not after what Williams pulled. One of the girls might need me."

Mercer began to protest, but Scotia kissed him again, effectively shutting him up. He relaxed, and when she pulled away, he sighed again. "I'll have a little chat with him. Make sure he knows what he cost me."

"You do that," said Scotia, and she slid her hand over his

backside and squeezed. Disgusting. "If all of my girls survive tomorrow, then I'll see about staying the night."

With one last kiss, they broke apart, and Mercer walked through the gate and back up the drive to the manor. Scotia watched him go, and it wasn't until he'd disappeared into the darkness that she finally began to trudge back to the bunkhouse.

I trailed after her, trying to ignore the barrage of questions that flooded my mind, but there was only so much I could do to keep them at bay. Why did Scotia sound surprised the guards had searched the bunkhouse if she'd been the one to snitch on Chelsea? And why had Mercer insinuated that he had orders to protect me? None of the Harts or the Ministers of the Union had any interest in keeping me alive, unless Daxton intended on hunting me himself when the time came. But if that were the case, then why wouldn't he have just thrown me into the hunting grounds to start instead of wasting time by sending me to Section X?

Did Knox's sudden presence here have anything to do with it? No—he was only the son of a Minister for now, not the Minister himself, and he didn't have the power to give those kinds of orders. He was here to watch me die, not to save my life when he was the one who'd put me here in the first place.

Lost in my thoughts, I turned onto the street that led to the bunkhouse. I would find out eventually one way or the other, but until then—

A hand clamped over my mouth. "Scream, and you're dead," whispered a harsh voice in my ear, and my entire body went cold.

Scotia.

IX

COLD HOPE

Scotia shoved me against the side of a gray building, and the back of my head cracked against the bricks. "What the hell do you think you're doing?" she whispered harshly. She must have been convinced I wasn't going to scream, because she dropped her hand from my mouth.

I gulped in a deep breath of cold air. "You're the one who told them about Chelsea, weren't you?" I said. "You're the snitch."

Scotia rolled her eyes and grabbed my shoulder, steering me away from the wall. I tried to fight her, but my wet boots had frozen in the cold, and my feet were numb. "Stop trying to think for yourself, Lila. You'll get wrinkles."

She pushed me into a narrow alleyway between two gray buildings, away from the bunkhouse. "Where are we going?" I said.

"Someplace where you can't get us killed," she said, taking another sharp turn. "Now shut up and walk before I decide to gag you."

I trudged on, debating whether or not it was worth trying to take her out. I was still injured and almost too cold to walk, let alone fight Scotia and live, and it was a maze back here, even more so than the wider streets of Elsewhere. Within minutes, I was completely lost. If I wanted any hope of returning to the bunkhouse without running across a guard, I had no choice but to stick with Scotia.

At last we arrived at a nondescript door in an alley behind a large building that smelled vaguely like grease. The dining hall. Scotia pushed it open and shoved me inside. "Watch your step," she said, and once the door closed securely behind us, she flipped on a light switch.

We stood at the top of a stairway that led down below the dining hall. I frowned, and Scotia nudged me forward. "We don't have all night."

"What're you going to do, kill me and serve me with tomorrow's lunch?" I said.

She snorted. "Please, like you have enough meat on your bones to make a sandwich, let alone feed everyone. Now either you can walk down those stairs, or I can push you. Your choice."

Reluctantly I descended the steps, taking them one at a time so I didn't trip over my numb feet. Wherever we were going, it was the last place I wanted to be right now, but I refused to let my fear show. I was Kitty Doe, not Lila Hart. I wasn't a coward.

At the bottom of the narrow staircase was a single metal door. Scotia reached around me and punched a series of numbers into the keypad beside it, and a lock clicked. "In you go," she said, turning the knob and pushing it open.

I didn't know what I expected, but a small crowd of several dozen prisoners wasn't it. No, not just prisoners—among the red and orange jumpsuits, I also spotted a few black uniforms. Guards. And scattered across every surface were dozens upon dozens of weapons. Guns, knives, bows and arrows, grenades—things no upstanding citizen could get their hands on, let alone prisoners.

"What's going on?" I said nervously, and every pair of eyes in that room turned to look at me. Most of them were older, in their twenties and thirties, but in the corner stood a handful of boys who looked barely old enough to take their test, and seated around a rickety table were half a dozen grizzled men and women. Two of them I recognized from the dining hall at dinner.

"You didn't think the Blackcoats only existed out there, did you?" said Scotia, hovering over me. I gaped at her.

"This is a Blackcoat meeting?"

"Isn't that what I just said?" She nodded to a stack of old wooden crates near the door. A machine gun leaned against it casually, as if someone had left it there and would be back for it at any moment. "Sit down, Lila, and let the adults do the talking."

I gingerly moved the gun so it leaned against the wall, and then I took a seat and glanced around the gathered crowd. Several of them stared back, but most refocused their gaze on Scotia, who moved to the center of the room. It took me several seconds to realize what I was looking for—rather, who.

Knox. And he wasn't there.

"We have two days," said Scotia in a voice that seemed to permeate every corner of the room. "Two days until everything we've worked for will be for nothing. I don't need to tell you what will happen if we don't get the codes, and we are teetering dangerously close to failure."

"Even if we were suicidal, we'd have no chance of sneaking in anymore," said a man dressed in a guard uniform. His blond hair was long and tied back in a ponytail, and his fingers tapped out a faint rhythm on the wall he leaned against. "Security's been raised now that Minister Creed's son has decided to go cherry-picking."

Several of the women shifted uncomfortably and glanced at one another. I frowned. "Cherry-picking?" I said.

The guard gestured to the crowd gathered. "Anyone he wants, for any purpose. They mostly have their fun and only stick around for a night or two, but a few of them have some twisted tastes." He tugged his collar down, revealing the start of a thick red scar that ran down his chest. "On the plus side, if you pretend to enjoy it and survive, they'll usually give you a uniform."

I stared at him in horror. No matter how much I hated Knox, I couldn't imagine him ever being that cruel. But the other Ministers…

"Rivers, stop it," said Scotia sharply. "The princess has had enough of a dose of reality for one day."

"I'm not a princess," I said, even though she was right. Elsewhere had been bad enough when I'd thought it was just a hunting ground, but the more layers I saw, the more I wished Knox had put a bullet in me like he'd promised. One more reason to enjoy watching the life drain from his eyes when I had the chance.

But even amidst the dizzying horror swirling in my mind, one thing became crystal clear: they had no idea Knox was one of the leaders of the Blackcoats. Or if they did, they didn't trust him.

"Has he chosen someone yet?" said a man whose face I couldn't see.

"Not that I know of," said Rivers, and his clear blue gaze settled on me. "Can't imagine who he might set his sights on."

CAPTIVE

"Enough," said Scotia, sharper this time. "Just because security's been raised doesn't mean it's impossible. We have *two days,* people. Start getting creative."

"I've searched Mercer's office high and low on my cleaning rounds," said one of the elderly women, whose white hair was twisted up into a braided bun. "If the codes are hidden in there, they're behind lock and key."

"That might be, but your eyesight's shit, too," said Scotia. The older woman sank into her seat and averted her gaze, folding her gnarled hands. "I can't do everything myself, people."

"You'll have to eventually if you keep treating everyone like that," I said before I could stop myself. Scotia turned slowly to face me, her mouth set in a thin line.

"If you're so eager to help, then why don't you take the Mercers up on their offer?" she said. "You can't be completely useless."

"What offer?" said Rivers, and his tapping abruptly stopped. Once again, all eyes in the room turned toward me.

"The offer for her to stay in Mercer Manor as their guest," said Scotia. I gritted my teeth.

"Did Mercer tell you that before or after you shoved your tongue down his throat?" I said.

The news of her affair with Mercer didn't seem to surprise anyone in the room, and Scotia shrugged. "Does it matter? If we don't get the codes in two days—"

"What codes?" I said. "What are you talking about?"

Dead silence. Several prisoners exchanged nervous looks, and Rivers sighed, resting his head against the wall. Scotia, in the meantime, narrowed her eyes. "I'm not in the mood for games."

"Neither am I," I snapped. "If there's some conspiracy or plot going on, I'm not aware of it."

"How could you not be?" she said, and for the first time since I'd met her, Isabel Scotia looked stunned and confused. "Isn't that why you're here? To make sure the plan goes through?"

"I'm here because Daxton caught me breaking into his office, not because of some plan." But even as I said it, the pieces clicked into place. This was what Sampson and the others had been plotting. "What are the codes to?"

Scotia frowned. "If the higher-ups didn't tell you—"

"The central armory," said Rivers. She shot him a warning look.

"Rivers…"

"You're sleeping with him, and you still can't get the codes," he said. "She might be our last shot."

Scotia took a long, deep breath, her dark eyes burning into mine. I refused to look away, and at last she nodded curtly and stepped aside, allowing Rivers room in the center. He took her place, directly facing me now.

"The Blackcoats need weapons, and nearly three quarters of the nation's artillery is stored here, in Elsewhere," he said. "The Mercers aren't just overseeing the section. They're also tasked with protecting the armory. We need those codes to get inside, overthrow the Mercers, and arm the rebellion."

The weight of what he was saying settled over me, and my mind spun. The Blackcoats were going to break everyone out. Thousands of ex-prisoners loyal to them, with three quarters of America's weapons at their disposal—that could be enough to rival the Shields and the armies Daxton had at his.

He'd said that Knox was behind the failure of the first raid—was that why he was here? To stop the second? Was that why Daxton hadn't killed me in the first place? So I would be Knox's excuse to come here and *cherry-pick* without raising suspicions?

"You can't trust him," I blurted. "Knox Creed—whatever you do, don't trust him."

Scotia scoffed. "Why the hell would we? He's one of them."

Yes, he was. I glanced at the weapons scattered carelessly throughout the room. "Don't you have enough weapons here to get started?"

"There are hundreds of sections in Elsewhere just like Section X," said Scotia. "Not even the guards know exactly how many there are. These weapons might be enough to hold the dining hall for a few days, but we might as well be ants against giants."

"We need the codes if we're going to have any chance of succeeding," said Rivers. "Not just us, but the entire operation. The entire *rebellion*. And if the Mercers offered you a spot in their home—"

"Knox Creed is her fiancé," said Scotia, crossing her arms as her stare settled on me. "There's a chance he knows where the codes are hidden."

"*Was* my fiancé," I said, "and even if he does know, I'm the last person he's going to tell. There's no point."

She scowled. "I saved your life today. This is the least you could do to try to repay me."

"I never asked you to save it," I snapped. "And I don't owe you a thing. Knox Creed won't tell me anything you won't be able to kiss out of Mercer, and even if he did, you can't trust a word out of his mouth. He swore he'd protect my b—my best friend, but Benjy's dead. He swore he'd kill me before he ever let me wind up Elsewhere, but here I am. Dying's the only thing he's good for anymore, and I owe him a bullet."

"If you raise a hand against a guard, let alone a senior official, you'll be dead in a second," said Rivers quietly.

"Good." I clenched my fists. "It'll be worth it. Knox Creed is a spy, and not only did he kill my best friend, but he sabotaged the last raid, too. He knows everything you're planning, and I guarantee you he's here to stop it. Might as well let me kill him. You'll be doing all of us a favor."

A ripple of murmurs rose up among the crowd, but Scotia raised her hand, and they quieted. "You want to die?" she said dangerously. "Fine."

Without warning, she pulled a pistol from the inside of her jacket and pointed it directly at me.

Bang.

I ducked half a second too late. By the time I fell to the concrete floor, crashing into the machine gun and another pile of crates, the plaster wall beside my head had already exploded, leaving white dust clinging to my hair.

My heart pounded, and adrenaline rushed through me as images of white and crimson flashed through my mind, blinding me. Every inch of me felt as if I were on fire, and my muscles tensed, ready to run if she tried again. I groped around for something to use against her, and my fingers wrapped around the handle of the machine gun. I had no idea how to work it, but I would be damned if I was going down without a fight.

Scotia laughed. It was a dark, humorless sound that could've easily come from the depths of my nightmares, and I cringed. "What are you going to do with that, princess? Shoot me? You couldn't find the safety on that if I gave you an instruction manual and circled it in red."

I clutched the gun to my chest anyway. It was better than nothing.

She huffed, and my vision began to clear in time to see her

tuck her pistol back into her coat. "You might think you want to die, princess, but you want to live as badly as the rest of us."

"You're crazy," I said, my voice laced with residual panic.

"*You're* crazy." She moved toward me as if she were the predator and I were the prey. "Do you know how many people die in here every day? Hundreds, if not thousands. Do you know how many of them would've killed to be in your shoes and have a chance to stop it all? Every last one of them."

"Then let one of them do it," I spat, struggling to my feet. The machine gun fell to the floor, and I winced, but it clattered harmlessly against the concrete. "They'd have a better chance anyway."

Scotia was silent for a long moment, as still and cold as if she were made of ice. "You're right," she said at last. "They probably would. And this close to the raid, the last thing we need is another liability. We can manage just fine without you."

"And that's what you're going to have to do," I shot. "Because I'm through."

I stood in the corner for the rest of the meeting, hugging my freezing body and trying not to look as exhausted as I felt. No one else tried to convince me to ask Knox for the codes, but every once in a while, I caught someone staring at me. They all hastily looked away, except for the guard with the long blond hair. Rivers.

Our eyes locked as Scotia barked a list of orders for the next meeting tomorrow night. I was only half listening, distracting myself with fantasies of how it would feel to wrap my hands around Knox's throat and squeeze, but Rivers's blue eyes were impossible to miss. They were the color of the ocean, like mine.

I held his stare, and he watched me openly, not the least bit ashamed of being caught. There was a question in his expression I couldn't read, and the moment Scotia ended the meeting, he crossed the room to join me.

"You don't have to ask Knox directly to help," he said, and I blinked at him.

"Are you incapable of listening, or do you just not understand the word *no?*"

"I'm not going to try to threaten or persuade you into helping," he said, leaning in so only I could hear him. "But if you want to get back at this bastard Knox for what he did to you, then wouldn't your best bet be to make sure the very thing he doesn't want to happen does?"

I glared at him, and he straightened, patting me on the cheek.

"If you need me to smuggle anything in for you, all you have to do is ask," he added. "First round's on the house."

With that, he melted into the steady stream of others leaving through the door, calling out, "Twos and threes, remember! If you're caught after curfew, it's your head, not ours."

Scotia stalked toward me and grabbed my elbow. "You say anything about this meeting to anyone, you'll be in the cage tomorrow night," she said. "*Please,* go ahead and test me on that."

"I'm not going to tell anyone," I said wearily. "I'm not stupid."

"Sure could've fooled me," she said, and with that, she dragged me back up the narrow staircase and back into the freezing alleyway.

The crowd quickly dispersed, leaving us alone in our journey back to the bunkhouse. She dragged me the entire way, her nails digging through my coat. Scotia was a master at melting into shadows and hiding around corners until she was sure the coast was clear, but it all seemed like a long-winded charade, as the streets were once again abandoned, leaving me to wonder if the cold had chased away the guards or if Scotia had done something to take care of them, too.

"I want my necklace back," I whispered half a block away from the bunk. Scotia scoffed, her breath visible in the freezing air.

"And I want the armory codes. Not all of us get what we want whenever we ask for it, princess."

"A friend gave it to me," I said. "A really good friend."

"Is that so?" She glanced at me, her dark eyes narrowed. "Funny, a *really good friend* gave it to me, too."

I prickled at the suggestiveness in her voice. "Mercer stole that from me, and it's mine."

"You want it back? Then get me my armory codes."

"No."

"Then I guess it's mine now, isn't it?"

I tightened my hands into fists. "It means nothing to you."

"Maybe thirty seconds ago, but now it means plenty." She stopped in the middle of an alleyway and faced me. "I don't know why you're refusing to help us, but I do know about the speeches you gave. I know what you've done for the rebellion in the past, and to see you piss it all away just because you wound up here—do you have any idea how badly you're hurting morale?"

"Give me my necklace," I said, ignoring her. She continued on as if I hadn't even spoken.

"I've heard the recordings they smuggled in. The speech you gave in New York City—you're the reason half of these people agreed to risk their lives and join us in the first place."

I opened my mouth to insist they were idiots, but stopped

suddenly. The speech in New York—that hadn't been Lila before she'd faked her death. That had been me.

"You're an inspiration to those people. Just you being here, in our section—it gave them hope. More people risked their asses getting to that meeting tonight than we've ever had before, just on the off chance you might be there. And come to find you're not here to help us—" Scotia shook her head ruefully. "You might've already ruined any chance we had of ever being free again."

"The only reason I'm still alive is so Knox can use me against you," I said, my voice trembling with cold and fury. "If I ask him about those codes, you won't stand a chance of ever finding them."

"So don't ask," she said. "Stay with the Mercers. Search for it while they're sleeping. I don't care what you do—but if you want to prove you're more than just a princess, then you have two days to help us before the entire rebellion fails. If we can get those codes, we might have a real shot at winning. But if we don't, then not only are we all dead, but no one's going to dare lift a finger against your family for generations to come." She leaned down until our noses were nearly touching. "We need a leader, Lila. You can be that leader. You can change millions of lives for the better. All you have to do is care enough to try."

I stood absolutely still as the cold seeped into my bones and the air turned to ice in my lungs. I'd tried caring. All it had gotten me was a one-way ticket to Elsewhere and a front row seat watching Benjy die. Now I had nothing left to lose, and no matter where I was—Elsewhere, D.C., that cabin in the woods—my life would never get any better than it was in that moment, cold and empty and worthless.

"Whether or not the rebellion succeeds or fails, it won't

have anything to do with me," I said. "And I'm not going to help someone who turns on the people she claims to protect. The only difference between you and Daxton Hart is that he has an entire country behind him, and you have a few dozen supporters who haven't yet realized you'll only care about them as long as they can do something for you." I backed away. "Keep the necklace. I hope every time you look at it, you see Maya's face, and Poppy's, and Chelsea's. And I hope you remember that the only reason they died is because you snitched on them for a chance to give Mercer your dignity."

I turned away and stalked down the street toward the bunkhouse. I couldn't do this, not again—I couldn't hope only to see it all burn. But even as I slipped into the bunk and curled up underneath my thin blanket, my mind whirled with plans and possibilities, leaving me staring into the darkness and wondering if maybe I had one last try left in me after all.

X

HUNTED

The morning bell rang at sunrise, and unlike in the group home where I'd been raised, not a single girl grumbled or complained as they pulled themselves out of bed and trudged into the communal bathroom. I joined them, remaining on the fringes while they went through their routines and whispered to one another, doing everything they could to avoid meeting my eyes. Only Noelle acknowledged me with a squeeze of my elbow and a friendly smile.

I was in the middle of brushing my teeth when a familiar voice boomed through the bunkhouse. "Lineup!"

Williams, the guard who had shot Chelsea the night before. I nearly dropped my toothbrush. "Lineup?" I said, my mouth full of toothpaste. "For what?"

Noelle paled. "No one knows," she said, her voice trembling. "They choose as many as they want. When you're taken, you never come back."

I started to ask who *they* were, but she and the other girls hurried into the bunk room, and I rinsed my mouth and followed them. Like the night before, each stood in front of their bunk bed, hands hanging at their sides as they looked straight ahead. Even Scotia stood in front of her curtain, her stance wide and her hands behind her back. Our eyes met, and her cold glare made it clear that if I got another girl killed this morning, I would be next.

My heart pounded as I took my place in front of my bunk. Williams burst through the door, and a handful of other guards joined him, crowding the small space. His gaze found mine, and he smirked. I stared back, refusing to flinch.

I waited for him to say something, but instead he remained silent. As the seconds passed, my chest tightened, and I dug my nails into my palms. The other girls all shifted nervously, some hanging their heads so their hair obscured their faces. I glanced at Noelle. She raised her chin as if she wanted them to see her.

Half a minute passed. At last heavy boots echoed against the steps that led to the front door, and Mercer stepped inside the bunkhouse. Towering over us, he scanned each face, his eyes lingering only on mine. To my surprise, he smiled. I didn't smile back.

"I think you'll like your pick here," said Mercer, and at first I thought he was talking to Williams—until a second set of footsteps clunked against the stairs, and Knox walked through the door, his black wool coat dusted with snow.

My entire body tensed. Rage burned through me, setting me on fire, and it took everything I had to remain still. Standing at the head of the aisle, Knox was less than an arm's length from me. Close enough for me to see the stubble forming on his jaw. Close enough for me to smell his soap. Close enough for me to reach out and snap his neck in the seconds before every single guard put a bullet in me.

My fingers twitched. It would be worth it if I knew I could

do it, but I didn't have the upper body strength Knox did, and I was still sore and bruised from the day before. If I killed him—*when* I killed him—I would need to be alone with him if I wanted any chance of succeeding.

"A great selection," said Knox quietly. He strode slowly up the aisle, eyeing each girl as he passed. "They're strong?"

"The strongest Elsewhere," said Mercer. "Fast runners, too, I'd imagine. They'll be the challenge you're looking for."

My stomach turned, and if I had eaten anything the day before, I had no doubt I would've been sick all over Mercer's shoes.

Knox was going hunting.

"This one," he said, tapping a redheaded girl on the shoulder. "And this one."

The black girl beside her let out a strange choking sound, and I turned away, biting my tongue to keep myself from blurting out something that would only get more killed.

"One more, I think," said Knox as he leisurely meandered back up the aisle toward me, now examining each girl on my side of the room. I would be the last.

I forced myself to relax and accept what was coming. My building hadn't been chosen at random; Knox was here for one person and one person only. Me. This was how he would finally kill me.

Let him try. If I was going down, I was taking him with me.

Knox stopped in front of me exactly as I expected him to, and our eyes met. I saw no hint of familiarity in his—no indication that we knew each other at all, much less that he regretted how things had come to pass.

For a moment I wondered if he, too, had been Masked. I wouldn't have put it past Daxton, especially if he had discovered the role Knox played in the Blackcoats. It would have been a perfect *in* into the rebellion. And it would have explained why Knox suddenly seemed to have no desire to keep a single promise he had made to me.

But then his lips curled into that secretive smile no one could have possibly duplicated, the same smile I had once thought was meant to reassure me that I was doing the right thing. Now all I could see was a mocking smirk.

He parted his lips as if he was about to speak to me, but instead he said nonchalantly, "This one."

He raised his hand to claim me, and rather than playing it cool the way I desperately wanted to, I flinched as if he were about to knock my teeth out.

Instead, he never touched me.

The girl beside me let out a choked sob. When I opened my eyes, Knox's hand rested on her shoulder, not mine.

"You three, with me," barked Williams. "The rest of you, get to work."

Knox stepped back, his eyes locked on mine until he turned away. Silence seemed to permeate the cabin as the three girls walked down the aisle to join the guards. Two of them were crying, but the third glared at me as if to say *this is your fault*.

She wasn't wrong, and I couldn't watch anymore. This was just another sick, twisted game I could never win, and the more Knox tortured me, the more I wanted to rip his throat out and feed him to the wolves.

More heavy footsteps echoed against the porch steps as the men exited, leaving us three fewer than we had been before they'd come. Before I had a chance to move, Scotia slapped the wall beside her, startling half the bunkhouse.

"You heard him," she called. "Dining hall now, and if any one of you is late for work, you'll have to answer to me."

The girls grabbed their coats and began to filter out. As I

pulled mine on, someone took my elbow, and I looked up to see Noelle standing beside me, her wide eyes glassy with unshed tears.

"I thought for sure he was going to take you," she whispered.

"Me, too." Judging by the way everyone glanced at us, we weren't the only ones who thought so. I stepped into my boots, too shaken and furious to bother being annoyed by the fact that they were still damp. "I'm sorry."

"For what?" she said. "This isn't your fault."

Yes, it was, but there was no use trying to convince Noelle, who only seemed to be able to see the good in people. "Is this how it always is? You wake up with twenty girls, and by lunch, you're down to fifteen?"

"By dinner, we'll be back to twenty," said Scotia from behind her curtain. "Get out of here, both of you."

Together Noelle and I ducked out the door and into the snowy street. The sun strained to shine through the clouds, leaving a weak light to fall on us as we trudged toward the dining hall. Others joined us, and Noelle slipped her arm into mine. At first I thought she was trying to comfort me, but when she hugged my arm to her chest, I realized it was the other way around. I was her security blanket.

The dining hall was only marginally warmer than the bunkhouse. I shivered as Noelle and I stood in line with the others, waiting our turn and soaking up what little heat crept toward us from the hot plates and ovens in the kitchen. As a woman served us pale pancakes and limp bacon, I tried not to think about the room beneath my boots, stockpiled with more weapons than I'd ever seen in my life. If one of those grenades went off, we'd all be dead. As if we weren't already.

"It's warm in the dollhouse," said Noelle as she slurped weak, pulpy orange juice from a plastic cup.

"The dollhouse?" I said, too busy rubbing my hands together and trying to breathe heat back into my fingertips to eat.

"Where we work," she said. "I guess it's not really warm there, technically, but the suits we wear keep the warmth in."

All of my questions died on my lips as I finally started on my breakfast. The pancakes tasted like paste, and the bacon was so salty that I nearly gagged, but it was food. I'd eaten worse.

We finished our meal in silence, and when another bell rang, Noelle leaped up and led me back outside. Groups of men and women in orange and red uniforms ducked into the buildings, stripping the streets of their color until only gray remained.

"In here," said Noelle, and we stopped beside the large three-story building I'd noticed the day before. Despite the size, the only entrance I could see was a single door. There were no windows, and the only hint I had as to what might be inside was a long chimney where white wisps escaped.

Beyond the first door was a second with a metal lock attached, and when Noelle opened it, I peered inside, expecting the same kind of interior—gray and dark. Instead I was greeted with a bright white hallway and a woman sitting at a desk, sorting something on a screen. She looked strangely familiar, and I tried to place her, but my brain had gone numb with the rest of me.

"Noelle, dear," she said warmly. "You're late."

"Sorry," said Noelle, her cheeks flushing. "I had to show Lila around."

The woman's gaze settled on me, and her eyes widened. "Oh—Lila! Yes, yes, of course. It's a pleasure to meet you."

She beamed, and suddenly I remembered where I'd seen her before. The meeting the night before—she'd been among the fringes of the group. I'd caught her staring at me twice.

"Can she work with me?" said Noelle hopefully. "Now that Maya…"

"Of course, of course," said the woman, and she typed something into the screen. "Why don't you show her the way, dear?"

With her arm still looped in mine, Noelle led me through a third door, one that looked much heavier than the others. It opened at her touch, however, and we stepped into a long hallway. It was just as bright as the room before, and there was a sterile feel about it that made me uneasy.

"What is this place?" I said. "Why do you call it the dollhouse?"

She shrugged. "I don't know—that's just what everyone calls it. Come on, we're through here."

We entered through a door that boasted a long word I couldn't read, and on the other side was the strangest room I'd ever seen. The walls on either side of us were made of the normal solid materials, but the one directly in front of us was made of clear plastic. The only way through was a thin slit in the center, and I saw several more layers of plastic beyond it, creating an odd tunnel.

"You have to strip," said Noelle, who had already taken off her jacket and was working on unzipping her jumpsuit. Half a dozen lockers lined the left wall, and I opened the one Noelle pointed to.

Growing up in a group home, I wasn't shy about nudity, but it was still unnerving to undress like that in front of someone I'd known for less than a day. Noelle didn't seem to notice—or maybe she had no idea that being naked was anything to be shy about—and once we had both stripped and shoved our dirty jumpsuits into our lockers, she led me over to the plastic wall.

"Go ahead," she said. "It's the sanitizing chamber. It's a little loud, but it doesn't really hurt."

With that ringing endorsement in mind, I slipped through the tight plastic, wincing as it rubbed against my skin. As soon as I was fully inside, the plastic seemed to close in on itself, and a red light above my head began to blink.

"Noelle, what—" Before I could finish, thick steam spilled into the airtight chamber, engulfing me until I couldn't see. On instinct I held my breath, and my skin began to tingle. If this was some kind of joke and I was about to melt into a puddle of blood and bone—

As quickly as it had come, the steam disappeared. The X on the back of my neck stung, but other than that, it had been painless. I glanced down at my hands. All the dirt that had accumulated under my fingernails over the past day was gone, and my skin was as pristine as it had been the day I'd woken up and discovered the Harts had had me Masked.

"My turn," said Noelle brightly, poking her head through the plastic. "Just go into the next chamber and put on a suit. I'll be right there."

I slid through the second slit into another section, this one full of plastic suits, shoes, and masks. Frowning, I pulled on the one nearest the entrance, unnerved by the way it crinkled every time I moved.

By the time I'd managed to finish tugging up the zipper, Noelle stepped through, looking as clean as I felt. "There you go, you have the hang of it already," she said, and she quickly dressed in a second suit. "You pull the hood over your head like this—you have to make sure you have every single hair inside, else they'll reprimand you. And then you put on the shoes and mask."

By the time we were both fully dressed, I felt like we were about to jump into a vat of toxic waste for a swim. But at least Noelle had been right about the heat—I hadn't been this warm since arriving in Elsewhere.

"What is all of this for?" I said.

"So we don't contaminate anything," she said. "Come on, we're already late."

She slipped through the final piece of plastic, and I hesitated. This one was opaque, making it impossible to see what was on the other side until I was there. My heart hammered. If Noelle did this every day, then it was fine. I'd be fine.

Before I could figure out when I'd regained my survival instinct, I reached the other side of the plastic, and I stopped. It was a simple white room, completely unlike anything I'd expected. It was mostly empty, except for a pile of small containers stacked neatly along several shelves and a guard dressed in a similar suit, holding a long thin club made entirely out of plastic. In the middle of the far wall was a window with a plastic barrier separating us from what lay beyond it, and beside the stack of containers was the start of a conveyor belt.

But the strangest thing of all was the boy who sat on a plastic stool in the center of the room, dressed in the same suit we wore. He had no mask, however, and his hood was pulled back, revealing his bald head.

"Good morning, Teddy," said Noelle cheerfully. The boy—Teddy—didn't acknowledge her. I frowned. Her voice had been muffled behind the mask, but even when she hadn't been facing me, I'd understood her. She turned and gave me a significant glance, one that was obvious even if I couldn't see most of her face.

"Hi," I said. "I'm Lila."

Teddy didn't answer me, either. I looked at Noelle uncertainly, but she didn't seem fazed in the least. Instead she was sorting through the containers, setting several up on a long white table beside the conveyor belt.

"Did I do something wrong?" I said quietly, ducking my head near hers.

"Wrong? What do you think you did wrong?"

"I—" I hesitated, my gaze darting toward Teddy.

"Oh!" Noelle giggled. "It's okay. He doesn't talk to anyone. I've never heard him say a word his whole life."

"His whole life?" I glanced at Teddy again. He sat perfectly still on the stool, his eyes focused on something I couldn't see. His lips moved as if he were speaking to himself, but no sound came out.

Noelle nodded. "We grew up in the same section. We were in all the same classes, but he never did anything. He just sat there. Everyone knew he was going to be declared a I, but then a couple years ago, when we were learning about what we'd be doing once we left Section J, they discovered he was really good at—"

Before she could finish, a buzzer went off. I jumped, but no one else batted an eye. The plastic barrier in the strange window in the wall opened, and a pair of gloved hands emerged, holding a lumpy red thing that looked like a piece of raw meat.

"What the hell—" I began, but Noelle jumped into action, delicately taking it from the gloved hands. She turned toward Teddy, whose eyes focused on the thing she was holding for a moment before unfocusing again.

"Open up that container," said Noelle, nodding to the nearest one on the table. "Hurry!"

My fingers trembled, and it took me two tries to undo the

complicated latch. At last I opened the top, and cold vapor poured out of the container while Noelle gently placed whatever it was inside.

"Secured," she called, closing the latch. "Number?"

"M042853," said a female voice through the half door before closing the plastic again. Noelle gestured to a blank square on the metal container.

"Can you write that down?" Her hands were covered in what looked like blood. I blinked.

"With what?" I said.

"The tip of your finger. It'll show up, trust me."

I couldn't distinguish whole words, but I did know enough to be able to slowly trace out each symbol on to the square. As promised, they appeared, though in shaky, barely legible writing. Noelle sighed.

"Never mind, I'll do it from here on out. Just let me wash my hands."

She moved to a sink I hadn't spotted in the corner, and using pedals on the floor, she made blue-tinted water spurt out from the faucet. I hadn't felt so incompetent and clueless since I'd first become Lila Hart.

"What was that?" I said. The blood from her hands mixed with the blue water, turning a sickening shade of purple before running down the drain.

"A heart," she said. My stomach contracted.

"You mean—a *human* heart?"

"Haven't you ever seen one before?"

I stared at her. "What are we doing with a human heart?"

She placed the container on the conveyor belt, and within seconds, it disappeared through another layer of plastic. "That's what we do," she said. "Once they harvest the hearts, we package them up for shipping. The doctors on the outside give them to people who need them. They do all kinds of stuff in the dollhouse—I've only ever worked hearts, but the others do lungs and livers and eyes, and Scotia's lucky enough to work hair."

I gaped at her. I really was going to be sick. "Human—human lungs and livers and eyes and—and hair? But where do they come from? Whose heart was that?"

She shrugged. "Probably not a I. The number's their birthday—April 28, 2053. It's really rare a I makes it that long, so he was probably a prisoner."

I stood rooted in place, trying to process it. Somewhere in the back of my mind, I'd known the organs of Is were harvested. Daxton had mentioned it when he'd taken me hunting Elsewhere. But I'd never let myself think about it too hard before, preferring to pretend it was just a story Daxton had told me to scare me into going along with his plans.

Now, after what I'd just seen, there was no pretending anymore.

"And—and Teddy?" I managed, my throat tightening. "What does he do?"

"He can tell the bad ones from the good," she said, her brow furrowing. "I'm not sure how, exactly, but they found out he could pick the hearts that would survive being transplanted from the ones that would likely fail. That's why they let him live."

"How is that even possible?" My voice broke, and it took everything I had not to lean up against the table of containers waiting for their inhabitants.

"Lots of Is can do stuff others can't," she said. "There was another one in my group that could draw anything from memory. Buildings, faces, trees down to the last leaf—it was amazing. He drew me a picture for my ninth birthday."

"Where is he now?" I said. "Does he have a job like Teddy?"

Her expression fell, and she busied herself with the latch on another container. "No. I don't know. Maybe. I never saw him again after graduation."

The buzzer went off again, and this time I didn't jump. There was no *maybe* about what had happened to the other boy.

"Here, you take this one," she said as the plastic window opened again, and another pair of gloved hands held out another human heart.

I wanted to say no, but the guard in the corner leered at me, and I gently took the organ from whoever was on the other side of the wall. It was still warm and much firmer than I'd expected, and I could've sworn I felt it beat.

The room began to spin, but I forced myself toward Teddy, holding it up for him. "Is this—" My mouth felt like sandpaper. "Is this okay?"

Teddy focused on it for a second, then looked away. "That means it's okay," said Noelle. "Here, put it down gently. Make sure it doesn't touch the edges."

She already had a container open, and I carefully—very, very carefully—set the heart inside. As soon as Noelle closed the lid, I exhaled and swayed on the spot. "Secured," she called, giving me a concerned look.

Whoever was on the other side either couldn't see us or didn't care that I was about to pass out, and a male voice called back, "F111964."

Female. November 19, 2064.

"Oh," whispered Noelle, her eyes going wide as she set the container down on the conveyor belt. She didn't say anything else, but it was obvious she knew whose heart I'd just handled.

The edges of my vision went dark, and in that moment, something inside me shut down. Together we watched the container roll away, and it wasn't until I felt something warm disappear behind my mask that I realized I was crying.

Noelle didn't say a word for the next hour, and I kept my mouth shut. There was nothing I could say to make any of this easier for her, and there was nothing Noelle could say to me to make me feel like any of this was okay.

Only once did Teddy open his mouth like he was trying to say something, and he slapped his hand to his thigh, his whole body squirming. This must have been the signal Noelle had been waiting for, because she immediately handed the heart back to the man on the other side of the plastic barrier.

"Defective," she said. The man didn't say a word; instead he took the heart back, and the plastic door shut, leaving us once again in silence. Teddy calmed down after that.

I wanted to ask what they did with that human heart—if it was tested to make sure Teddy was right, or if they simply threw it away on his word. The loss of life was hard enough to take, but not even being able to provide a viable heart that could help someone else live—somehow that made the whole miserable situation even more hopeless than it already was.

After that, I was sure things couldn't get worse. But this was hell, and of course they did, when a woman on the other side of the wall handed me a tiny heart that belonged to a little girl born that day. I consoled myself by rationalizing that the baby must have died at birth from an unrelated condition, but I couldn't shake the feeling that this heart had been requested from a VI with their own dying baby.

An hour later, a crackle from the communication device strapped to the guard's shoulder interrupted the silence. We'd packaged eleven hearts by then, and I couldn't make out the garbled speech, but the guard seemed to understand it clearly enough. "Hart," he barked. "You've been requested."

"By who?" I said, startled, but he didn't elaborate. Instead, Noelle shot me a frightened look, and I swallowed the lump in my throat.

It would be fine. If Knox had wanted to hunt me, he would have picked me before breakfast. But even the most airtight logic couldn't calm the fear churning within me, and I mumbled my goodbyes to Noelle and Teddy, who seemed as oblivious to me as ever, before heading back through the plastic walls.

By the time I reached the locker room, I was naked and shivering despite the blast of warm air coming from somewhere above me. I opened my locker and discovered a fresh set of clothes, and I'd managed to put on my underthings before a guard opened the door.

"Miss Hart?" he said. A rifle was strapped to his back.

I nodded, resisting the urge to shy away and insist he come back when I was fully dressed. "A moment, if you would," I said in the most Lila-like tone I could muster. I must have still had it, because the guard nodded, and though he didn't close the door, he didn't hurry me, either.

A minute later, I emerged in a clean jumpsuit, dry boots, and a heavy winter coat that actually had a prayer of keeping me warm now that it wasn't soaked through. The guard wasn't alone—another stood beside him, also holding a weapon, and I took a deep breath. Everything was okay. If they were going to kill me, they would have done it already.

Unless they were waiting for me to get outside, where they wouldn't have to sanitize the area.

"Miss Hart, if you'd follow me," said the first guard with an air of politeness I hoped no one intent on murdering me would bother using. He led me back down the brightly lit hallway toward the entrance, even opening the door for me to step through, but I stopped suddenly when I saw who was waiting for me on the other side.

Half a dozen guards stood in a semicircle, including one with an all-too-familiar pair of blue eyes—Rivers.

But he wasn't what caught my attention. Instead it was the woman in the center, hands on her hips and a scowl on her face, who made me wish I was still in that room handling warm human hearts.

Hannah Mercer.

XI

HEARTBEAT

Hannah's dislike hadn't dissipated in the eighteen-odd hours since we'd been introduced. She eyed me like a cat sizing up a mouse, and for the first time since Knox had spared me that morning, I let myself acknowledge the fact that I was terrified.

"Heard you had a bad night," she said. "Still want to refuse my husband's offer?"

Mercer's offer, not hers. The significance wasn't lost on me. "I'm happy here," I said stiffly.

She snorted. "Happy? Is that what the kids are calling it these days?" She jerked her head and started toward the door, indicating I should follow. I hesitated, but the guards on either side of me left me with no real choice.

It wasn't until we were both outside and walking through the cold that she spoke. "Jonathan also heard what happened, and he's insisting you remain with us for your own safety. The girls in this section can be dangerous, and he has no desire for anyone to hurt you."

"But he's fine sending three other girls off to be hunted

like wild animals," I said before I could stop myself. To my right, I sensed Rivers stiffen, but Hannah barely glanced at me.

"Consider yourself lucky. Every single one of these girls would kill to be you."

That was because they had no idea what my life was really like. Hannah did, though—she'd felt the III underneath my VII, yet as far as I knew, she still hadn't said a word to anyone about it. I could come up with a dozen reasons why she might want to keep that between us, but at the end of the day, because Hannah knew the secret that had so far kept me alive, that made her the biggest danger of all.

"There's possibility here, you know," said Hannah half a block later. "It may not seem like much, especially compared to the lifestyle you're used to, but your stay here doesn't have to be miserable. If you let us help you, you could have a life here. A family. A real shot at happiness. It's not all gloom and doom."

"Which one of us are you trying to convince?" I said. A strange expression flickered over Hannah's face, and she paused.

"I was in your position once," she said, gesturing for the guards to give us space. They backed away, forming a wide circle around us. Enough to offer some semblance of privacy, but not far enough to give me the chance to make a run for it. As if I had anywhere else to go. Though why we had guards today and not the day before, I couldn't fathom.

"What position is that?" I said. "The one where you went from a VII to an X because your uncle decided you weren't useful anymore, or the one where everything in your life worth loving vanished because you took a gamble and lost?"

A faint smile tugged at the corners of her mouth. "You think you're so alone, don't you? You think you're the only person in the world with your problems. Wake up, darling. You're surrounded by people who lost everything because they took a gamble. You sleep inches from people who your uncle decided weren't useful anymore."

She turned, and I thought the conversation was over until she swept her thick braid aside, revealing a scarred X on the back of her neck—one covering a faded V.

"I was seventeen years old when I was arrested," she said. "I'd been a V for a week. A Shield decided I was pretty, and when I knocked out his teeth for putting his hand where it didn't belong, I was the one who was punished, not him. I was lucky I made it here at all—most of the other Shields would have shot me in the alleyway and left me for dead. But I started out just like you, Lila. Bottom rung. Punching bag for the rest of the girls. And I didn't have a famous face to protect me from the worst of it."

She gave me a knowing look, and I kept my expression perfectly neutral. If she hadn't spilled yet, then she wasn't going to do it in front of a bunch of guards.

"Someone helped me out when I was a little older than you," she said. "Kept me safe. Gave me an opportunity to advance and, ultimately, have a life worth living. Let me return the favor."

"Why me?" I said. "Daxton hates me. I won't be able to get you any special treatment."

"This has nothing to do with him," she said, her brow furrowing. I thought I saw something flash across her face again, but it was gone before I could be sure. "I'm doing this because I'm willing to bet your journey's been more difficult than the rest of us know, and because I think you have an enormous amount of untapped potential. Now that you're here—now that you're just another inmate instead of the beloved Lila Hart,

I want to give you an opportunity to discover who you really are. And I think your best bet would be to stay with us."

I barely managed to hold back my snort. "The only thing I have that's worth a damn is my face and my name. No one cares about the rest of it."

"I do," she said. "Jonathan might want you to come to the house because he thinks it'll buy him a favor somewhere, but I'm much more interested in the side of you no one else sees. Let me help you, Lila. I promise you won't regret it."

I held her stare for several seconds, my mind racing. I would hate to leave Noelle in that damp, dank place with the likes of Scotia, but Rivers's words the night before ran through me, drowning out my doubts.

Even if Hannah was lying through her teeth, at least this might get me close enough to Knox to slit his throat and watch him bleed. And maybe—just maybe—getting him out of the way would give the Blackcoats a chance to get the arsenal codes and start a real revolution. My life was over either way. That didn't mean it was over for everyone else, too.

"I guess it wouldn't hurt to see the house," I said, and Hannah straightened, squaring her shoulders in an oddly victorious way.

"It wouldn't," she agreed. "This way."

As we walked down the street, several of the men and women going about their duties stared at us. Now that they knew who I was, I supposed this was even bigger news, and part of me hoped it would reach Noelle before dinnertime. When I didn't come back to the dollhouse, she would worry, and I had no desire to put her through that.

The rest of the walk to Mercer Manor went by quickly, and Hannah punched a sequence into a keypad at the entrance, allowing the gate to open for us. Several of the guards lingered, staying off the property, but a handful joined us, including Rivers.

The small hill was covered in untouched snow, unlike the gray and muddied slush that soaked the other streets. Someone had meticulously plowed the drive to leave a perfectly even trail upward, and we passed several large trees that probably provided ample shade in the summer. If this yard hadn't been in the middle of Elsewhere, it would have been picturesque.

"Here we are," said Hannah as we reached the front door. She punched a code into another keypad, and this time she also scanned her handprint. "I'll get your prints into the system tonight if you decide to stay. Shoes off."

We stepped into an enclosed porch, and I toed off my boots, too busy looking around to care that my socks were soaking up some of the muddy water. Hannah eyed my feet dubiously, and only then did I pull them off, too.

When we moved into the massive foyer, I understood—everything was clean in a way that made it sparkle. The floor was made of white marble, the walls seemed to shimmer in the light, and a chandelier hung overhead, swaying gently once Hannah closed the door. It was as beautiful as any of the Hart properties, and as I spotted an ornate gold H imbedded into the marble entranceway, I had the sneaking suspicion it *did* belong to my supposed family.

A grand staircase wound up to the second floor, splitting off and going in two different directions halfway. Off to the right of the foyer was a pair of tightly closed double doors, and to the left was an open and airy sitting room. Beyond that, I made out signs of a dining room, and I thought I heard the faint sounds of dishes clattering in the distance.

"Lunch will be served soon," said Hannah. "You should join us. Come—I'll give you a tour."

She led me around the first floor, showing me the main rooms. There was another, more casual sitting room deeper within the mansion, and the hallways felt like a maze as they turned in on themselves, leaving me as lost as I felt on the streets. On the bottom floor alone, Hannah pointed out three bathrooms, and she walked me through a magnificent dining room meant to seat at least fifty.

"Your family has dined here many times, along with the Ministers of the Union and their loved ones," she said, gesturing to the dark wood and silver candlesticks. Rich oil paintings hung on the walls, and I recognized a man in one—Daxton's grandfather, the original ruler of the new United States. The one who had put the ranking system into place and, according to Augusta, saved the country from economic ruin.

Even back then, in the darkest hours of history, it had to have been less barbaric than this place.

"Does my family own this home?" I said as we approached the back of the house. Hannah nodded stiffly.

"Daxton—the Prime Minister allows us to stay here while we watch over the prisoners," she said. "Another reason why we feel it only appropriate you stay with us. I have one more room to show you down here."

She opened another door, and I stepped inside what was probably the simplest room of the house, but I instantly understood why she'd saved it for last. All three outer walls were made of glass, and the ceiling was angled, allowing for an uninterrupted view of the sky. A line of trees cut off most of the view of Elsewhere, giving it the illusion of being nothing more than a home in the middle of a beautiful forest.

"This is what's called a solarium. It's my favorite place," said Hannah, her voice low, as if she were admitting some kind of embarrassing secret. "It's especially beautiful at night."

"It—looks like it would be," I said tightly. The thought of there being any kind of real beauty in this place seemed so diametrically opposed to the ugliness and horror that I couldn't wrap my mind around it. But maybe that was the point. Maybe this was how Hannah stayed above it all. If what she'd told me was true, I couldn't blame her, not really.

We lingered for another minute before she led me to a staircase in the back of the house, and we headed upward. "The third floor is mostly mine and Jonathan's," she said. "The second floor is meant for guests. Jonathan took the liberty of having a room set up for you. I hope you like pink."

She led me down the hallway toward a door marked The Augusta Suite. I nearly gagged at the thought of staying anywhere Augusta had slept, but my disgust grew less vehement when Hannah opened the door.

Inside lay a bedroom that would have been more appropriate for a preteen girl than for Lila Hart, decorated in shades of pink and gold with decals of three-dimensional butterflies glued to the far wall. The gold canopy bed was hidden by a shimmering fabric, and a stained-glass window depicting a sunset cast hues into a mirrored wall, making the entire room explode in color.

"It's...younger than you may be used to, but you have your own bathroom, and I made sure the servants removed the dolls." Hannah's voice had a nervous edge to it, as if she was afraid I was going to judge it harshly after spending the night in a room half this size crammed with twenty other girls.

"It's beautiful," I said. "Thank you. Do you have a daughter?"

Hannah shook her head. "Jonathan and I don't have any children."

There was a wistful look to her that made me wonder if

she had wanted children, or if she'd had them once and lost them. Asking outright was likely to shatter whatever tentative peace we'd created between us, but another question popped into my mind.

"If you had children," I said, "would they be allowed to leave Elsewhere and become part of society?"

She pursed her lips, not meeting my eye. "If you're born Elsewhere, you stay Elsewhere. No one except Jonathan and the other appointed officials ever leave, not without executive order."

"So you haven't...?"

"No. Not since I was arrested." She stepped into the room and opened the drawers. "I've set aside some of my old clothes. They might be a little loose, but they should fit. If you're staying here, I don't want to see you wearing that damn jumpsuit."

I glanced down. The red had seemed to stick out like a sore thumb the day before, but now I knew it was the only way for me to blend in. No one else wore regular clothes. Even Hannah wore a white uniform. "I'll change later. I need to go back to the bunkhouse and—get my things."

"Your things?" said Hannah, eyebrow arched. "What things?"

I'd tucked the napkin Benjy had drawn for me underneath my mattress for safekeeping, but more urgently, I needed to make sure Noelle knew I was all right. "Just—something sentimental," I said. "It doesn't have any real value. I just want to have it."

She took a long breath and released it sharply. "If you insist. At least wait until after lunch. I suppose I'll be able to stomach one meal with you in that thing."

I had to bite my lip to stop myself from a retort I'd likely regret. "Thanks," I managed, and I stepped out of the pink-and-gold room. "Which way?"

Hannah led me farther down the hallway, presumably toward another staircase. Before we reached it, however, we passed an open door, and out of habit, I glanced inside.

It was another guest room—this time marked The Edward Suite—and it was decorated in navy and silver. A four-poster bed and other mahogany furniture dominated the room, and unlike the Augusta Suite, this had no stained glass. It was comfortable, but there were no frills or personal touches.

Except for one. On the bedside table was a gold frame with a labyrinth etched into the metal—the exact same one Greyson had given me for Lila's birthday.

I stopped in the doorway. This must have been the room Knox was staying in, only a few yards from mine. It would be incredibly easy to sneak into his room and slit his throat in the middle of the night. If I did it right, he might even think I was there to ask his forgiveness. It would be simple. One piece of that stained glass, one slash to the throat—

"He misses you," said Hannah over my shoulder.

"Knox?" I said, too startled to hide my surprise. "He doesn't miss me. He never loved me in the first place. It was all some twisted political arrangement."

"Maybe that's how it started, and maybe that's what it is for you, but I know love when I see it. That man would move heaven and earth to keep you safe."

The ludicrousness of her statement fueled me with an insane kind of courage, and I stepped into the room, heading straight for the picture frame. I picked it up and examined the photograph of Greyson and me inside. I'd been Elsewhere for a single day, but already that felt like another lifetime ago.

My finger twitched toward the switch on the back, the one

that would reveal the picture of my real face and Benjy. But with Hannah lurking behind me, I couldn't risk it. Not even for a split second.

"Knox is the reason I'm here," I said, tracing the golden labyrinth. "He killed my—he killed my best friend and sent me here all because he thought he couldn't control me anymore. If he loved me the way you think he does, I'd be back in D.C. right now, and you wouldn't be on babysitting duty."

"I'm always on babysitting duty." She stepped beside me. "Who is that?"

"Greyson. My cousin." It took me a moment to remember that until his older brother had been killed last year, Greyson had been the spare and had spent his life out of the public eye. I'd barely known anything about him before being Masked as Lila, and someone Elsewhere likely wouldn't recognize him at all. "He'll be Prime Minister next, after Daxton."

"Right." Hannah hesitated. "I'm sure we'll meet him soon enough."

"I hope not." I set the picture frame down gently. The knowledge of what lay behind that photograph would have to be enough for now. Maybe later, when Hannah wasn't trailing me, I would have the chance to sneak in and see Benjy's face one last time.

Instead of leading me back out, Hannah remained standing in the room for a long moment, her gaze focused on me. "Whatever happened between you and Knox...I'm sure he had his reasons for it, and I hope you find it in yourself to forgive him. That kind of love is rare in this world, and if you're lucky enough to find it..." Her lips pursed, and for a moment, she looked away. "You shouldn't throw it away all because of a stupid mistake."

I opened my mouth to tell her that it hadn't been a

mistake—that Knox had known exactly what he'd been doing when he'd pulled the trigger and murdered Benjy, but my protest died on my lips. Hannah was focused on something far beyond this room, and it was obvious we were no longer talking about me and Knox.

"I'll talk to him once I'm settled," I said, trying to sound like I was really considering the option. Inwardly I began to wonder if there wasn't more to Hannah than I'd already assumed. Whoever she was thinking about, it was obvious it wasn't her husband.

At last she led me to the grand staircase. The steps were cold and sharp, made of marble with no carpet to protect them, and as I followed Hannah down to the foyer, I fantasized about pushing Knox down the stairs. It would work just as well as a shard of glass to the throat, and this way, I could reasonably claim innocence. No doubt Hannah would suspect me, but without any proof...

Hannah knocked on the double doors that had remained shut throughout her tour. "Jonathan, Lila's here."

"Come in," called a muffled voice. Hannah pushed the door open, revealing an office with a long desk in the middle and a pair of uncomfortable chairs facing it, clearly meant for guests. Mercer stood in front of a wall of wooden filing cabinets, and he hastily closed a middle drawer, locking it with something hanging from a cord. Before I could get a good look at it, he hung the cord around his neck and dropped the key underneath his shirt.

"Ah, Lila," said Mercer, and he moved around his desk to join us. Kissing Hannah on the cheek, he wrapped his arm around her shoulders possessively before focusing on me. Up close, I could see the fine lines on his face and the bags under his eyes. He looked like he hadn't slept in a week. "I'm so pleased you've decided to join us."

"Thank you for inviting me," I said, forcing a smile. Whether Mercer could tell or not, he didn't seem to care.

"Lunch is about to be served," said Hannah. She slumped underneath his weight, and though she snaked her arm around his waist, her hand was clenched in a fist. "Is Knox back from his hunt yet?"

The reminder of what had happened that morning made a block of ice form in my stomach, and I dug my nails into my palm. How could Hannah insist he loved me when he was in a forest nearby hunting three of the girls I'd shared a bunk with?

"He canceled," said Mercer with a sigh. "Got an important note from D.C., something he had to take care of right away. I gave him use of your office for the morning."

As Hannah's displeasure settled clearly over her face, I struggled to hide my relief. There was still time to talk him out of it. I didn't want to die, not until he was dead right alongside me, but if I could spare just one of those girls' lives, it would be worth it.

"I take it he'll be joining us for lunch, then," said Hannah.

"I will," said another voice from behind me—Knox. I stiffened and stayed still, refusing to turn around. "I see I'm not your only guest."

"Lila decided to join us after all," said Mercer. "It seems your allure was too much for her to resist."

Knox chuckled, and I could feel his warmth directly behind me. His hands settled on my shoulders, and I struggled not to wince. "I'm sure it has less to do with me and more to do with the warmth and food."

Mercer laughed as if this was some sort of hilarious joke—as if men and women in his section weren't freezing to death at night and eating food most IIs wouldn't serve to their pets. At least Hannah didn't crack a smile as he led the way into the dining room, where a hot lunch of turkey, potatoes, crisp vegetables, and biscuits with gravy waited for us. Compared to the pale pancakes and questionable bacon I'd had for breakfast, it was a feast fit for a king.

Knox sat beside me at the table, and though I could feel his stare on me several times, I refused to look up from my plate. He and Mercer carried on a conversation about hunting—deer, I was relieved to figure out only a minute in—and later on, the various issues Mercer had been facing with Elsewhere lately.

"Everyone wants to be a guard," he said. "We have to be careful who we pick—can't put a weapon in the hands of anyone who might use it against us."

"Is there some kind of test or screening you do?" said Knox as he dipped a bite of turkey and potato in gravy. "How do you determine the rebels from the obedient?"

"We watch them." Mercer tapped his temple. "That's what we do here—we watch. I know everything that goes on in this place. If anyone steps a toe out of line, I'm right there. Thinning the herd is important—without it, we'd be overcrowded, with too many mouths to feed and not enough beds."

"Hence the nightly entertainment," said Knox. Mercer nodded.

"It's especially important during the cold months. Not many of the Ministers want to spent hours in subzero temperatures hunting, so we have to make do. We tend to receive an influx of citizens during that time period, too—Hannah suspects it has to do with people growing more desperate during the winter. So we have to get creative. Anyone with a rare or needed blood type is sent to processing, of course, but the rest—the more miserable they are, the more willing they are to play nice. Make an example of a few, and the rest fall into place."

He said this all in a tone that implied he was talking about cattle, not human beings with lives and feelings. I gripped my fork, resisting the urge to leap over the table and stab him in the eye. Across from me, Hannah looked pale.

"Do you have security cameras set up so there's hard evidence against them?" said Knox.

Mercer snorted. "We don't need hard evidence. The moment they step foot here, their lives are a privilege, not their right. But, yes," he added. "We have cameras set up around the administrative and manufacturing areas, and regular patrols in the residential quarters. We also have informants—most of our information comes directly from them."

Informants like Scotia, who had been all too happy to rat out Chelsea, Maya, Poppy, and the others. "What do they get in return?" I blurted.

Mercer's gaze fell on me, and the corners of his eyes crinkled. "My favor, of course. Privileges the others don't. We ensure they're never at risk for being selected for hunts. And we choose our guards from our pool of informants, so it's quite a lucrative choice for them. Most days we have so many willing to inform on others that we have no need for security."

"How do you know they're telling the truth?" I said.

Mercer blinked. "The truth about what?"

"About what they saw. How do you know they're not just making it up to get on your good side?"

He shrugged and stabbed at a carrot. "Does it matter? Either way, it helps thin the herd. As I said, their lives are a privilege, to be taken away at our discretion. We don't need a reason. Most of them have already committed crimes after all."

So that was it, then. The prisoners weren't people to the

Mercers. They were something to be managed—a product that, in the end, they would send back to society in pieces, meant to save the lives of citizens who hadn't been desperate enough to steal an orange or a loaf of bread.

"I need to go to my bunk," I said, standing abruptly. "I have to pick up my things before the other girls take them."

"If they do, we'll find them. Don't worry," said Mercer, but I shook my head.

"I'll be quick."

"I'll escort her," said Knox, and he folded his napkin and stood, too. "I'd like to take a look around without the guards hovering anyway. See what it's really like for the prisoners."

"Of course," said Mercer, though he sounded dubious. "If anyone gives you trouble, I'll make sure they're handled."

Anyone would have to be suicidal to hassle Knox, a Minister's son, but he nodded anyway. And though I would've rather chewed off my fingers than let him touch me again, he set his hand on my shoulder and guided me out of the room.

We dressed in coats and boots in silence, and it wasn't until we were halfway down the Mercer's drive that he spoke. "Are you all right? You look terrible."

I gaped at him. "Am I all right? Today, after I watched you pick out your prey among my bunk mates, I handled eleven human hearts—still warm, by the way. Yesterday a pack of girls beat me up, and a guard shot a girl named Chelsea in the head because I tried to help her. The day before that, my supposed fiancé killed my boyfriend, and the Prime Minister tried to break my spine. Which part of that is supposed to make me feel like anything other than shit?"

Knox stared straight ahead as we reached the Mercers' gate. The guards had dispersed, and no one else was stupid enough to linger nearby. "The girls are fine. I didn't go hunting."

"Yeah, because Daxton had something more important for you to do," I spat. "Why didn't you pick me?"

He raised an eyebrow and finally glanced at me. "Do you want me to kill you?"

"You promised you would. You swore you'd put a bullet in my brain before you ever let me wind up here."

"Is that what you really want?"

"I want you to stop playing games and tell me the truth for once." My eyes began to burn, and despite my best efforts at bottling my fury, my throat tightened. "Why did you do it? If you wanted to punish me, then you should've killed me instead. Benjy never did anything to you. He didn't deserve to die."

Knox pushed the gate open for me, and it was only through a supreme act of willpower that I resisted the urge to knock his head into one of the spikes. "I did what I did to save your life."

Tears blurred my vision, and I wiped my eyes angrily. "You think I care about my life anymore?"

"You should," he said. "It's the only one you've got."

Before I could stop myself, I drew my arm back and punched him directly over the heart. My wrist buckled under the force of it, bending awkwardly, and pain shot up my arm. "You're sick," I said, my voice breaking. "You're no better than the rest of them. You don't care about anyone but yourself, do you? You didn't just kill Benjy—you betrayed the Blackcoats, too. How many people are dead because of you, Knox? A dozen? A hundred? A thousand? How many people are going to die before it's all over because you care more about your own worthless life than the freedom of millions?"

His expression remained blank. "Believe what you want, but I did what I did because it was my only option. Sometimes pawns have to be sacrificed for the game."

"I'm not a pawn, and my life isn't yours to sacrifice."

"No, it isn't," he agreed. "You did a fantastic job of securing that fate for yourself. And for Benjy."

"Say his name again, and I'll show you sacrifice."

Knox sighed, and for the first time since I'd spotted him the evening before, he looked like the same Knox who had pretended to care about me in D.C. "I'm sorry, Kitty. I really am. If I could've done it any other way…"

"But you didn't," I said. "And now this is my life. Thank you for that, by the way. I'm sure I'll find some way to repay you eventually."

"I'm sure you will, too," he said with a resignation I didn't expect. I eyed him, and a few seconds passed. My fingers grew numb in the cold, and I shoved my hands in my pockets.

"Why are you even here, Knox? If you want to kill me, just get it over with already. Stop playing with your food."

He tilted his head and peered at me curiously. "Is that how you really see me? As one of them?"

"What do you think?"

Knox raked his leather-gloved hand through his hair. "I needed an excuse to be here, Kitty. When I saw an opportunity to gain Daxton's trust and get you out of D.C., I had to take it. I had no other choice, not if I wanted to keep you safe."

"This is what you call keeping me safe?" I gestured wildly. "Do you have any idea how many people have threatened to kill me in the past day?"

"But they won't, because you're Lila Hart, and even if they hate you, they value their life more," said Knox. "The Mercers took you in at my request. They'll continue to keep you safe until everything's over."

"Until what's over?" I said. "What's going on, Knox? Why was Augusta keeping a file on me? What's in it that makes me so important that you have to babysit me even after you've had me arrested?"

He shook his head. "I'm keeping you safe for the same reason you were chosen to replace Lila in the first place. But this is bigger than you, Kitty, and right now, all you need to know is that you're my excuse to be here."

"Why? Because it gives you the perfect opportunity to betray the Blackcoats a second time and make yourself look good in front of Daxton?"

He eyed me. "Who told you?"

I clenched my jaw. As angry as I was at Scotia, I couldn't betray her and the Blackcoats here, not to Knox. "You answer me first. What's going on? What plan is so huge that it's worth Benjy's life?"

Knox shook his head. "I want to show you something."

I snorted and wiped my nose with my sleeve. "I'm not going anywhere with you."

"Yes, you are." He fished a tissue from his black wool coat and offered it to me. "Just because you're here doesn't give you the right to act like anything less than a Hart."

"I'm not a Hart, or have you forgotten?" I shot, snatching the tissue from him. Instead of using it, I stuffed it in my pocket.

"You're more of a Hart than the rest of them combined," he said. "Now come on. This won't wait forever."

To my surprise, he took my hand, his grip like iron around my fingers, but not tight enough to hurt. Just tight enough to make it impossible for me to wriggle away. I briefly considered causing a fuss, but he was clearly a visitor, and I still wore the red jumpsuit that marked me a prisoner. There was no way I was going to win that war.

Instead of leading me toward the bunkhouses, Knox made

a sharp right toward the edge of Elsewhere, where I'd met Elliott the night before. It was a short walk to the fence, and he led me down the length of it to the nearest guard tower. It was made of stone and metal, rising above the rest of Elsewhere to give the guards patrolling along the perimeter a clear view of everything that was happening.

"I'm sure it's no prettier up here than it is down there," I said as Knox led me up the winding staircase.

"You'd be surprised," he said mildly. When we reached the door that opened onto the top of the tower, he paused. "Everything I do is for the greater good, Kitty. I hope you understand that, because I need you to trust me."

"Then I guess you're shit out of luck, because if you think I'm ever going to trust you again, you're delusional," I said.

He shrugged.

"Maybe so, but I'd like you to keep an open mind regardless."

He pushed open the door before I could reply. Despite the heavy clouds, the light hurt my eyes, and I blinked.

And then I blinked again.

And a third time.

"What?" I said breathlessly, and this time there was no holding back the flood of tears.

Standing on the circular platform, wearing an orange jumpsuit, was Benjy.

XII

GUARDED

I didn't remember crossing the platform. One second I was standing in the doorway beside Knox, and the next I was in Benjy's arms, sobbing into his shoulder.

"Shh, you're okay. It's okay," he murmured in my hair. "I'm right here. Everything's going to be fine."

Hearing his voice again was enough to make up for everything that had happened the past two days, and suddenly the part of me that had gone numb the moment Knox had put that bullet into Benjy came alive again, flooding me with a rush of uncontrollable emotions I couldn't begin to sort. Relief—elation—terror he would be taken from me again—and the crushing reality that Benjy was here, in Elsewhere, and didn't have the face of a Hart to protect him.

"What—what's going on?" I managed to choke out half a minute later. I didn't pull away from Benjy, but I did glance to the side where Knox stood. "How is this even possible? I saw you kill him. I *saw* it."

"What you saw was a plan we concocted months ago, in case Daxton decided to get rid of you permanently," said

Knox. "I knew the only thing he would accept in place of your death was making you watch Benjy die and having to live with that memory."

"I'm sorry," said Benjy, his warm arms wrapped so tightly around me that I could barely breathe, but I would've rather had him over oxygen any day. "We had no other choice."

Knowing Benjy had been in on it lessened my anger only slightly, and I glared at Knox. "You could've told me."

"No, I couldn't have," he said. "Your reaction had to be authentic. If I'd told you, you would have given it away even if you hadn't meant to. I tried to tell you earlier—I'd hoped you would be with the Mercers when I arrived, but of course you were too stubborn to listen to them."

I shook my head, clutching Benjy and inhaling his scent. Even here, he still smelled like home. "Why did you side with Daxton if you were going to save me and Benjy?"

"Because Daxton needs to believe someone is on his side," said Knox, leaning against the rail. "I'm the best candidate. He trusts me, and that trust is invaluable. It could mean the difference between losing and winning this war."

"But you betrayed the Blackcoats," I said.

He hesitated. "Under Celia's orders, yes. Sampson didn't know it, but the raid was always meant to fail."

I stared at him. "You sent those people to their deaths."

"And I would do it again if it meant gaining Daxton's trust."

The part of me that had begun to thaw toward him froze solid again. "Why are you even here, Knox?" I said coldly. "Can't the Blackcoats break everyone out of Elsewhere without your help?"

He leveled his stare at me. "The Blackcoats aren't breaking anyone out, Kitty."

I frowned. "Then what—"

"The Blackcoats are breaking in."

He straightened and took a step toward us, leaning in as if he were afraid of someone else hearing. A pair of guards stood at the far edge of the circular platform, barely visible beyond the door, but when one of them glanced over, I recognized his face from the Blackcoat meeting. Maybe they didn't know who Knox was, but Knox knew who they were.

"We're going to war, Kitty. A real war this time, not just random bombings and guerilla tactics under the cover of night. If we can gain control of Elsewhere, we have a real shot. We'll have resources, weapons, an entire army at our disposal—"

"You're not going to make the prisoners fight, are you?" I said, horrified.

"No one will be forced," he said. "But this is their chance at a normal life. Enough of them will pick up a weapon, and we'll have the numbers we'll need to give the Blackcoats the edge."

I hesitated. "Not everyone's in here for stealing food or not paying taxes. Some of them—"

"We'll sort that out when we get there," said Knox. "For now, we need numbers, and we need weapons. This place has both, and it's designed to keep prisoners in, not upstanding citizens out. This is our best shot, and I'm here to make sure it happens."

I pressed my lips together. "Do you have the armory codes?"

He grimaced, not looking surprised that I knew about those. "Not yet. We're working on it."

"Do you know where they are, at least?"

"In Mercer's office, corner drawer. It's in a black folder. The codes are changed every three days, which is why we've cut it close."

"I know what you're thinking, Kitty, and you're not going

to do it," said Benjy, running his fingers through my hair. "You can't risk it, not when we're this close."

"I don't have a choice," I said. "If Knox can't get them—"

"Then you'll have no chance, either," he said. "For once in your life, would you please listen to me?"

Knox cleared his throat. "Benjy has a point. The Mercers respect me. They've given me free run of the house, and if I'm caught lurking around at night, they won't question it. You, on the other hand—you might be a Hart, but I can only protect you so much. We're going to lose enough people during the war. I'm not throwing anyone away unnecessarily."

"How many—" I swallowed hard. "Do we really have a shot? Elsewhere against the rest of the country?"

"Anything I tell you right now would be a guess. Daxton might have reserves I'm unaware of. The armories might have been cleared out. We have no way of knowing for sure."

He and Benjy exchanged a look, and Benjy's grip on my shoulders tightened.

"What?" I said, glancing back and forth between them. "Don't tell me there's more."

"We might have one way to avoid a bloodbath," said Knox. "It's not a guarantee, but as you so astutely pointed out, it's our best shot of overthrowing Daxton as peacefully as possible."

I opened and shut my mouth. The file on Daxton—the one that had gotten me arrested and Benjy supposedly killed in the first place. "You haven't found it yet."

"You know we haven't," said Knox. "You were right, Kitty. If we can get our hands on it and prove Daxton isn't the real Prime Minister, we could strip him of his support. The army, the navy, the generals, the Ministers of the Union, everyday citizens—if they know he isn't who they think he is, they'll rebel right along with us. He'll be arrested in a matter of hours."

"And Greyson will be Prime Minister," I said. "No."

Knox reached for me, and I slapped his hand away. He might not have killed Benjy, but he'd still put both of us through this. "You're willing to get countless people killed just so Greyson won't have to be Prime Minister for a few days, until we get it all settled?"

"The Blackcoats will kill him," I said. Knox opened his mouth, but I cut him off before he could speak. "You can pretend all you want that the Blackcoats will leave him alone, but he isn't one of them. He's a Hart. They'll string him up right alongside Daxton, and I'm not going to let that happen."

"Neither will I."

"Then prove it. Get Greyson to safety—bring him here so I know for sure you're telling the truth—and then I'll tell you where the file is."

Knox's frown deepened, and suddenly he looked much older than he really was. "You're going to get people killed."

"So are you, so I guess that makes us even."

He huffed. "Fine. I will bring Greyson here once we've overtaken Elsewhere, and then you'll be able to see for yourself that he's safe. The instant he arrives, you tell me where the file is. Deal?"

"And you're going to tell me what was in mine, too."

A low growl escaped him, but at last he nodded shortly. "Deal."

The three of us spent the next few hours on the guard tower as Benjy and I curled up against the wall, keeping each other warm as we talked about nothing and everything. Knox pretended not to listen, but I could see the way his head tilted toward us whenever we whispered to each other, and part of me wondered if what Hannah had said back in Mercer Manor was true—if Knox really did love me the way she claimed.

It was ridiculous. I was a pawn to him in a game he was determined to win, and he'd proven time and time again that he was willing to sacrifice me for the greater good he claimed to believe in. At this point I wasn't sure he was capable of loving anything more than that, and even if he did, I wasn't it. Benjy was my home. He was my other half, and that was the love I was fighting for. That was the love I believed in.

At last the sun began to dip below the horizon, and it was time to go. Benjy was in the section beside ours—the one Noelle had grown up in before she'd come to Section X. "It's safer there," said Knox as I hugged Benjy one last time. "The guards are gentler, and the section leaders don't allow violence in front of the children."

"I'll be fine," said Benjy, nuzzling the top of my head. "Take care of yourself, all right? Don't do anything crazy. I can't lose you again."

"You won't," I said fiercely, and I stood on my tiptoes and kissed him. His lips were chapped, but it was the same familiar kiss I would have crossed mountains to find. He hadn't been Masked.

One of the guards led Benjy down the stairs first, and as soon as he was out of sight, something inside me began to ache. I told myself again and again that this wouldn't be the last time we would be together, but I wasn't sure what to believe anymore.

"If he has so much as a scratch on him next time I see him, I'll slit your throat," I said to Knox as we descended the steps a minute later, once Benjy and the guard had disappeared beyond the fence into the other section.

"I know," he said. "Come on, we'll stop by your bunkhouse

before we go back to the Mercers'. They're probably wondering where we are by now."

I yanked my arm from his grip. "I know the way. I'll be back in time for dinner."

"Kitty—"

"We're not friends," I said, walking backward and putting several feet between us. "After what you put me and Benjy through, we're never going to be friends again. So you might as well stop pretending, all right? There's no point anymore."

I turned and hurried away, shoving my hands in my pockets and ducking my head. Knox didn't call after me, and by the time I worked up enough courage to look over my shoulder, he was gone.

I tried not to think about him as I wound through the gray, slushy streets of Elsewhere, instead focusing on the fact that Benjy was alive. Every time I remembered the warmth of his arms around me, my heart skipped a beat, and it was all I could do to hold it together. There was still a chance. We still had a chance at the future we wanted together, and this time I wasn't going to let anyone, especially Knox Creed, steal it from us.

When I reached the dining hall, I turned a corner to cut through an alleyway I remembered from the night before. Instead I nearly tripped on a girl curled up against the wall, sobbing.

"I'm sorry, I—" I began, but as soon as she looked up, I dropped to my knees beside her. "Noelle? What's wrong?"

Her dark hair hung in a limp curtain, hiding her features, and I brushed it back so I could see her face. Her cheeks were red and streaked with tears, and her entire body shuddered with sobs as she forced herself to speak. "It—it's Elliott," she cried. "He—he wasn't at the fence today. I think—I think—"

I hugged her thin shoulders. "Hey, it's okay. I'm sure he's

fine. His schedule probably got shifted around or—something. Maybe there was an incident, and he didn't have time to meet you."

She shook her head. "You don't understand—he never misses a day. Ever. Something happened to him. I know it."

"But he's a guard. No one's going to hurt him."

Another choked sob escaped her. "Sometimes, if the guards are caught doing really horrible things—sometimes they—they—"

"Would Elliott do anything really horrible?" I said gently.

She sniffed and rubbed her eyes with her sleeve. "No. I don't know. He's the nicest person I've ever met."

"Then I'm sure he's fine," I said. But that only made her break down all over again, her body trembling as she hid her face in her bare hands.

I inched closer, pressing my side against hers for warmth and running my fingers through her hair, trying over and over again to reassure her. But the more I spoke, the harder she cried, until finally she gasped, "How do you know it'll be okay? You're here, just like the rest of us. You don't know anything for sure."

I bit my lip. She was right, but at least when I was wrong, that meant my nightmares hadn't completely come true yet. "I do know we aren't nearly as alone here as they want us to think," I said quietly. "There are people out there—lots of people, powerful people—who know what we go through. They want to help, and they're going to. You just have to hang in there and trust that nothing's going to happen to Elliott."

"There are?" She sniffed again and finally looked at me. Her face was blotchy and her eyes swollen, but at least she had stopped crying for a second. Seizing the opportunity, I nodded.

"Out there, everyone thinks Elsewhere is some sort of—" I hesitated. I knew what I'd thought Elsewhere was before Daxton had brought me here to hunt, but no one had ever really talked about it. It was a mythical, far-off place we'd never see, if we were lucky and behaved ourselves—but at the same time, it had been a constant threat hanging over our heads, ready to uproot us from our lives at any moment. "No one really knows what it is," I admitted. "It's just this—place. Some people think it's somewhere warm, because they send the elderly here. Others think it's…what it is, I guess. But no one really knows how horrible it is, not unless they've gone hunting. And even then—"

"Hunting?" she said. I silently cursed myself.

"Nothing—never mind," I said quickly. Noelle was scared enough as it was. "There are people out there who know how bad it is, though, and they've told others. And people are rising up against the Prime Minister. They want to break us out of here—they're going to really soon, so you just have to sit tight, okay?"

She looked at me dubiously, and I couldn't blame her. I wouldn't believe me, either. "Who?" she said. "No one cares about us."

"Yes, they do," I said firmly. "I care. I cared before I came here, and lots of other people do. Powerful people who can change things and help us—*really* help us." I lowered my voice. "Have you ever heard of the Blackcoats?"

"The Blackcoats?" Her frown deepened. "What are those?"

"They're a group of people who are going to get us out of here," I said. "I'm here because of them—because I'm going to help them. And I'm going to help you, too, Noelle. I prom—"

"Lila," said a sharp voice over my shoulder. I jerked around.

Scotia stood only a couple feet away, close enough to hear everything we'd just said. My face grew hot.

"Hasn't anyone ever told you that eavesdropping is rude?" I snapped.

She ignored me. "I need to speak with Noelle," she said, looking past me and staring directly at her instead. "Go back to Mercer Manor, Lila, and enjoy your dinner."

"I—" I began, but Scotia grabbed me by the arms and hauled me to my feet, her fingers digging into bruises. I yelped.

"That wasn't a request," she said. *"Go."*

Noelle sniffed and rubbed her eyes. "It's okay, Lila," she said, offering me a faint smile. "Thank you."

"You're welcome," I said, and I glared at Scotia. This wasn't over. She barely looked at me as she helped Noelle to her feet—much more gently than she'd been with me, I noticed—and led her deeper into the back alleys.

I watched them until they disappeared around a corner, and with a huff, I shoved my hands in my pockets and returned to the street. The bunkhouse wasn't far, but the bottom of my jumpsuit was soaked with dirty snow, and the biting wind felt worse than usual. I hated myself for joining the Mercers, as necessary as it was, but I couldn't deny it would be much more comfortable.

That wouldn't fix the problem for the rest of the prisoners, though. The only thing that could possibly help them was finding those armory codes and giving the Blackcoats a fighting chance to overtake Elsewhere. Knox and Benjy were right—if I was caught searching for them, I'd be dead in seconds, and this time my face wouldn't help me, not when everyone thought Lila was leading the rebellion in the first place. But that only meant I couldn't get caught.

And in order to break into the filing cabinets and steal the codes, I needed my necklace. The chances of Scotia handing it over if I asked politely were slim, even if I explained myself, and I didn't trust her enough to do that anyway. Not after all she'd done. She might have been working for the Blackcoats, but that didn't mean she wasn't willing to rat me out in a second if it meant distracting the Mercers long enough to further her own agenda. Ratting me out meant potentially ratting out Knox and Benjy, too, and I couldn't let that happen.

So that was it. I had to find the codes myself. If Knox could have done it, he would have already, and Scotia herself had admitted she stood no chance.

I had to steal back my necklace.

I slipped into the bunkhouse, relieved to see it abandoned. Everyone must have been at the dining hall already. The napkin Benjy had drawn was where I'd left it, underneath the thin mattress, and I slipped it into my coat pocket, where it stood the best chance of staying dry.

After I ducked into the bathroom to make sure it was empty, I stood in front of the curtain that separated Scotia's room from the rest of us. My heart hammered, but I had no idea when she'd be back, and I didn't have any time to waste. Now or never.

The curtain was heavier than I expected, and to my surprise, her room was almost warm. It was small—barely big enough for a bed, a tiny desk and chair, and a nightstand—but it was a palace compared to the rest of the bunkhouse.

In the group home, we had a strict no-snooping policy. Anyone caught looking through someone else's stuff voided their right to privacy, making their possessions fair game for the rest of us, and I wasn't stupid enough to give up what little I had. And even though I'd had no trouble going through

Daxton's and Lila's things, being in here without Scotia made my skin prickle with the wrongness of it.

But I was on a mission. I hadn't spotted the necklace on Scotia in the alleyway, and it could have easily been hiding underneath her jumpsuit. I silently prayed it was around here somewhere instead.

I started with the single thin drawer on the desk. It was empty, save for some scraps of paper with scribbles I couldn't read. I found a handful of pencils, all worn down to the nubs, but there was nothing else there. I turned to the nightstand.

The top drawer was small and full of pictures of girls I didn't recognize—smiling faces wearing white jumpsuits instead of red, which I could only guess meant they were from a different section. My eyes lingered on a younger-looking Scotia, with longer hair done in braids and a wide smile. Part of me was stunned to see anyone looking that happy Elsewhere, but most of me was relieved Scotia wasn't a heartless monster after all. She had people she cared about, too, and at least now I had some glimmer of understanding as to why she'd risked her own safety and a cushy position all to help out the Blackcoats. We all had someone we were fighting for, even if that someone was ourselves.

I was careful not to disturb anything in the nightstand as I searched for the necklace. The second drawer was stuffed with an extra jumpsuit and wool socks, and among them I discovered a batch of folded notes bundled together with an old shoestring. I tried to make out the names on the top and bottom of each page, but the letters didn't form any word I recognized. Not that that was hard. I bit my lip. Maybe if I took these, Scotia would be willing to trade.

Or she'd kill me. That was a much more likely outcome.

Without warning, the door to the bunkhouse opened, and

I froze. For an instant, I couldn't move as panic overcame me, but I forced it aside. The odds of it being Scotia were slim, but that was a chance I couldn't take. As silently as I could, I shut the drawer and slid under the bed.

Uneven footsteps echoed from the doorway, almost as if whoever it was couldn't keep her balance. Underneath the edge of the curtain, I spotted prisoner-issued boots, and I silently willed them to walk away from the curtain. Just one step, and I would be able to relax.

Instead they turned toward me, and a gloved hand pushed the curtain aside, revealing Scotia.

I remained absolutely still, not even daring to breathe. Scotia's coat and jumpsuit were soaked in fresh blood, and she stumbled forward, groping around until she reached the nightstand. She was only a few inches from my hiding spot under her bed, close enough for me to hear her labored breathing.

Where had the blood come from? I searched for any sign of injury on Scotia, but all I could see were a few scratch marks across her neck. Nothing deep enough to cause that much blood to soak into her clothes.

I spotted something else, too—a delicate silver chain hanging around her neck. I bit back a hiss of frustration. The most I could do at this point was yank it off her and make a run for it, but even in her condition, she could probably take me. I couldn't risk it.

Scotia stood with effort, crying out softly as she did so. She was hurt, and worse than it first appeared—maybe I could outrun her after all.

Clutching a fresh change of clothes, she stumbled out of her room and to the left, toward the bathroom. Moments later I heard the shower running, and I cautiously slid out from underneath the bed. Nudging the curtain aside, I peeked into the bathroom, relieved to see Scotia's bloodied clothes discarded on the floor.

Her pile of fresh ones sat on the long counter beside a sink, and I tiptoed across the tile, careful not to make a sound. Sitting on top of a fresh shirt was the silver necklace Greyson had given me, half the face tinged red with blood.

I snatched it from the pile and didn't bother washing it off. Within seconds, I slipped through the door of the bunkhouse and out into the snowy street, careful to keep a straight face. Finally, something was going my way. I could sneak into Mercer's office while everyone was asleep, get the codes, and deliver them to the Blackcoats. The thought of facing Scotia again after what I'd just done made me queasy, but if I had the codes, maybe she'd forgive me for stealing the necklace. If she figured out it was me in the first place.

Feeling lighter than I had in days, I knelt beside a clean pile of snow a couple blocks from the bunkhouse and scooped a handful into my glove. I scrubbed the face of the necklace clean and pulled it apart to make sure the individual pieces were also free of blood. I had no way of knowing if the electric lock pick would still work, but I couldn't imagine Greyson creating something this incredible and not waterproofing it. I hoped.

Once the disk was clean, I fastened the chain around my neck and paused, looking at the pink-tinged snow beside my boot. Now that my heart wasn't in my throat, I realized I had no idea where the blood had come from. How had Scotia managed to get so messed up in the few minutes she'd spent with—

Noelle. The edges of my vision went dark, and I scrambled to my feet and looked around, as if she would be right there waiting for me to notice her. But of course she wasn't there. Whatever Scotia had done to her, it must have been bad.

I ran through the street toward the dining hall, hoping against hope she would be there. As I passed the alleyway where I'd last seen her, I darted down the path in hopes of spotting her, or at the very least finding a trail of blood. I found neither, and after a minute of searching, I doubled back. The dining hall. She had to be inside the dining hall. If she was injured, she would have gone somewhere warm nearby, and in the sea of gray administrative buildings, that was the only option.

I burst through the doors and searched the crowd. Several people stopped eating and stared, but I ignored them as I scanned every face in there. Noelle wasn't with them. She wasn't anywhere.

I swallowed a screech of frustration before darting back outside. I didn't feel the cold anymore, even with my jumpsuit still wet, and I hurried through the darkening streets, searching every building nearby with an open door. Bunks I didn't recognize, buildings with cold entranceways and locked hallways—she wasn't in any of them. And no matter how hard I searched, I couldn't find the trail of blood that had to be somewhere.

Just as I decided to head back to the bunkhouse and see if I could trace Scotia's boot prints, an air horn went off, and my entire body went numb. This time it had nothing to do with the cold.

I was one of the first to reach the railing around the cage. I found a spot where I had an unobstructed view of the rooftop where the Mercers and Knox had viewed the matches the day before, and I waited anxiously, fighting the fear that crept into my thoughts. It would be okay. Everything would be okay.

At last the Mercers appeared, and it was only then that I became aware of the crowd surrounding me, trapping me against the railing. Everyone in the section was here, just as they'd been the night before, and they were all ready to watch someone else die.

I looked up at Knox, waiting for him to notice me. He cast his gaze around the crowd, but at last our eyes met, and he shook his head minutely. I didn't have to hear him to know what he was thinking: I'd missed dinner, and the Mercers weren't pleased.

I didn't care about the Mercers right now. All I could think about was that cage, and as the trapdoors opened underneath, I held my breath.

It would be okay. It would be okay. It would be okay.

But as the familiar mop of floppy brown hair appeared, my blood turned to ice, and I knew it wouldn't be.

Elliott stood on trembling legs inside the cage, still in his guard uniform. And across from him, wearing a blood-soaked jumpsuit with no coat, knelt Noelle.

XIII

MERCY KILL

"Noelle!" I screamed. *"Noelle!"*

Even though she couldn't have been more than twenty feet from me, she didn't look my way. Her head lolled forward as if she were barely conscious, and her dark hair was matted with blood. Elliott knelt beside her, and for one terrible moment I thought he was going to kill her—until he wrapped his arms around her and buried his nose in her bloody hair, the same way Benjy had held me only hours before.

Desperation clawed at me from the inside out, but there was nothing I could do. They were already inside the cage. Guards holding rifles surrounded the base, making it a suicide mission at worst to even try to get to them.

But the crowd was dead silent. My scream had echoed through the streets, and even Mercer had glanced my way.

They could hear me.

"They did nothing wrong!" I shouted, climbing onto the railing so the Mercers could see me, too. Hannah averted her eyes, but Mercer stared straight at me, his gaze unblinking.

Beside him, Knox leaned in and whispered something in his ear, but Mercer didn't react. No one said a word.

"It's okay, Lila," said a small voice. I turned around. Noelle's head was resting on Elliott's shoulder, but she was looking at me, her eyes slightly unfocused. Her face already showed signs of bad bruising, and a gash ran from her temple to her chin. That must have been where most of the blood had come from. Even now, I could see it dripping down her cheek.

Tears stung my eyes, and without thinking, I tried to climb over the railing. "No, this isn't okay—Noelle, this isn't okay. *Knox!*" A guard grabbed my waist, and I began to kick. "Knox, *do something!*"

A second guard grabbed my flailing legs, and I stood no chance of fending off both. Their arms were strong and their grips unbreakable, and no matter how I twisted and moved, neither of them let go. I didn't pay attention to them, though—instead I stared up at the rooftop where Knox and the Mercers stood, all three of them now pretending I wasn't there.

"Lila, please," said Noelle in that same broken voice. "I don't want you to die, too."

A choking sob escaped me. "I'm sorry," I managed. "I'm so sorry."

"It's okay," she said again. "This is as good a way out as any. At least now we'll be together."

Elliott held her tighter and turned away from me, and I forgot how to breathe. The defeat in Noelle's eyes—she didn't deserve this. She hadn't done anything wrong.

"This is your only warning," boomed Mercer from the rooftop, and I stared at the pair inside the cage, unable to look away. Noelle whispered something I couldn't hear in Elliott's ear, and he shook his head, his arms tightening around her.

It wasn't hard to imagine what she had asked and what he

had refused to do. Elliott looked uninjured, and with his physical strength, he could have easily snapped her neck. It would be painless—a mercy kill, and he would have another chance at survival. Maybe not as a guard, but he would still be alive. And by this time tomorrow, we'd all be free or dead anyway.

But if it had been Benjy and I inside that cage, I knew without a doubt that neither of us would make a move no matter how close to death the other was. I'd already had a taste of what life would be like without him, and there was nothing in the world that could make me go back there.

No matter how much sense it made for Elliott to kill her to save himself, he wasn't going to do it. He loved Noelle more than his own life. And in that moment, I hated Scotia more than I thought I could ever hate anyone, even Knox.

"I'm sorry," I sobbed as Mercer raised his rifle. "I'm so sorry."

Noelle wasn't listening to me anymore. Instead she focused on Elliott, her fingers tangled in his hair, her lips brushing against his ear, and her entire body molding against his, as if she were trying to be as close to him as possible. This was how she wanted to spend her last moments, and I had no place in it.

I turned away. Two shots cracked through the streets, one right after the other, and then—

Silence.

It was over.

There were no more fights that evening. Guards cleared Noelle's and Elliott's bodies away as the crowd dispersed, and the two men holding me set me down on the other side of the railing with a stern warning to get to my bunkhouse. I stood there for a long moment, as numb as ever as the world seemed to cave in on me all over again.

"You shouldn't have told her about the Blackcoats."

I turned slowly. If I moved too fast, everything would shatter, and my grip on the here and now was fragile enough already. Scotia stood two long strides away, her arms crossed loosely over her chest. Nothing about her blank expression or relaxed shoulders indicated she had just watched two innocent people die because of her.

It was her apathy that made something snap inside me, and before I realized what I was doing, I crossed the distance between us and grabbed her jacket, shoving her as hard as my wrung-out body could manage.

"I was trying to *help* her!" My voice rang through the empty streets. "She needed hope—she needed to know things were going to be okay, and instead you *killed* her."

Scotia tried to grab my hands, but I pulled back against her thumbs, releasing her grip. For several seconds we grappled for control, me trying to shove her again while she tried to subdue me. She lurched, and suddenly my feet disappeared out from under me.

I hit the ground hard, and the air whooshed out of my lungs, leaving me breathless. I struggled to inhale, the pain and pressure in my chest making it impossible, and Scotia knelt beside me. She pinned my arms to the ground, and when I tried to kick, she sat on my thighs, pressing my legs into the freezing dirt. Her movements were labored, but she was still strong, and I went limp underneath her.

"Noelle was the snitch," she said, hovering over me. "She's been snitching to Williams ever since she moved into the section. She was the one who ratted out Chelsea, and she's responsible for another sixteen deaths in the past year."

My lungs burned, and I struggled to speak. "But—"

"In this place, you've got to look out for yourself, and that's what Noelle was doing. I'm not saying she didn't have her good side, and I'm not saying I'm any better than her. But I am saying if she'd told Williams about the Blackcoats, Williams would have gone to Mercer, and everything would have been ruined."

My vision blurred, and I stared at Scotia as her words sunk in. "She wouldn't have said anything." I had to believe that as much as I needed air. "She—she wouldn't have told anyone."

"And you know that for sure?" Scotia leveled her stare at me. "You're willing to risk the entire rebellion on your opinion of someone you've known for a day?"

"I—" I faltered, and although I hated myself for it, my eyes welled up. "She wouldn't have done that to me."

"Yes, she would have," said Scotia. "And she would have skipped all the way to Mercer Manor. You were her big fish. The moment she spotted you doing something out of line, you would have been in that cage, and she would have been putting on a crisp new guard uniform. The sooner you accept that, the easier this will be for you."

Hot tears rolled down my cheeks as a battle waged inside me. The rational part of me that could step back and see the situation for what it was knew Scotia was almost certainly right. Noelle herself had admitted that she wanted to be a guard, and she'd even told me exactly what she had to do to become one. I'd been naive to trust her as much as I had—it wasn't a coincidence she'd befriended me, and as I ran through the past day in my mind, I couldn't remember a single instance of her having a conversation with someone else. Everyone had known she was the snitch, and they'd steered clear of her. I hadn't been so lucky.

But the part of me that understood her—that looked at her and saw the person I would have been if I hadn't been lucky enough to wind up in society despite being an Extra—that part of me had just witnessed my own death, mine and Benjy's, and I couldn't process it. Noelle hadn't been a bad person to me. She'd been the only friend I had in this place—and even if her friendship had been a charade, it had felt real to me. It still did, and the pain of watching her die wasn't lessened by learning the real story behind her warmth. If anything, it only made me feel worse for mourning someone who had caused so many others to die.

No. Noelle hadn't created the system. She'd taken advantage of it, but she wasn't the enemy. She was a product of her environment, and all she'd wanted was the same thing I did—to be with the person she loved most.

It was this place that was the problem. It was Elsewhere. It was the guards, the Mercers, the Harts—they were the ones responsible for taking decent people and turning them into the worst versions of themselves. They were the ones responsible for this mass slaughter and waste of human life, and they were the ones who were going to pay.

"Did she tell anyone?" I said tightly. Scotia's grip on me lessened.

"No. I didn't give her a chance. I didn't enjoy it, but better one life lost than millions."

I blinked hard. "It was the only life she had."

"This is the only life any of us have," she said. "Noelle made her choices long before you arrived. She and Elliott both did. You messed up telling her, but you can't take it back now, so there's no point in feeling guilty about it."

But I did. No matter what Noelle's intentions had been, I was still the one who'd told her. I was still the one who'd set the ball in motion, and now she was dead because I couldn't keep my mouth shut. I had to believe she would have changed once she'd had her freedom. She wouldn't have had to snitch on anyone anymore, and she would have had a real chance at a good life. Now, because of me, that was gone.

Scotia stood and offered me her hand. I ignored it. Hauling myself to my feet, I shoved my fists in my pockets and trudged off down the street, guilt burning through me. No one was blameless in any of this—not Noelle, not Scotia, not me. But Noelle was the one who had paid the price.

"Hey, Hart," called Scotia. I paused, but I didn't turn around. "I hear you're staying at Mercer Manor now."

I tensed. The codes. After all that had happened, all she really cared about were the damn codes.

As if she could hear my thoughts, she stepped in front of me, her dark eyes piercing. "Make sure Noelle and Elliott died for something," she said as she touched a lock of my hair. "Not everyone gets to be so lucky, you know."

I jerked my head away, but she grabbed my shoulder and held my stare. A shiver ran down my spine. "I'm not your pawn."

"Then start acting like a queen before we lose the game for good." Scotia nodded to the necklace peeking out from underneath my collar. "If Mercer sees it and asks, I gave it back to you. Steal from me again, and I'll break your neck."

I yanked my arm from her grip and stalked off. She could threaten me all she wanted, but in the space of two days, I'd already faced my worst fears and seen what rock bottom looked like. And just as I'd started to crawl back from it, someone else had died because of me. There was nothing Scotia could do to hurt me more than this place already had.

The walk back to Mercer Manor was long and bitter. I passed several guards on the way, but none tried to stop me, and every prisoner unfortunate enough to be in the vicinity kept their head down and increased their pace. I was as much of a pariah as ever, but at least this way, no one would get close enough for me to hurt them no matter how good my intentions were.

Rivers stood guard at the gate to Mercer Manor, and he offered me a small smile when I approached. "Good to see you're all right, Miss Hart."

"Why wouldn't I be? I wasn't in the cage," I said, my voice shaky to my own ears, but Rivers didn't seem to notice. He punched a code into the gate, and it slid open for me.

"No, you weren't," he said, his words heavy with meaning I chose to ignore.

He ushered me inside and led me up the drive, his rifle strapped to his back. Idly I wondered how many people he'd shot with it. The scar snaking up his neck was a reminder I sorely needed that he, at least, hadn't snitched out his friends in order to gain a uniform. But it was also one more aspect of Elsewhere I was no longer ignorant about, and I averted my eyes, concentrating on the frozen ground instead.

"You did a good thing for those two, showing them they weren't alone," he said quietly. "Not to say it wasn't a stupid move, because it was—but it was also brave. Very brave. That kind of courage is rare around here."

"Guess Mercer hasn't had the chance to beat it out of me yet," I muttered. Rivers smiled at me in a pitying sort of way and set his hand on my shoulder.

"Don't sell yourself short. You're a better person than you know."

I shrugged him off. He had no idea what had happened. "Why are you doing this?" I said. "You have the cushy job, the privileges—and now you're going to risk it all for some rebellion that probably won't even work. I don't get it. You seem smarter than that."

He drummed his fingers against his shoulder strap. "You're a little ray of sunshine tonight, aren't you?"

"That's not an answer."

"No, it isn't," he agreed, and he paused underneath one of the massive trees twenty feet from the Mercers' front door. "I should ask you the same question, you know. Why did you risk your perfect life as a VII and a Hart to stand up for the rest of us? Why did you try to save your friend's life knowing it was entirely possible Mercer would shoot you, too?"

"Stupidity," I grumbled. He chuckled.

"Maybe to you. To the rest of us, you're a hero." Rivers nodded toward the manor. "Tonight's our last chance. What do you think? Are we going to make it?"

"You tell me. What does Scotia have planned?"

"You," he said. "She has you planned. If you're not following through, tell me now. I prefer to know if it's going to be my last night."

I shrugged. "Guess you'll just have to wait and see, won't you?"

"Guess I will." His grin returned, and he ruffled my hair. "We're counting on you. No pressure, though."

"Yeah, no pressure." I started toward the porch and stopped. "That scar—who gave it to you?"

For the first time since I'd met him the night before, Rivers faltered, and he touched the bit of it that crept over his collar. "Daxton Hart."

"When?"

He shrugged. "Eight months ago, maybe? He and Mercer—" Rivers paused. "Not sure what I did to piss them off, but whatever it was, must've been a doozy."

The real Daxton Hart had died over a year ago, which meant it had been the man Masked as him instead. "Did Mercer have a—brother or a best friend?" I said. "Someone who died or disappeared a year or so ago?"

Rivers furrowed his brow and shifted his gun. "Victor Mercer, his older brother. He ran the place before he had a heart attack. Dropped dead in front of Augusta Hart and everything."

"I bet he did," I mumbled. Victor Mercer. That had to be him. "Thanks, Rivers. Don't freeze your feet off tonight."

"No more than any other night," he said, tilting his hat to me. "Take care of yourself, Miss Hart. Hope to see you tomorrow safe and sound."

He headed back down the drive, and I climbed up the porch steps and knocked on the front door. There was a significant chance my stunt had made the Mercers change their minds, and I was mentally preparing myself for the walk back to the bunkhouse—where Scotia would be waiting, no doubt ready to lay into me for failing to get the codes—when Hannah opened the door.

"There you are!" she said, relief saturating her voice. But why she had been worried about me in the first place, I couldn't fathom. "Look at you—were you rolling around in the mud?"

I hesitated. "Someone knocked me over."

"Who?" she said, her eyes flashing. I shook my head.

"It was an accident."

She didn't look entirely convinced, but she still helped me out of my muddy boots and socks before leading me into the warm foyer. My muscles shuddered as they began to thaw, and I padded after Hannah as she led me into the kitchen.

"No, don't sit down," she said, cringing. "Here—take that thing off. I'll fetch you a robe and have a servant draw you a bath."

She held out her hand for my muddy jumpsuit, and I stared

at her. "Right here? You want me to get naked in the middle of the kitchen?"

"Well, you're certainly not tracking that thing around my house," she said. I sighed and began to strip.

Thirty seconds later, Hannah shoved my mud-caked clothes into a trash chute as I stood in the middle of the kitchen, shivering in a plain T-shirt and underwear. Her change in mood continued to baffle me, and I watched her as if she were about to grow a second head.

"I see you found your necklace." Hannah poured boiling water from a kettle into a mug, and she dropped a tea bag inside. "Here, drink this—it'll warm you up."

I took the hot cup and wrapped my hands around it. The heat burned my cold skin, but I refused to set it down. "Why are you being so nice to me?"

"Why wouldn't I be?" she said, but there was a note of tension that hadn't been there before.

"I'm sure Mercer wasn't happy with—what happened earlier."

A muscle in her jaw twitched, and she poured a cup for herself. "No, he wasn't. I take it that girl was a friend of yours."

I took a sip of tea. It burned my tongue, and I could feel it slide through me as I swallowed. "Yes. Or at least I thought she was."

"Jonathan could have shot you, you know," she said. "If Knox hadn't asked him to be lenient, he might have. He doesn't appreciate acts of rebellion."

"And yet you're offering me tea and warm clothes."

She glanced at me out of the corner of her eye. "I don't mistake loyalty for revolt."

"You still shouldn't have done it," said another voice from behind me. Knox. I glared at him over my shoulder.

"I'm half-naked, in case you didn't notice."

"Oh, I noticed."

Hannah set her tea aside. "You should head upstairs before Jonathan walks in, too. He's due back any minute."

"I'll show her the way," said Knox, setting his hand on the small of my back. I scowled.

"I know how to get to my room, thank you."

"I'm sure you do. Through here."

The harder I tried to shake him off, the closer Knox seemed to get, so at last I let him follow me up the back stairs and to the second floor. The hallway was empty, and I stopped in front of the Augusta Suite, not bothering to hide my sneer at the name this time.

Instead of making the lighthearted quip I expected, Knox stooped toward me. "Are you okay?"

I opened my mouth to tell him yes, I was fine, but a lump formed in my throat before I could do anything more than squeak. No, I wasn't okay. I hadn't been okay even after finding out Benjy was still alive, and now, with the weight of Noelle's and Elliott's deaths on my shoulders, along with the responsibility of getting the codes—it was a miracle I was still standing.

"How do you do this?" I managed, my voice cracking. "How—"

"Get inside," he said quietly, pushing open the door. I took one look at the childish room named after the woman I'd killed, and my stomach turned.

"No. Not in there." I slipped past him and moved down the hallway toward the Edward Suite. That morning, I'd been planning the best way to kill him in that room without anyone finding out it was me. Now it felt like the only safe place in Elsewhere.

I didn't understand why until I reached the room and spotted the gold frame Greyson had given me. I sank onto the edge of the bed beside the nightstand and, setting my hot mug of tea down, I picked it up instead.

"What did Greyson say when you had me hauled off?" I said. Knox stepped into the room and closed the heavy wooden door behind him. The click of the lock reverberated through my chilled bones, and even though I knew I shouldn't have trusted him, I didn't have enough left in me to care anymore.

"I'm afraid father and son aren't getting along very well at the moment," he said. "Greyson is confined to Somerset for the foreseeable future."

"You should tell him what's going on."

"And risk Daxton finding out? No." Knox shook out a dark quilt and draped it over my shoulders. "The less Greyson knows, the safer it'll be for him."

"Didn't you say the same thing about me?" I glanced up at him, and in the low light, I spotted lines on his face I hadn't noticed before. "What's the endgame, Knox? Why are we all doing this?"

He eased down onto the mattress beside me, leaving enough room between us so it didn't become awkward. "Ideally, by the time my father's generation is dead, we would like to see the country returned to some form of democracy, where the people decide on issues and a majority rules. Right now, the VIs are a small percent of the population—"

"Two percent," I said. "Benjy told me that once."

"Yes, two percent. Yet they're the ones dictating what everyone else's lives are going to be. It goes against basic human rights. Everyone should have freedom and choice, and that's what we're going to restore first and foremost. It won't be an immediate change. We can't have one, not without throwing the country into chaos all over again and creating an opening for another form of government that will only repress the people even more. Change and reform have to come from within, and I plan on helping it along."

"So that's it," I said. "You're going to be the Prime Minister."

"Celia, more than likely," he corrected. "If she's stable enough for it. If not, then we'll talk to Greyson. See if he's willing to take the lead."

"He won't be." I touched the glass over his face in the picture. "Not everyone wants to rule the world."

"But everyone wants to live in their perfect version of it."

I was quiet for a long moment. "If someone from the future came here tonight and told you that the only way for the rebellion to succeed was to kill me and Benjy, would you do it?"

"Yes," said Knox without hesitating. I snorted. Somehow I wasn't surprised.

"Would you bother to think about it at all? Even for a second?"

He shook his head. "I would hate doing it, and I would carry the burden of guilt for the rest of my life. But if it meant freedom and choice for every single person in this country, then I would. And you would let me."

"Would I?" I said coolly.

"Yes. Because no matter who you pretend to be, you're Kitty Doe. You put your life on the line again and again to protect the people you love, and you would never let millions die just so you could live."

Seconds passed, and I was silent. He was right. In the end, everything was temporary, and a few more decades of breathing was nothing compared to a future where no one's worth would be decided by a number on the back of their neck.

"Would you kill yourself?" I said. "If you knew it would make the rebellion succeed, would you put a gun to your head and pull the trigger?"

He exhaled and raked his hand through his hair. "I ask myself that every night. And every night I remember that death is inevitable for all of us. The only thing that really matters in the end is how we choose to live."

Knox reached for the frame, but instead of taking it from me, he touched the switch on the back until Greyson and Lila melted away, and Benjy and I filled the screen.

"I don't expect you to ever trust me again, Kitty. I don't expect you to say a word to me once this is over one way or the other. But I see what being Lila puts you through day after day. I see your courage. I see your sacrifice. And I see you when I look at your face—not her. Not anymore." He set his hand on my arm. "You're not alone. You've never been alone, and I'm immensely grateful for all you've gone through to help us. I should have said it more before. But since I can't go back, just like no one is coming from the future to tell us what to do, I'm going to say it now. Thank you."

A lump formed in my throat, and I nodded tersely. Anything more and I would break down, and I'd done enough of that today to last me a lifetime.

I would never trust him again, and when this was over, Benjy and I would disappear inside our future together, and Knox would be nothing but a memory we never talked about. But right now, in a place full of people who would have been happy to watch us burn, he was my only real ally. And I suspected I was his.

"Can I keep this?" I said, staring at Benjy's face.

"I brought it here for you." Knox cleared his throat. "Kitty,

I need you to promise me you won't try to find those codes tonight. If you're caught—"

"There's nothing you can do or say that will save me from the Mercers. I know." I looked at him—really looked at him for the first time since I'd arrived Elsewhere. Our eyes met, his so dark they appeared to have no irises at all, and I smiled faintly. "But it's not the dying that matters, remember? It's how we choose to live."

"I mean it," he said, frowning. "Everyone here still thinks you're Lila Hart. You can help us in a way no one else can, and I need to know you're safe. That's why I brought you here in the first place."

"Directly into the line of fire? How thoughtful of you."

"To a place where I can *protect* you. The war isn't over, Kitty. It hasn't even begun. And when it does, the Blackcoats are going to need you. Benjy's going to need you, Celia's going to need you—*I'm* going to need you. Promise me you won't try to find those codes."

I scowled. "Fine. I promise."

Knox eyed me as if he didn't believe me, and I held his stare, silently daring him to challenge me. At last he relented. "All right. Come on, back to your room. Unless—"

"I am *not* sleeping in here with you," I said. Even the Augusta Suite was better than that. I stood, taking the blanket with me. "Good night, Knox."

"Good night, Kitty."

He followed me to the door, but he stayed there as I trekked back down the hallway. Now that I'd had time to compose myself, I slipped into my room without any fluttering panic. Augusta had lived her life, and she'd made her choices. I wouldn't let her ghost haunt me when I knew I was doing the right thing.

I sat on the soft bed for hours, staring at the picture of Benjy and replaying the memory of that afternoon in my head over and over again, until I could feel the weight of his arms around me and the warmth of his breath tickling my cheek. It wouldn't be the last time he held me. And if for no other reason than that, I knew I was doing the right thing. For Benjy, for our future, for the happiness we both deserved. Now that I had him back, I wasn't going to lose him again, and if the Blackcoats failed, that was exactly what would happen.

Scotia and Knox had had their chance to get the codes. Now it was my turn.

When the clock struck two in the morning, I slipped out of the bedroom and crept down the hall. I paused in front of Knox's room, listening for any sign he was awake, but I heard nothing. Relieved, I headed to the grand staircase, taking two at a time. Once again I paused at the bottom, waiting for a cough or soft footsteps to indicate I wasn't alone.

Silence.

Mercer's office door creaked as I slid it open, and I held my breath, waiting for someone to appear. No one did. My luck wouldn't last forever, though, and I fumbled to unclasp my necklace. Corner drawer, black folder. I could do this.

There had to be two dozen drawers lining Mercer's back wall, but there were only four corners. I started at the bottom right. The lock wasn't a standard one—there was something strange about it that made it much harder to pick, and I had to use all three lock picks on the necklace before I managed. As quickly as I could, I flipped through the folders, but they were all manila. No black in sight.

Muttering a soft curse, I ducked over to the other corner, making quick work of the lock now that I knew how to do it. But to my dismay, there was no black folder in that one, either.

That left the two drawers in the top corners. I wouldn't be able to reach either on my own, and I carried Mercer's chair over instead, careful not to make a sound. I climbed up and undid the third lock, and once again, it was full of manila folders.

"You better be it," I muttered as I dragged the chair over to the fourth and final drawer. Close up, I could see that this one was different. Over the spot where the lock had been for the other drawers, there was a shiny black square exactly big enough for a fingerprint.

I mentally kicked myself for not noticing earlier, and without hesitation, I passed the silver disk over the drawer. A light beside the square turned green, and the lock clicked.

Butterflies fluttered in the pit of my stomach, and I pulled the drawer open. It was lighter than the others, and I immediately saw why. Only one thing lay inside: a single black folder.

I opened it. Inside was a small strip of paper no bigger than a name tag, with a series of symbols I couldn't make sense of. This had to be it. I carefully folded the paper, and, realizing too late that I had no pockets, I slipped it snugly under the waistband of my underwear instead. Good enough.

Returning the black folder to the drawer, I closed it and climbed down. I moved the chair back into place, but just as I took my hands off it, something clicked.

Light flooded the room, causing a stabbing pain in my eyes, and instinctively I ducked underneath the desk. But it was too late. Unless the dark figure in the doorway was blind, he had already seen me.

"Lila?" said a familiar voice, and I exhaled. Knox.

"What are you—" I began to straighten, but as soon as he came into view, I froze.

Knox stood in the doorway, holding a glass of amber liquid, and he wasn't alone.

Standing beside him was Mercer.

XIV

TORTURE

"What are you doing here?" said Mercer, his voice harsh and his words slurred. The glass of alcohol in his hand clearly wasn't his first.

"I—" I glanced at Knox, silently begging him to say something, but his expression remained stony. "I got lost—"

"You got lost?" Mercer scoffed and advanced on me, liquid sloshing over the edge of his glass and onto the gleaming wooden floor. "What were you looking for, girl?"

Any trace of the friendly man who had insisted I stay with him and his wife was gone. Instead his eyes were bloodshot and his mouth curled into a snarl, and he grabbed my shoulder.

"You don't want to talk? Fine. I enjoy a challenge."

With his nails digging into my skin, he dragged me past Knox and into the foyer. At first I thought he was going to throw me out the front door and into the frozen night, but instead he pushed me deeper into the manor.

"Knox!" I cried. "Knox, please—"

"Jonathan," said Knox, his voice tinged with annoyance, like this was nothing more than a moderate inconvenience to him. "She said she was lost. Nothing in your office is disturbed—"

"I brought her here as a favor to you," said Mercer. "You swore you'd keep an eye on her, and here we are. Are you in on this, too, Creed?"

Knox sighed and set his glass aside. "I was down here with you."

"Distracting me, making sure I didn't come in here and find her."

"Convenient, considering you're the one who asked me to have a drink in the first place."

Mercer's grip on my shoulder tightened, and my knees buckled as pain shot through me. "Think it's time you took your leave. I'll have a driver escort you to the perimeter as soon as I'm through with this one."

"Don't bother. I know the way." Knox glanced at me, and for a moment I thought I saw a flash of pity in his eyes. Terrific. "I hope you're right about this, Mercer, because you will pay dearly for stealing my property for your own enjoyment."

His *property?* I sputtered, but before I could form intelligible words, Mercer interrupted. "You'll have your pick next time you come. This one's defective anyway."

Knox said nothing to counter him. Instead he turned and headed up the grand staircase, not bothering to spare me one last look.

And then I was really alone.

"Need two in the workshop," muttered Mercer into a communication device, and he opened a door I hadn't noticed before. A narrow staircase descended into darkness, and he shoved me inside. I stumbled down the steps, losing my balance halfway there and pitching forward the rest of the way.

I hit the concrete floor with a crack, and my shoulder exploded in pain. I scrambled to my feet as quickly as I could, but Mercer was already there, grabbing my uninjured arm and yanking me forward.

"I invite you into my home, feed you my food, let you sleep in a warm bed, and this is how you repay me?" He flipped a switch, and yellow light filled the room, revealing walls lined with rack after rack of gleaming metal objects. Some I could name—knives, saws, screwdrivers—but others looked like they were relics from some ancient time.

That wasn't the worst part, though. Three metal tables large enough to hold a full-grown adult stood evenly spaced from the center of the room, where the stained concrete floor slanted toward a drain. I'd seen enough dried blood to know it when I saw it, and panic joined the pain pulsing through me.

We stood in a literal torture chamber.

"The workshop," said Mercer proudly. He dragged me toward the nearest table, which gleamed in the low light. "Last chance, little girl. Tell me the truth, or you'll turn this into a night to remember for both of us."

Footsteps thudded down the stairs, and my insides clenched. "I told you, I was looking for the kitchen to get something to eat, and in the darkness, I got mixed up. I didn't realize where I was until I ran into your chair. I was on my way out when you found me."

"If you could see well enough to reach the foyer without tripping, you could see well enough to know it was my office." Two guards spilled into the room, and Mercer barked, "Tie her to the table."

"No—don't—I'm telling the *truth*," I said, trying to wriggle out of his grip. "It was an accident."

"I guess we'll find out, won't we?" A sickening smile spread across Mercer's face, and in that moment he reminded me so much of Daxton that, in my panic, I saw him standing there in Mercer's place.

"Please—*please*," I begged as the guards hoisted me onto the table, wrenching my shoulder so badly that white-hot agony burned through me. I screamed, but they ignored me, wrapping thick leather straps around my hands and ankles. Another burst of pain shot down my spine as they tightened the straps, rendering me immobile.

"The more you struggle, the more it's going to hurt," said Mercer. He stood in front of a rack filled with knives, running his hands lovingly over each handle. Without a word, the two guards disappeared, leaving us alone in that torture chamber together.

As the reality of the situation set in, my veins pumped full of adrenaline, and I began to tremble. "You don't have to do this," I said. "I'll cooperate. I'll never come here again. I'll be the best citizen you've ever had—please. I'll do anything."

Choosing a scalpel and a pair of tongs from his collection, he then turned to face me. "What I want you to do right now is tell me which you value more—your teeth or your toes?"

"Jonathan," said a voice from the staircase. Hannah. "You need to see this."

Mercer narrowed his eyes. "I'm busy."

"Even if she's lying, there's a greater chance of her passing out than telling you," said Hannah. She appeared in my line of sight, and something glinted in her hand.

The gold frame.

Frantically I tried to remember if I'd switched the picture back to the one of Lila and Greyson. I must have—I wouldn't have left out a picture of me and Benjy for anyone to see.

Desperate hope pulsed through me as Hannah held up the

frame for Mercer, and as soon as I caught sight of the picture, I had to bite my lip to keep myself from crying out.

Benjy. She was showing him the picture of me and Benjy, with no idea they were looking at my real face, too.

"Knox said there's a boy in Section J—Benjamin Doe," she said. "His former assistant. They had a relationship behind his back. You'd be better off using him to get her to talk."

"No—*no!*" I shouted, fighting the restraints. Agony ripped through me, but I didn't care. "He has nothing to do with this!"

Mercer's sickening grin returned, and he took the picture from Hannah. "Fascinating. Truly fascinating. I'll alert the guards. Watch her, darling. She'll say anything to get out of here."

"They all will," said Hannah, and Mercer took the frame and headed up the stairs, leaving the pair of us alone.

"Why did you show him that?" My voice broke, and hot tears stung my eyes. "Benjy had nothing to do with any of this."

Hannah didn't answer. Instead she moved toward me, and before I could ask what she was doing, she began to undo the straps.

"Listen to me—we don't have much time," she said. "There's an emergency tunnel underneath the cellar. It's several miles long, but it'll lead you to the edge of Elsewhere. Knox is arranging for someone to meet you there."

I stared at her. "What?"

"You need to go." She freed my good arm and started on my ankles. "He'll be back any minute."

I undid the buckle holding my second arm hostage, wincing as it pulled my shoulder the wrong way. "I'm not leaving. He's going after Benjy—"

"I'll make sure nothing happens to him." She pulled my left leg free. "Jonathan won't hurt him anyway, not until you've been found. He means something to you, and Jonathan won't risk losing that leverage."

I shook my head and sat up. "He's going to kill him—"

"He's going to kill *you* if you stay here."

"I don't care."

"I do." Her deft fingers undid the final strap, and I swung my legs off the side of the table. "I don't know what you were doing in his office, and I don't care. Right now, all I want is for you to get somewhere safe so he can't kill you."

"Why do you even care?" My voice broke, and I cradled my bad arm. "Yesterday, you didn't want me anywhere near you or your husband."

"And I still don't, but for an entirely different reason now." She pulled the silk belt of her dressing gown through the loops and began fastening it around my shoulder.

"What are you talking about?" I said, wincing as she eased my arm into the makeshift sling. It wasn't perfect, but it was something. "I'm not going anywhere until you tell me exactly what's going on."

Her expression grew pinched, and she glanced at the stairwell. "Fine. That girl in the picture, the one with your friend—that's you, isn't it?"

I bit the inside of my cheek and nodded. No point in lying to her. She had already felt the III on the back of my neck. "A year ago. Before I was Masked."

Hannah took a deep breath and exhaled sharply. "So he was telling the truth."

"Knox?" I said. "Hard to say for sure. What are you talking about?"

She moved into a corner of the workshop and pushed aside

a creaky old cabinet. The wood screeched against the concrete floor, and I winced. "That girl in the picture—her name's Kitty Doe. *You're* Kitty Doe."

I blinked. "How did you—"

"Daxton told me," she said, and I grew still. "No, not that Daxton. The real Daxton."

My mouth dropped open. "Wait, you *know*—"

"Daxton used to come here all the time," she said. "I met him when I was twenty, and we formed a—bond."

The idea of Daxton—real or fake—forming the kind of *bond* she was implying made me gag. "Sorry he forced you to do—whatever it is he made you do."

"He didn't make me do anything." Her voice grew hard and defensive, and she shoved the cabinet a few more inches before crouching down in the corner. I hopped off the table to join her. "I loved him. He loved me. If circumstances had been different—if he hadn't been married already—if I hadn't been a prisoner—"

"He would have carried you off to his castle in the sky, and you would have lived happily ever after," I said. "I get it."

She rooted around in the corner searching for something I couldn't see. "He was a good man. His mother was the real problem, you know. He wanted to start imposing sentences that fit the crime. Releasing Extras and giving them a chance. But she insisted he couldn't do it, not if he wanted to remain in power—"

"I know what a terrible person she was," I said. "I'm the one who killed her."

She paused long enough to twist around and eye me. "Thank you."

"You're welcome. Thought you said we didn't have a lot of time."

"We don't." She yanked on something, and suddenly a square piece of wall swung out, revealing some kind of trapdoor. It was large enough for a man to crawl through, and darkness permeated the space beyond it. "Long story short, we had a baby. And even though she was born here, Daxton made a deal with his mother and found her a place to grow up out in the world."

My mouth went dry, and a block of ice formed in my stomach. "No. Whatever it is you're trying to say—"

She pushed a wisp of hair out of her eyes and stepped back from the opening. "He sent me updates—pictures, reports, that kind of thing. Took care of me even after she was gone. Introduced me to the Mercers, and they took a liking to me." She shook her head. "Anyway. I wasn't supposed to know Victor replaced him. No one was. But I'm not stupid—and when Daxton came to visit Elsewhere a month after Victor died, it was obvious. He wasn't my Daxton, and I recognized the way he was looking at me. And when he threatened to hurt you, I knew it wasn't him."

The cellar spun around me. I had to lean against the old cabinet to keep my balance, and a splinter slid into my palm. "You're not my mother. Daxton—Daxton isn't my father. I'm not your kid."

"You're not," she agreed. "But that girl in the picture, Kitty—she is."

A knot formed in my throat, making it impossible for me to speak. I'd never known my parents—I'd assumed I was an Extra like the others in my group home, because that's what we were. I was nobody. Nothing until I earned my rank and proved I was worth something to the rest of them.

But I had the Hart eyes. I had Hannah's hair. And even though the thought of being biologically connected to Daxton Hart made me sick to my stomach, Hannah had no reason to lie. She had no reason to risk her own life helping me, either, unless I meant something to her.

Unless I was her daughter.

"You—you're sure?" I said in a choked voice. Hannah fished a gold chain out from under her nightgown, and at the end dangled a tiny locket. She pushed a button, and it flipped open, revealing two pictures: one of a baby with bright blue eyes, and one I recognized as me on my fifteenth birthday.

"I'm sorry. I didn't know until now." Her eyes grew glassy, and she tucked the locket back underneath her nightgown. "When Knox showed me that picture, I thought it was a prank. But it's really you, isn't it?"

I nodded wordlessly, and the room tilted around me, nearly taking me with it. I had a mother. I had family.

Greyson was really my brother. Lila was my cousin.

I really was a Hart.

And Knox had known.

"I need—I need—" I gestured helplessly at the tunnel. Hannah stepped aside.

"Of course." She hesitated and briefly wrapped her arms around me. She was warm, and for a split second, I let myself imagine what it would have been like to grow up with a mother. "There's a flashlight attached to the wall a few feet inside. Run. I'll distract Mercer for as long as I can."

"Thank you. For everything," I said.

Neither of us managed anything more. I slipped inside and

waited on the rough concrete while she sealed the tunnel again, watching as the last sliver of light took her from me.

Once I was surrounded by darkness, I took a deep breath, forcing myself to calm down. This changed nothing. I still had to get out of there before Mercer figured out what she had done, and if he took it out on her—

No. Hannah was capable of taking care of herself. If I showed my face to protect her, it would only make things worse for both of us. She was smart, and she knew Mercer better than I ever would. She would figure something out.

I groped around until I found the flashlight, and light flooded a long tunnel that curved out of sight. At first it was concrete, but after only ten minutes of walking, it shifted to dirt. I gulped in the stale air. I was fine. There had to be an end to the tunnel, and when I found it, I would join Knox and the Blackcoats and make damn sure they got to Mercer before Mercer could hurt Benjy and Hannah—or worse.

Everything would be fine.

I stopped suddenly. It wouldn't be, not without the codes. If the Blackcoats couldn't get into the armory, they didn't stand a chance. And I was the only one who knew where they were.

I touched the waistband of my underwear, relieved when I felt the paper crinkle against my skin. I still had it. And if I wanted the Blackcoats to have any chance at all, I needed to get it to them.

But Hannah had said the tunnel ran for miles. There was a chance no one would be there when I got there, or even if they were, they might not be able to communicate with the people inside Elsewhere, where the armory was hidden.

I silently cursed. My life or the lives of millions.

Once again, Knox was right.

I turned around and darted back down the tunnel, the beam

of light from the flashlight swinging in time with my strides. When I reached the concrete, I flipped the light off in case Mercer had sent a guard down to see if this was where I'd gone, but as I crept back to the cellar, it was as dark as ever.

I stopped at the entrance into Mercer Manor, crouching beside the opening and holding my breath, listening for any signs of Hannah or Mercer on the other side. My legs began to ache, and soon my feet grew numb as I waited. Eventually I lost all sense of time in the darkness, and instead I began to count my heartbeats.

When I reached a thousand, I took a breath and set the flashlight down. I couldn't risk waiting any longer, not if I wanted to get the codes to Scotia in time. With Knox gone, she was my only option, even if she'd likely turn me in on sight. At least the Blackcoats would have a fighting chance.

I pushed against the door, but to no avail. The cabinet must have been blocking it. With a grunt, I shoved the door with my good shoulder, wincing as pain radiated down my injured side. The cabinet hadn't been that big. I just had to push and—

Crash.

I jumped away from the door, and it swung open, revealing the smashed cabinet in the middle of the cellar. I swore and leaped out, grabbing a pair of knives from the nearest rack. Ducking underneath the stairs and into a dark corner filled with cobwebs that tickled my skin, I waited for Mercer to come thudding down the stairs. This time I wouldn't hesitate. One knife to the gut, another to the throat—if one of us was going to die tonight, like hell I would let it be me.

But nothing happened. Either the cellar was soundproof, or the manor was abandoned.

At long last I dared to climb the steps. Two of them creaked underneath me, but still no one came. I didn't wait around and wonder how I'd gotten so lucky—if this was a trap, then I had no choice but to walk straight into it. And at least this time I was armed.

The entrance hall of Mercer Manor was dark and abandoned. A knot formed in the pit of my stomach at the thought of what Mercer might be doing to Hannah for letting me go, but I didn't have the luxury of looking for her. She'd known the risks involved when she'd released me, and she'd done it anyway. If I had the chance to help her, I would, but not until the codes were safely in Scotia's hands.

I paused long enough to tug on my boots and a thick black coat that must have belonged to Hannah. Without my red jumpsuit, I would stick out like a sore thumb, which meant disappearing in plain sight wasn't an option. But the sky was still an inky-black, and the moon was only a sliver. As long as I stayed off the main streets, I had a chance of making it to the bunkhouse without being seen.

I jumped from shadow to shadow until I reached the gate of Mercer Manor. The cold cut through my pajama bottoms, but my heart was pounding hard enough to keep me warm for now. With my shoulder injured, I had no chance of climbing the gate, and when I tried to push it open, it remained shut.

Terrific.

"Thought I saw someone lurking by the tree," said a low but jovial voice. I spun around.

"Rivers." I swore softly. He stood on the other side of the gate, rifle still strapped over his shoulder. "Think you could help me out?"

"The entire section is looking for you," he said. "Mercer's livid."

"Good. He tried to cut my toes off."

Rivers's eyebrows shot up. "Would've been more than that,

sweetheart. If they catch you, you stole my gun and forced me to open this for you, all right?"

I shook my head and held up one of the knives. "Knifepoint."

He grinned and punched a code into the keypad of the gate. "Smart girl."

I darted into the grid of gray buildings, taking alleyways when I could and sticking to shadows and darkened streets when I couldn't. I knew the way between Mercer Manor and my old bunkhouse well enough by now to avoid the cluster of guards that seemed to be gathered at every crossroad, and at last, I reached the right block.

I peeked around the corner, and my heart sank. No less than a dozen guards stood up and down that street, with two stationed in front of the bunkhouse alone. There was no way I could slip past them, not if I valued my internal organs. And even if dying was worth it, I had to get to the bunkhouse alive to give Scotia the codes in the first place.

As I was trying to work out whether or not I could get there by jumping roofs, a cold hand clamped over my mouth, and another wrapped around my chest, narrowly missing my broken shoulder.

"Don't say a word," whispered a rough voice. Scotia.

I remained still, and together we waited in the darkness. Suddenly a beam of light filled the alleyway running perpendicular to ours, and a guard shouted, "Clear!"

The light disappeared, and Scotia eased her grip. "Where the hell have you been?" she whispered. "Mercer's on the warpath—said you attacked Hannah and disappeared. I've been out here for an hour looking for you."

I blinked. "Attacked Hannah? How? Is she all right?"

"Don't know, don't care. What the hell happened?"

I slipped the folded piece of paper out from my waistband and handed it to her. "The armory codes."

Scotia's mouth fell open. "How did you—"

"Doesn't matter. You'll make sure the Blackcoats have it?"

She nodded and tucked it into her pocket. "I will. Thank you."

"I didn't do it for you."

"I know." She glanced up and down the alleyway. "You should go now, before they come back. Stick to the shadows. If anyone catches you—"

"I'll be dead anyway, so there's no point thinking about it," I said. "Whatever you do, don't die before using those codes."

"I'll do my best." She looked at me for a long moment, her brow furrowing. "I'm sorry about Noelle."

I swallowed hard. "You did what you had to do. I just wish—" I shook my head. It didn't matter.

Scotia found my hand and squeezed it. "Stay alive. Come find me after it's over. I'll make sure the Blackcoats know what you did."

I nodded, and we both took off in opposite directions. Now that the codes were in safe hands, the crushing weight of responsibility lifted off my shoulders, and I briefly considered returning to Mercer Manor. They must have searched every inch of it if they'd left it unguarded, which meant it was likely the safest place for me to go. But getting back there without being seen—that was the real problem.

I turned down another alleyway. I'd done it once—I could get back there again. I just had to be—

"Aha," said a voice, and this time it wasn't Scotia's. I whirled around, gripping a knife in my uninjured hand.

Williams stood in the alleyway behind me, brandishing his rifle like a club.

"Everyone's looking for you, you know," he said, and a deep, booming laugh echoed from his chest. "You're worth a promotion."

I didn't wait for him to make the first move. There was no way I'd be able to outrun a bullet, so I did the only thing I could do—I rushed forward, hoping to catch him by surprise and stab him in the side.

I managed three steps before he pivoted easily despite his size, sending me flying toward a gray wall. Before I could run headfirst into it, he caught my good arm and whirled me around, pinning me against it instead.

"Nice try," he said, grinning. I shoved my knee to his crotch, but instead of finding soft flesh, I hit something hard and plastic instead. A protective cup.

Perfect.

"Nighty-night," said Williams, and as I struggled against his grip, he slammed the butt of his rifle into my temple, sending me spiraling back into darkness.

Voices murmured around me, and cold hands pulled at my bad shoulder, sending a white-hot shock of pain down my arm. I opened my eyes. My vision was blurry, but I could make out a shadowy figure standing in front of me, while two others hauled me to my feet.

"Knox?" I mumbled. My head pounded, and the world seemed distorted, as if I were looking at it through a piece of curved glass.

The shadowy figure didn't answer me. Instead he called out, "Ready in five, four, three, two, one…"

A buzzer went off above my head, and the two figures on

either side of me shoved me upward through a trapdoor, into bright light that might as well have shoved shards of glass into my eyeballs. A strange whooshing sound echoed in my ears, louder than it probably was thanks to the pounding in my head, and I squinted enough to see the opening in the floor close up completely.

What was going on?

Tears flooded my eyes, but I forced them open, and slowly my vision swam into focus. I was on some kind of platform at least six feet off the ground, with looming gray buildings surrounding it. Weak morning light filtered through the clouds, but there was something else above me, too.

Metal bars.

My chest tightened, and suddenly I could barely breathe.

I was in the cage.

"Kitty?" said a trembling voice only a few feet away. I turned my head slowly, and my heart dropped to my knees.

His face was covered in purple bruises, and his lank hair hung in his eyes as he hunched over, cradling his ribs, but I would have recognized him anywhere.

Benjy.

XV

THE CAGE

"Benjy?" My voice sounded weak and muffled, and I wasn't sure if it was me or the concussion. "What—"

He limped across the cage and collapsed beside me, wrapping his arms around me the same way Elliott had embraced Noelle. I hugged him back with my good arm, and as I looked over his shoulder, the rest of the world came into focus.

Hundreds of prisoners in red and orange jumpsuits stood around the platform, staring up at us with blank expressions on their faces. But something wasn't right—the sun was coming in from the wrong direction. It was still morning.

I looked up at the rooftop where Mercer stood, tall and proud and holding his automatic weapon with a sneer. Hannah stood beside him, and even from a distance, I could see the cuts and bruises decorating her face. Even if she'd managed to make it look like I'd injured her while escaping, there was no way she could have done that amount of damage to herself.

Mercer knew she'd let me go. And this was her punishment.

This was our punishment.

"Benjy," I whispered. He was warm and solid against me,

and I closed my eyes, breathing in his scent. So this was it. This was how we were going to die.

I exhaled, and relief crept through me, numbing the pain from my head and shoulder. I'd never had a chance of surviving Elsewhere, and Benjy was always paying for my mistakes, too. But we were together, and now there would be no more wondering when the final axe would drop.

"I'm sorry." I kissed his stubbly cheek, and his grip around me tightened.

"You have nothing to be sorry for," he whispered. "I love you, and I would rather die with you than live a single day without you. This is exactly how I want to spend my last seconds—with you."

I buried my face in the crook of his neck and took a slow, deep breath. I was okay. We were okay. Death was inevitable, and this was our time.

"This is your only warning," called Mercer, but his voice sounded distant, as if he were somewhere at the other end of a long tunnel. My fingers curled around Benjy's jacket.

"You know where we're going to be when we wake up?" I whispered. "In a field by our lake, tangled together under the warm sun. There's going to be a picnic basket full of all kinds of food, and we're going to have our cottage together, right next to our lake."

Something warm and wet dripped down my cheek. I couldn't tell if it was Benjy's tears or mine.

"It'll be perfect," I murmured as the click of Mercer's rifle echoed through the square. "Just you and me for the rest of forever."

"I can't wait," he said, and though his voice was rough, I could hear his smile.

Bang.

Everything went gray. We both tensed, and Benjy curled around me instinctively, shielding my body from the shot. But it was half a second too late. Time seemed to stand still, and in that infinite moment, I waited for pain to blossom.

It never did.

Maybe this was what dying was like. Maybe, in our last moments, our bodies gave us a chance at peace, and the pain of death would never register at all.

Bang.

A second shot rang out, and this time a chorus of screams rose from the crowd. Benjy jerked me toward the center of the cage, and I cried out in pain.

"What—"

On the rooftop, Mercer had dropped his weapon and doubled over. Hannah was on the far side of the building, huddled in the corner and covering her head with her arms. The crowd around us continued to scream, trampling each other in an attempt to get out of the square.

"Lie flat!" said Benjy, and he shoved me to the floor, once again covering my body with his. My face pressed against the cold platform, and several more shots rang out.

It wasn't until I saw a group of prisoners running toward us with weapons drawn that I understood.

The rebellion had begun.

The smell of gunpowder permeated the air around us as shot after shot echoed through the square. Most of the prisoners managed to run from the fighting, but even from my narrow vantage point, I spotted several bodies lying motionless on the ground. The guards surrounding the platform fired back, but they were hopelessly outnumbered, and soon the gunfire ended.

"Lila!" called a woman, and it took me a moment to realize the voice was coming from underneath me.

The trapdoor in the platform opened. Scotia. "In here," she said. "Hurry, before the rest of the guards come."

Benjy lifted himself off me and shoved me down into the holding area. Scotia caught me, and he quickly joined us, breathing heavily as he collapsed beside me.

"What's going on? Are the Blackcoats here?" I said. Had Knox come back after all?

Scotia shook her head and began to reload her weapons. "The cavalry's taking their sweet time, but you got us the codes, so consider us even." She gave Benjy a handgun. "Know how to use this?"

"I do," I said, taking it from him. She raised an eyebrow.

"I'm not sure you should be shooting anyone right now."

"Then make sure I don't have to."

Scotia smirked. "That's the spirit. The other guards will be here soon. I'll lead them away, but don't move, got it? This thing is bulletproof."

She gestured to the holding area beneath the platform, hollow and dark. I hadn't gotten a good look before, but now I could see chains and shackles hanging from the walls, presumably where they kept the prisoners before forcing them to fight.

"It figures that the safest place in Elsewhere is where you wait to die," I muttered. She patted my shoulder, and I cried out. With a frown, she gently probed the tender area.

"Your shoulder's out of place," she said, taking my arm. I winced. "There's nothing I can do about it, not until—"

She wrenched my arm, and I screamed. White-hot pain

exploded through my body, causing my vision to blacken for a moment, and Benjy lunged toward her.

"What the hell do you think you're doing?" he growled, but it was over in an instant. Suddenly the pain began to lessen, and Scotia eased my arm back into my lap.

"It's back in the socket now, but you'll need medical attention once this is over," she said, and she looked at Benjy. "It's easier when they don't know it's coming. She'll be fine."

He glared at her, but he stepped toward me, touching the small of my back protectively.

"I have to go," she said. "Take care of that arm, and don't do anything stupid."

"We'll try our best," I muttered, and she slipped through a metal door at the base, shutting it firmly behind her. A lock slid home on the other side, and I exhaled.

"Are you okay?" he said, and I nodded. It still ached, and my fingers tingled unpleasantly, but at least I could move them again.

Benjy pulled me into his lap, and we stayed there in the darkness, ignoring the echoes of gunshots and screams as Scotia and her band of misfits fought the guards for control of Section X.

Neither of us spoke for what must have been over an hour. It was freezing underneath the platform, but he held me, and I curled up against his chest, trying to burn this moment into my memory. Even if we died today after all, at least we had a little more time.

"You know, I'm almost mad at them," said Benjy, his voice a low rumble. "I was looking forward to that picnic."

I snorted in spite of myself. "We'll get there eventually. No need to rush it."

He ran his fingers through my hair, gently working out the tangles. "If the Blackcoats succeed, can you promise me something?"

"What?" I said, my head resting against his shoulder.

"Promise me you won't be Lila anymore."

I blinked up at him, confused. "Why—"

"Because everyone cares about Lila Hart," he said. "They either love her or they hate her. There is no in between. And I can't stand to go through losing you again."

I was quiet. After everything that had happened, I'd nearly forgotten that before Knox had hired him as his assistant, Benjy had thought I was dead, too, after I'd been kidnapped and Masked as Lila. At least I'd only thought Benjy was dead for a couple days. He'd had to mourn my death for over a month.

"Please, Kitty," he said softly. "Just be you again. For me."

I took a deep, shuddering breath. Now that the adrenaline was gone, the pain in my shoulder was nearly unbearable, but I would put up with anything to be there with him. "Okay," I said. "I promise. But only if you make me a promise, too."

"What?" he said, and I laced my fingers in his.

"Promise that no matter what happens to me, you won't do anything stupid," I said. "You won't die to protect me, or die to avenge me, or—anything. If I'm going to be safe, then you have to be, too. Because I want that picnic in this life. I want that cottage. I want our future, and I'm not going to let anyone, not even you, take that from me again. Got it?"

He hesitated. "Kitty—"

"Yes or no?" I said, pulling away enough to look at him. "If we make it through today, then I swear to you I'll stop being Lila. I'll never leave you again, and we'll weather this together. Either we're going to survive together, or we're going to die together. That's the only way I'm going to let this end. I just have to know that you're with me, too."

He clenched his jaw, but at last he nodded. "All right. I promise."

"Thank you," I whispered, and I settled back against him. I would never stop worrying about him, and he would never stop worrying about me, but at least now we would be at each other's side until the end. One way or the other.

Finally the sounds of gunshots ceased, and the door opened, revealing Scotia. Several wisps of hair had slipped out of her sleek ponytail, and her coat was stained with blood spatter, but at least she wasn't dead.

"You two all right?" she said, and I nodded.

"You?"

She nodded, too. "We've taken over Section X and Section J. The Mercers are still alive, we think, but they've retreated into the manor. We have them surrounded."

I swallowed tightly. "Don't kill Hannah."

Scotia frowned. "Excuse me?"

"Please," I said. "She's as much of a victim as the rest of us. You saw what her face looked like. Mercer did that to her because she helped me escape."

"Do you have any idea what she's done to people like you and me?" said Scotia, her mouth curled into a sneer. "She's one of them."

"Because it was the only way she could survive," I said. "And I know exactly what she's done to me. She saved my life. She's the reason we have the codes in the first place. You're the one who was letting Mercer stick his tongue down your throat for a chance at survival—she was doing exactly the same thing. It's not her fault she was better at it."

CAPTIVE

Scotia clenched her fists. "Fine. But if I'm doing you a favor, then you're going to do one for me, too."

"What kind of favor?" I said warily.

"You're going to work your Lila Hart magic on the crowd out there and convince them to fight with us."

I gaped at her. "What?"

"You heard me," she said. "My people are gathering everyone now. We don't have much time before reinforcements come from the other sections, and we're down a dozen people. We have the weapons we'll need, but we can't hold them off on our own until the Blackcoats arrive. We don't have the manpower."

I stared at her. "And you want the prisoners to fight?"

"Oh, I'm sorry. Did you have a secret cache of soldiers ready to die for us?"

I opened and shut my mouth. I was no stranger to speeches. In my three months as Lila Hart, I'd stood in front of a dozen crowds in various cities and encouraged them to stand up to the Harts and fight for true equal opportunity. I could recite that speech in my sleep if I had to, but never had I tried to convince anyone to walk straight toward their death.

"If they don't want to fight, then there's nothing I can say to convince them," I said. "They have a right to protect their lives."

"If we lose, they will bomb the entire section," she said. "Prisoners, guards—everyone who's left will be burned alive. If they fight, we have a chance. If they choose to act like cowards and let the rest of us die for them, then they're dead anyway."

I gritted my teeth. "If I get up there and convince even one person to stay and fight, their blood will be on my hands."

"If you get up there and convince enough people to stay

and fight, and we win, then they'll have their lives because of you. They'll have their freedom." Scotia shook her head. "We all have blood on our hands already. Now it's your job to make sure those people didn't die for nothing."

There's no such thing as a bloodless revolution.

Knox's voice echoed in my mind, and I closed my eyes. He was right. Scotia was right. I had gotten the codes, and now I would have to live with the consequences, both the good and the bad. People were going to die no matter what I did—they'd died already. I owed them a chance to survive.

"Okay," I said. "On one condition. Benjy doesn't fight."

"And neither do you," he said, touching my temple gently. It was enough to feel like someone was hammering a nail into the side of my head.

"I know how to use a gun. You don't."

"You've used a gun once. That doesn't count."

"But none of them have used weapons before at all," I said. "I can't just send them to their deaths without fighting beside them."

"If you're with them, they'll be too busy trying to protect you to do any good," said Scotia. "No one injured is going to fight. Period. And that includes you, too, lover boy."

I squeezed Benjy's hand. "We do this together. You promised. I won't do this unless I know you're safe."

He grumbled. "Okay. As long as you're not fighting, either."

"I won't."

"I'll put you with the kids," said Scotia. "Chances are the guards will go after them to get us to back down, but if we have a few plants—"

"Kids?" I said. "From where?"

"Section J. We've got them grouped together right now,

but Rivers wants to break them up and scatter them so the guards won't be able to get them all at once—"

"I know a way out."

She stopped. "Excuse me?"

"It's not very big, and it won't fit many people," I said. "I don't know where it leads. But I do know it lets out somewhere that isn't here. Except—"

"What?"

I hesitated. "You said the Mercers are holed up in the manor?"

She nodded. "We've got them surrounded."

"I need you to figure out a way to get them out of there," I said. "The tunnel's in the cellar."

Someone knocked twice on the door, and Scotia swore. Loudly. "I'll figure it out. But right now, I need you to get up there and get us as many fighters as you can. Deal?"

I nodded, and she tugged open the trapdoor again. This time, as she and Benjy hoisted me up, I shielded my eyes against the late morning sun. I could do this. I *had* to do this.

As promised, Scotia's people had gathered everyone back in the square. Unlike that morning, when everyone had stared up at Benjy and me with emotionless expressions, this time several groups huddled together as if they could shield one another from a shower of bullets. Many were limping or had their arms in slings, and as I gazed out across the crowd, I spotted a row of bodies laid out in the shadows of a nearby building.

My stomach turned. That was why I was doing this—to prevent these people from ending up like them. They had to have a chance, and right now, I was the only one who could give it to them.

I cleared my throat and, with effort, I forced myself to my feet. My legs trembled and my vision was still fuzzy around the edges, but they had come here despite their fear. The least I could do was stand.

"My name's Lila Hart," I called. "For the past two days, I've been one of you. But before that, I was on the other side—I was a VII, and I saw firsthand the horror that happens here. You don't need me to tell you what your lives are like. You don't need me to say how hard they are or how much you put up with just to survive. I've been here for forty-eight hours, but many of you have been here your entire lives. You know this place better than I ever will. And you know what's at stake if Jonathan Mercer and the guards retake this section."

I glanced down, and through the trapdoor, Benjy smiled up at me encouragingly. I took a deep breath. I had no idea what to say, but as I opened my mouth again, words spilled out without any conscious thought.

"Isabel Scotia won the first round of fighting today, with her selfless and brave soldiers who picked up weapons knowing there was a very good chance they could lose—not just the fight, but their lives, too. They've chased the guards back, but they won't stay there forever. The real battle is still coming, and as it stands right now, we're going to lose."

In the middle of the crowd, I spotted Rivers wearing an orange prisoner's jumpsuit and what must have been hundreds of rounds of ammunition around his body. Two weapons were slung over his shoulders, and he held another at the ready. Our eyes met, and he nodded once.

"We need your help. I know you're scared, and I know most of you have never held a gun in your lives. But you deserve better than this. There is so much more to this world than these damn gray walls and barbed-wire fences and the guards' whims dictating whether you live or die. Out there, there's hope. There's opportunity. There's love. There's a place where you belong. And every single one of you deserves the chance to see it."

Several men and women glanced at one another, and I pressed my lips together. I had to do this.

"I won't stand here and make you promises I can't keep," I called, my heart thumping painfully, "but I will promise you one thing—you have a chance, right here and right now, to change your lives completely. And it is the only chance like this that you will ever get. So, please—fight with us. Not for me, not for Scotia, but for yourselves. For your lives. For your freedom, and for the opportunity to walk out of Elsewhere and start a real life. Because if we fail today, there will be nothing left of Section X. Jonathan Mercer will not distinguish between those who hid and those who fought. And the more fighters we have, the better chance we have at walking out of here alive. We're in this together. We're all equals today, and we will survive together, or we will die together. There is no in between."

Silence. Those hundreds of prisoners stared up at me, their expressions unreadable. I stood there in silence, at a sudden loss now that the flood of words had stopped. Out of the corner of my eye, I spotted Scotia climbing up the platform, and she joined me, setting her hand on my uninjured shoulder.

"Anyone who's willing and able to fight, come up to the platform," she called. "You'll be given a weapon and shown how to use it. Consider my people your lieutenants, and listen to everything they say. We have a plan, and with your help, we can do this. Anyone who can't or won't fight—head to the dining hall. You'll receive further instructions there."

I stood beside her, barely daring to breathe. At first no one moved. Everyone looked around, waiting for someone to take the first step, and no one dared to meet my eyes. But at last, a man in his forties walked forward through the crowd until he reached the railing.

"If I'm going to die today, then I'm going down fighting," he said, looking straight at me. "I've waited twenty years to have my shot at those bastards. I'm not going to waste it."

I smiled, but a knot formed in my throat, and it was all I could do to stop my eyes from watering. "Thank you," I said, my voice hitching. He nodded, and a muscle in his jaw twitched.

Others began to step forward. Men, women—even a few who looked no older than me. One by one they joined us, each bringing us that much closer to victory. As they crowded around the platform, several men I recognized from the Blackcoats meeting handed them each a weapon. I leaned over enough to see that inside the railing, where guards usually stood, Scotia and her people had stored a cache of weapons and a dozen large crates of ammunition.

Slowly everyone began to sort themselves out. A thin trickle of men and women—nearly all limping or sporting visible injuries—headed toward the dining hall, but to my relief, the vast majority of the prisoners stayed and waited their turn for a weapon.

"It worked," I said, stunned. "They're really going to fight."

"It wasn't Shakespeare, but it got the job done," said Scotia. "Every death today will be worth it if we win. And I'm going to make damn sure we do."

I glanced at her. "We need to get the kids out of here before the fighting starts."

Scotia nodded, her mouth set in a grim line. "I have a plan. It's not pretty, but it'll get the job done. Right now I need you to go to the dining hall and make sure everyone capable of leaving goes with you. I'll have one of my men bring the kids to you as soon as possible. By then, we should have Mercer Manor cleared."

I bit my lip. "I'll need enough time to lead them there safely."

"I'll make sure you have it."

"Good." I hesitated. "I don't know what you have planned, and I don't want to know, but I fulfilled my side of the bargain. You fulfill yours. Don't kill Hannah."

Scotia scowled. "Like you said, none of us can make any promises right now."

"Just—try. Please."

She nodded, and with that, I headed back to the opening in the platform. Benjy helped me down, and together we opened the door and headed out into the square.

Walking away from the crowd and toward the dining hall was one of the hardest things I had ever done in my life. Everything inside me begged to stay there, to pick up a weapon and fight beside them. But I couldn't move my injured arm, and the farther we walked, the dizzier I grew. I wouldn't be able to help them. I'd be a hindrance at best, and at worst, I'd get several of them killed.

"I hate this," I said to Benjy. He slipped his arm around my waist, and I leaned against him as we walked. He still favored his right side, where it looked like he had a few bruises, if not broken ribs, but he refused to complain.

"You're doing the right thing," he said. "Everything you told them was the truth. They know you would fight alongside them if you could. What you *can* do is help get the kids to safety. That will mean more to them than a few shots fired."

Not if those shots saved someone's life, but I didn't argue. We trudged through the slush until we reached the dining hall, where several dozen people had gathered. Most were sitting down, and a few were laid out across tables while others tended to them. The smell of blood and death hit me like a sucker punch to the gut, and I steeled my stomach against it.

"Now what?" I said to Benjy.

"We help until the kids get here. Come on."

Together we headed toward the nearest table, where a woman was trying to stop the flow of blood from a bullet wound in an unconscious man's leg. I didn't know much about medicine, but I pulled off the makeshift sling Hannah had given me and handed it to Benjy. Wordlessly he created a tourniquet around the man's thigh.

"Can you do me a favor?" I said to the woman. Tears ran down her dirty face, and she nodded. "Can you go around and see who's able to walk? Everyone who's seriously injured needs to be brought downstairs—there's a room that will keep them safe during the fighting." I hoped. "We need everyone's help to move them there while there's still time."

She nodded, and shakily she began to walk around the dining hall, going from group to group and asking for help. Soon several people were using tarps and plastic sheets found in the kitchen to carry the injured and unconscious down to the room where the Blackcoats had had their meeting. It wasn't much, but at least they wouldn't be out in the open.

Twenty minutes later, Rivers arrived, leading a group of at least a hundred children. The ones who could walk held hands, forming a line that never seemed to end. Older men and women who must have been their caretakers carried the smallest ones—toddlers and infants who couldn't have been more than a few months old, and I bit back a curse. If the guards found us, we would be completely defenseless.

"Val," called Benjy as they entered. A blonde woman who

reminded me of Nina, the matron of our group home, looked up. "Over here."

She carried two sleeping babies in her arms, and when she joined us, Benjy took one. "What's going on?" she said.

"We're getting out of here." As he launched into the plan, I headed across the dining hall to join Rivers. He stood at the doorway, weapon in hand, as he kept vigilant watch over the eerily quiet street.

"How long before we can move?" I said. His steady stare didn't waver.

"Scotia gave me a ten-minute warning. Gather everyone together, and I'll lead you there."

"Any idea what she's going to do?" I said, and he grimaced, all traces of his boyish demeanor gone.

"Concentrate on doing your part. Let her handle the rest."

Worry fluttered in my chest, but for once in my life, I did as I was told. There was nothing I could do to help Scotia and Hannah, but I could help those kids, and I had to focus on that.

By the time those ten minutes were up, Benjy and I had sorted the children into small groups and assigned an able-bodied adult to look after them. I was kneeling beside a five-year-old girl on the verge of tears when a loud blast sounded nearby, rattling the dining hall. Several children screamed, and I flinched as the world seemed to tilt all over again.

"Rivers," I called, stumbling toward him as quickly as I could. "What's going on?"

He spoke into a communication device on his shoulder and glanced at me. "Time to go."

One by one, we ushered the groups out of the dining hall and into the freezing cold. It was early afternoon by now, but clouds had gathered, and as we made our way through the back alleys toward Mercer Manor, it began to snow.

As we passed each block, I spotted clusters of men and women holding weapons and standing on the corners, watching us. Several nodded, and one man—the first man who had volunteered—smiled.

"All right?" said Benjy, appearing beside me. Now he carried a toddler in his other arm, and despite his brave face, I could see him wince with each step.

"Yeah—are you okay? I can take the baby," I said, but he shook his head.

"You can barely walk in a straight line. I've got them."

I remained glued to his side. As we grew closer to Mercer Manor, I drew the gun Scotia had given me, holding it in my uninjured hand. The silence seemed to echo warnings all around us, and my skin prickled as if I could sense someone watching us. With every step I took, I readied myself for an onslaught, but miraculously, nothing happened. Despite the tension in the air, no one attacked us. Scotia really had secured the section.

"All right," said Rivers once we reached the street. "You have a clear shot. Go as fast as you can. Lila—up front. I need you to show them where to go."

I joined him, Benjy still at my side. "There's a tunnel in the cellar," I said to the others. Dozens of faces stared at me, and the children's weren't the only ones that were tear-stained. "Once we reach it, go as quickly as you can. It's several miles long, but it should let out in a safe place."

"Should?" said Val.

"It's our best chance. Unless you want to stay here."

Her face grew pinched, and she shifted the baby in her arms, but she didn't say anything more.

I led the way across the street and up to the gate of Mercer Manor. Half a dozen Blackcoats stood on either side of us, weapons at the ready in case someone attacked, and my heart was in my throat as Rivers opened the gate. I expected smoke and fire at any moment, but everything was unnervingly normal. The only sign that something was amiss was the unnatural quiet throughout the section, and I couldn't shake the feeling that something or someone was watching us.

The climb up the hill wore me down to the bone, but I pushed on, refusing to collapse no matter how badly my knees shook. I had to do this. This was their only chance at safety, and Scotia and the others wouldn't be able to fight a real battle if they had to worry about protecting us, too. I had to do my job so they could do theirs.

At last I reached the porch, and I unlocked the keypad securing the front door with my necklace, not caring who saw. As soon as the lock clicked open, I pushed open the door and led them inside the foyer. Dozens of footsteps echoed in the marble hallway, and several people gasped as they saw the splendor that had stood here all this time while they were only a hundred feet away, trudging through snow and mud.

"This way," I said, and I led them to the cellar door and down the creaky steps. Part of me expected to see Mercer in the workshop, waiting with knives in each hand, but it was empty. I flicked on the lights and hurried over to the opening in the wall. The wooden cupboard still lay smashed on the concrete floor, right where I'd left it, and I stepped around the pieces of wood before yanking the door open.

The tunnel was as dark as ever. I rooted around for the flashlight I'd left down there, sighing with relief when I found it. "Here—take this," I said to a girl who looked to be about ten. "Hold the flashlight so everyone can see where they're going."

She nodded and tucked her dark hair behind her ears. Nervously she stepped inside, and one by one, the others followed. Several of the adults stopped to pick weapons from the racks lining the walls of the workshop, and I noticed that Rivers hadn't joined us.

"We don't have much time before the reinforcements come," I said to Benjy as we stood together, watching everyone filter into the tunnel. They seemed to be moving as slowly as humanly possible, and I gritted my teeth impatiently. "If they attack Mercer Manor—"

"We have to trust that the Blackcoats will hold them off," said Benjy. The baby had fallen asleep in the crook of his arm, and the little boy he held sucked his thumb as he stared at me with wide brown eyes. "There's nothing more you can do, Kitty."

"Yes, there is." I clutched the gun in my good hand. "If anyone comes—"

"You're not holding off an entire army with ten bullets and a bad shoulder," he said, and he raised his voice. "Everyone, hurry up—we don't have much time."

The adults rushed the children through the tunnel, and at last the final group disappeared into the darkness. I looked at Benjy. "You first. I'll bring up the rear."

"Kitty—"

"I only have ten bullets, but that's ten more than you."

He muttered something that sounded suspiciously like a curse, but he ducked into the tunnel, the concrete ceiling a few inches too short for his tall frame. Tucking the gun into my pocket, I pulled the door shut behind me.

We were far enough away from the front of the group that the light from the flashlight didn't reach us. I groped around, wishing I'd thought to look for another one, when suddenly the tunnel shuddered, and a booming thud rattled me from the inside out.

Several children burst into tears, including the toddler in Benjy's arms. He soothed the little boy as much as possible, but his shrill screams pounded against my temple, making white lights dance in front of me.

"You're okay—you're okay," murmured Benjy, and as my eyes adjusted, I saw him rocking both baby and toddler with each step he took. "Everything's all right, I promise."

But it wasn't all right. The deeper we went into the tunnel, the more the walls around us shook. Once we reached the end of the concrete, clumps of dirt dislodged with each new tremble, and my throat began to close. Benjy was right—we were all okay. We just had to keep putting one foot in front of the other.

Suddenly a weak shadow appeared in front of me, and I stopped. The light bent around a curve in the tunnel we'd just passed, and it swayed in time with the shuffle of footsteps.

Without making a sound, I started back, slipping my gun from my pocket. If someone was following us, it would only be a matter of time before they caught up, and I was the group's last defense. I'd already sent enough people to their deaths today. No one else was dying on my watch, not if I had anything to say about it.

"Kitty!" Benjy's voice echoed back down the tunnel toward me, and I heard his footsteps mingle with the distant shuffle. "What are you doing?"

"There's someone back there," I whispered. "Go—catch up to the others. I'll be right behind you."

"I'm not leaving you," he said, but even as he spoke, the baby in his arms whimpered.

"Yes, you are. I can't protect all three of you, and they won't make it without you," I said. "Please, Benjy."

"I'll get one of the others to carry them," he said, and his voice hitched. "If we hurry, we can catch them and—"

"And whoever's following us will only get closer," I said. "Please, Benjy. *Go.*"

Even in the low light, I could see the desperation in his eyes, and he leaned forward to kiss me. "I swear, if you get yourself killed—"

"I won't," I said. "Not if I don't have to worry about you."

The baby in his arms began to cry again, and he winced. "I love you."

"I know. I love you, too," I said. "Now get out of here."

He took one last long look at me before finally hurrying to catch up to the others. As his footsteps faded, I crouched in the darkness, my palms growing sweaty as I waited.

The light grew stronger until the narrow beam reflected off the wall beside me, leaving me in shadows. Something crackled, and a man's voice murmured, "I hear something. Investigating now."

I tensed. A guard. I flattened myself against the wall as he came around the curve, and as soon as he appeared, I pointed the barrel of my gun at him, my finger resting on the trigger.

He didn't look much older than me—twenty at the most, with light brown hair and a narrow face with a gash running down his cheek. He wore a guard uniform—a dead giveaway, now that I knew Blackcoats like Rivers were wearing prisoner jumpsuits—and he limped through the tunnel, while his right arm was in a proper sling I would have killed for.

This was my chance.

He stopped suddenly when I came into view, and his eyes widened as he raised his good hand. "Don't shoot, please—"

"Call them back," I said. "Whoever you just spoke to—tell them you're wrong. There's no one else down here."

His Adam's apple bobbed, and he slowly reached for the communication device on his shoulder. "Never mind, it was just a rat. All clear down here."

Static burst from the device, and then a muffled voice said, "Angelo, confirm?"

Another voice said, "Guarding the entrance, sir."

So he wasn't alone. I held the gun steady, far enough away that he couldn't make any sudden moves, but close enough not to miss. "Kick your weapon over," I said. "No sudden moves, or I *will* put a bullet in you."

The guard pulled his weapon from its holster and, holding it with two fingers so I could see he didn't intend on using it, he set it on the ground and kicked it toward me.

"Do you have a tranquilizer gun?" I said, and he hesitated. "In sixty seconds, you're going to be unconscious. If you ever want to wake up again, I would recommend giving me everything you have."

With a frown, he reached inside a pouch and produced a handful of syringes. "This is it."

"Good," I said. "Kick them over, turn around, and strip."

Reluctantly he did so, and slowly he undressed, mindful of his bad arm. I waited impatiently and glanced over my shoulder, sure I would see Benjy at any moment. But he didn't come back. I couldn't decide whether to feel relieved or hurt.

No—he was carrying two innocent children, and the other adults had their hands full, too. He was doing exactly what I'd told him to do and staying safe. I wasn't about to get upset over that.

At last the guard stripped down to his underwear. "Kneel," I said. "And toss your sling over here, too."

"But—"

"Do you want a bullet in your brain, or do you want a nice nap?"

He grumbled but gingerly pulled the sling over his head. His arm was bandaged, and some blood seeped through the fabric. I felt a pang of guilt, but I was going to need this more than him.

Once he knelt on the dirt floor facing away from me, he put his good hand on the back of his head, and I finally dared to move. Picking up the nearest syringe, I uncapped it with my teeth and wasted no time crossing the distance between us. The needle was half an inch from his neck when he spoke.

"When I don't come back, they'll go looking for me," he said. "You can't hide down here forever."

"Luckily for you, you'll be asleep." With that, I shoved the needle into his neck and pressed the plunger. He groaned, but a heartbeat later, he collapsed face-first into the dirt.

I waited several seconds to make sure his chest was rising and falling steadily before I picked up the sling he'd discarded. I tucked my arm safely inside it, along with the syringes he'd dropped. I stuck his other weapon in my pocket, but when I turned to rejoin Benjy and the others, I hesitated.

He was right. Others would come looking for this tunnel when he didn't come back, and there was already someone guarding the entrance. If two guards had slipped through the Blackcoats' defenses, there was no telling how many more would join them.

I took a deep breath. Benjy or the Blackcoats. My own chance at survival, or theirs.

Death is inevitable for all of us. The only thing that really matters in the end is how we choose to live.

From the moment I'd handed Scotia those codes, I'd made my decision. Being a coward wasn't part of it.

I looked once more into the darkness and said a silent goodbye to Benjy. If I made it out of this alive, he was going to kill me.

With that, I picked up the guard's flashlight and started back toward the entrance to the tunnel. If anyone tried to go after those kids, they were going to have to go through me first.

XVI

EXECUTION

Ten feet from the entrance to the tunnel, I crouched in the darkness and eyed the guard who stood amongst the shattered remnants of the cabinet. He, too, was young, and he kicked a piece of wood, holding his hands above his head in victory when it skittered to the other side of the room.

Before he could lower them, I crawled out of the tunnel and jammed a second needle in his neck. By the time he turned around and saw my face, the tranquilizer was already pumping through his veins.

"You…" His eyes rolled back into his head, and he collapsed.

I closed the door of the tunnel behind me. There was nothing I could do to hide the guard's unconscious body, not when he had a good eighty pounds on me, but I could conceal the opening of the tunnel. Dragging one of the metal tables over to the corner, I shoved it against the wall and hastily scattered a few tools on the shining surface, doing my best to make it look used. It wasn't the best hiding job in the world, especially not with the guard lying unconscious right in front of it. But with any luck, if anyone else came down here, it would buy Benjy and the others a few more minutes.

Once everything was done, I looked around the workshop. I had two guns now, along with enough tranquilizers hidden in my sling to take care of anyone stupid enough to get too close. If I stayed at the base of the stairs—

A scream echoed through the house, and I tensed. Hannah.

My feet were moving before I had the chance to think. Adrenaline shot through me, and I scrambled up the steps, making as little noise as possible.

The foyer was empty. Heavy silence settled over me, and seconds ticked by. Maybe I'd imagined it, or maybe it hadn't been a scream at all. Or maybe Hannah was dead, and—

A muffled sob echoed down the grand staircase. Drawing my gun, I crept up along one side to the second floor, careful not to make a sound.

"Where is she?" Mercer's voice cracked like a whip in the distance. "This is your last chance."

"I don't know," sobbed Hannah. "I don't *know*."

"You do know—you know exactly what's going on. You've known the whole time, haven't you?"

"Of course not! How could you even think—"

"Don't lie to me."

The unmistakable sound of a slap echoed down the hallway, followed by silence. I tiptoed past Knox's room. The door to the Augusta Suite was ajar, and I peeked inside.

Hannah sat at the foot of the pink-and-gold bed, her knees drawn to her chest as she quietly sobbed. This close, I could see half a dozen bloody gashes running across her face, and one of her eyes was swollen shut. Mercer stood over her, wielding a butcher's knife.

Fury boiled inside my veins, and I gripped my gun. One shot. That was all it would take.

But as I raised the weapon, a shout echoed from the foyer, and a door slammed shut. "Mercer!" called a booming voice.

Mercer looked up, and I only barely managed to duck out of the doorway. "Up here," he called, and added in a mutter, "This better be important."

I darted into the second stairwell, the one that led to the back of the house, and crouched low. Heavy footsteps thudded against the carpeted hallway as someone came running, breathing heavily.

"Sir," he said, his voice much closer now. I hid my head between my knees, praying he didn't come down this way. "We have her."

I frowned. They couldn't have been talking about me, so who—

My breath caught in my throat.

Scotia.

"It's about time," said Mercer. "Watch my wife. If she tries to escape, kill her."

I listened as Mercer strode down the hallway in the opposite direction, toward the foyer instead of the stairway where I was hiding. I waited until the front door opened and shut, and then, once I was as sure as I could be that Mercer was gone, I rose and crept back down the hall.

The door to the Augusta Suite was wide-open now, and a guard stood in the doorway facing Hannah, his feet planted a shoulder width apart as he clutched his rifle. I sneaked closer, my footsteps silent as I came up behind the guard and peeked into the room.

Hannah sat on the bed, and her feet brushed the carpet as she stared off into the distance, her expression unreadable. I didn't wait for her to see me. Taking a third syringe, I stabbed the guard in the neck and dosed him. Once again, he fell to the ground, and I jumped over him.

"Are you okay?" I said, hurrying over to Hannah. She scrambled to her feet, her mouth hanging open.

"Lila—Kitty?" she said, stunned, and she wrapped her arms around me in a tight embrace. "It's really you? Jonathan said—I thought you were *dead*."

So they had been talking about Scotia. My determination turned to steel, and I hugged back before letting go. "I'm fine," I said. "Are you okay?"

"It's nothing. Just a few scratches."

The slashes across her face were anything but scratches. I didn't need to know much about medicine to know they would need stitches. "We need to get you someplace safe. Can you walk?"

"They know about the tunnel," she said, and she bent down to pick up the guard's rifle. "We were going to use it to escape, but Jonathan saw the smashed cabinet, and he thought there was an ambush waiting."

"If you put on a jumpsuit, they won't hurt you," I said. "Come on, let's get you downstairs."

Using the back staircase, we slowly made our way down to the kitchen, where I fished my jumpsuit from the night before out of the trash. It was small on Hannah, but she managed to fit it over her clothes. "What about you?" she said.

"I'm not going with you."

"Yes, you are." Her fingers wrapped around my wrist, as if chaining herself to me. I shook my head.

"I have to take care of something. I'll be along as soon as it's over."

"Kitty—"

"If you want to keep me safe, then you'll take that rifle, and you'll make sure the people in the tunnel get to safety," I said. "There's a boy, Benjy—the one in the cage with me. He's bringing up the rear. Tell him Kitty said to trust you."

Her blue eyes watered, and she stared at me. "I won't be able to live with myself if anything happens to you."

"And I won't be able to live with myself if anything happens to you or Benjy. Now, please—before they figure out you're gone."

Hannah's mouth formed a thin line, and she caught me in another hug. "Don't you dare die before I get the chance to know you," she said, her voice breaking.

"I'll do my best," I promised, but that was all I could manage right now.

At last she released me and headed toward the cellar without another word. Once I was sure she was gone, I crept into the foyer and pushed open the front door, my weapon drawn. I had no plan and no idea what was out there—but Benjy and I wouldn't be alive if it weren't for Scotia, and if there was anything I could do to help her, I owed her that much.

Even from the porch, I could see a crowd gathered on the street in front of Mercer Manor. Taking a breath, I sneaked down the steps and toward a nearby tree. Tracks zigzagged across the snow, and I was careful to step in them, not leaving any trace I was there.

"This is what rebellion looks like!" Mercer's voice cut through the cold air, and I peered around the massive tree trunk. From my vantage point, I spotted Mercer standing on a makeshift platform in front of the gate, surrounded by a small army of guards. And in front of them—

My stomach dropped. A dozen men and women dressed in jumpsuits knelt in the slush, each blindfolded with their hands tied behind their backs. I scanned them, looking for any familiar features. My gaze fell on the figure kneeling in front of Mercer. She raised her chin in defiance, and even from a distance, her sleek ponytail was unmistakable.

Scotia.

A strange buzzing rang in my ears, growing louder as the seconds ticked by, and my head pounded. This couldn't be happening. I had to do *something*.

"Countless are dead because of you," said Mercer, and while his voice carried through the street, he looked down at Scotia. I tried to map out a path closer to the gate, but it was all open space. "The snow is red with innocent blood, and now we have no choice but to punish the entire section, all because you decided to have a little fun. You were never going to win." He gestured to the sky. "I have the might of the American government behind me, and all you have are a few criminals, bastards, and useless invalids."

The buzzing grew louder, and I looked up through the branches. Helicopters. My heart sank. No matter how many weapons the Blackcoats had, there was no way they would be able to fight off the entire military. And there was no way I could sneak across the open lawn without someone seeing me before I had a chance to help. But there had to be a way—there *had* to be.

Despite everything, Scotia held her head high. She was blindfolded like the others, but she seemed to be staring straight at Mercer. "I would rather die beside my people than live with yours."

He scoffed. "As you wish. I hope it was worth it."

"It was," she said. "And I'd do it all again for a chance to kill you."

"Unfortunately you'll never have that opportunity. Enjoy hell."

"I'll see you there," said Scotia.

Before I could move, before I could think, Mercer pressed the barrel of a gun against her forehead, and he pulled the trigger.

A shot rang out, and she crumpled to the ground. I swallowed a scream. A chorus of gunshots followed, and the other prisoners joined her one by one, until none were left.

The buzzing of helicopters grew louder, the wind whipping up a frenzy by now, and my chest tightened. Mercer kicked Scotia's body hard enough for the crack of bone to echo over the sound of my heart pounding in my ears, and bile rose in my throat.

"Round up the others," he called. "Search the bunks, the buildings, the dining hall—everywhere they could possibly hide, and don't come back until you've found—"

A shout of alarm cut off Mercer's speech. The sound of unrelenting gunfire rang in my ears, close enough to turn the ache in my head into a roar, and suddenly a spray of bullets rained down upon the platform. The guards standing with Mercer collapsed in one fell swoop, and Mercer threw himself off the platform, into the small space beside the gate.

I gasped and crouched down beside the tree. The branches waved as if we were in the middle of a hurricane, and they parted enough for me to see more than a dozen black helicopters hovering above us in the cloudy sky. Like the first, each bore the Prime Minister's seal, but they continued to shoot into the crowd of guards, mowing them down unmercifully. It wasn't the military after all.

The Blackcoats had arrived.

I hid behind the tree, not daring to step out into the open.

Several men shouted, and one by one, soldiers dressed in black dropped to the ground, carrying weapons that made the guards' rifles look like toys. Some lingered, but most headed off down the streets and away from the manor, and I briefly considered darting back inside. Before I could move, however, I spotted a familiar figure in the middle of a group of soldiers, the silver lining in his uniform making him stand out.

Knox. He'd come back after all.

I opened my mouth to call out to him, but instead a movement in the corner of my eye caught my attention. Only twenty feet from where I stood, Mercer climbed up the hill toward the house, limping and holding his stomach.

I crouched down again and watched him pass. No doubt where he was going this time—the tunnel was his only way out. A potential ambush there was better than an absolute death here, and as he slipped inside Mercer Manor, I gathered my courage and raced after him.

Part of me expected gunshots to follow my path, but either no one in the sky saw me, or they didn't care. I skidded into the foyer, gun drawn and ready to shoot, but once again, it was empty.

Inwardly I cursed. Where—

"We need backup." Mercer's voice, laced with desperation and hysteria, filtered toward me from his office. "The rebels hijacked the helicopters and raided the armory. Elsewhere is falling. I repeat, *Elsewhere is falling.*"

I pushed open the door with my foot. He stood at his desk, hunched over a monitor. Minister Bradley looked back at him, his bushy mustache hiding his mouth from view.

"We're sending troops to assist you," he assured him, but Mercer wasn't paying attention to him anymore. Instead we stared at each other, his eyes locked on mine.

"Make it the entire army," said Mercer in a deadened tone. He switched off the monitor and straightened as much as his injuries would allow. The middle of his white uniform was stained scarlet with his own blood, and he held his hand to his stomach as if he were holding his innards in place. For all I knew, he was.

"Put your weapon on the desk, and walk toward me slowly," I said, keeping my voice as steady as I could. Through some small miracle, my hand didn't shake.

Mercer did as I said, setting a handgun on the desk before limping toward me. Despite his injuries, he never winced or took his eyes off me, and I didn't dare look away.

"My brother warned me about underestimating you," he said. "I was a fool not to listen to him."

"A dead fool," I said, and he chuckled.

"If you were going to kill me, you already would have, sweetheart. Which makes me wonder exactly what you plan on doing with me."

"Holding you here until the Blackcoats arrive," I said. "They can decide whether you live or die."

"Lucky me." His dark eyes glittered with amusement. "I've always hoped my executioner was a coward. It makes this so much easier."

"I'm not a—" I began, but before I could finish, he lurched forward, grabbing the barrel of the gun and pushing it away from him. In my surprise, I pulled the trigger, and plaster dust exploded from the ceiling.

Mercer wrestled the weapon away from me and shoved me to the floor, and I landed hard on my back, all the air leaving my lungs. He stood above me, still holding in his organs as a maniacal smile danced across his face.

"I would say that this is going to be harder on me than it

is on you, but that would be a lie," he murmured, pointing the gun Scotia had given me straight at my head. I fumbled for the one I'd stolen from the guard, but in the scuffle, it had fallen out of my pocket and lay at Mercer's feet. Perfect.

"You don't have to kill me," I said, swallowing my fear. This was the risk I'd taken, and it was worth it when it meant Benjy and Hannah and all those kids might live because of me. But it didn't stop the terror of the unknown from infiltrating every corner of my being until I was frozen, unable to tear my stare away from his. "I'd make a good hostage. My life for yours—it's a fair trade. The Blackcoats would take it."

He snorted with laughter. "Are you still telling yourself that lie, sweetheart?"

"What lie?" My mouth went dry.

"The one where you really believe you're Lila Hart."

So he knew, then. In the few seconds of silence between us, I debated my options. I could admit it and point out that I was still valuable to the Blackcoats, or I could deny it and hope to hell it was enough to plant a seed of doubt.

Before I could say anything, however, he leaned over, and a trickle of blood from his abdomen dripped onto my shirt. "The Prime Minister told me everything. I know exactly who you are, Kitty Doe, and I know exactly what you're worth to me. Nothing."

"She means something to me," said a voice, and my heart leaped. Hannah.

I craned my neck. She stood in the stretch of foyer between Mercer's office and the cellar door, holding the guard's rifle. Her swollen eye was purple now, but her other was wide-open and focused directly on Mercer.

He chuckled again, but there was a hint of nervousness in it. His grip shifted on the gun, and he set his finger on the trigger. "Hannah, my darling, don't be silly. We both know you would never—"

The gunshot was so loud that for a moment, I went deaf. Above me, a tiny red hole blossomed in the middle of Mercer's forehead, in the exact spot where he'd shot Scotia. His body went slack, and I rolled out of the way in time for him to come crashing down on the marble floor, close enough for me to feel the heat from his body.

His eyes stared at me, lifeless and empty, with his last unspoken word still on his lips. I stared back, too stunned to waste any witty remarks on a corpse.

"Come on," said Hannah, and she was at my side in an instant, helping me to my feet. "We need to get out of here before the rebels find us."

"No." I stood, my legs trembling underneath me as adrenaline rushed through my system. Everything seemed brighter, and my pulse raced so fast that I thought my chest would burst. "I need to stay here. Knox and the Blackcoats—"

"They'll kill us," she said, and I shook my head.

"I'm one of them. They won't hurt me." But Hannah wouldn't be so lucky. I glanced at the cellar door. "If they see you here—"

"I'm not going anywhere without you." She leaned the rifle against the staircase and sat down in the center of the marble floor. "If you're staying, so am I."

I hesitated. The only way to guarantee her safety was to be there when the Blackcoats found her and tell them exactly what she'd done. At least this way she would have a fighting chance.

"Okay." I tossed the remaining syringes aside and sat down beside her. "Thank you. For—" I swallowed hard and stared at the floor. I couldn't say the words.

"He stopped meaning anything to me the minute he hurt you," she said quietly, lacing her fingers through mine. "I'm just sorry I didn't do it before."

The image of Scotia and her smirk flashed through my mind, and I couldn't help but feel the same way. "Still. Thank you."

"You're welcome," said Hannah, and together we sat on the cold marble floor, waiting for the Blackcoats to find us.

XVII

VOICE

Fifteen minutes later, a group of soldiers flooded the entryway of Mercer Manor, guns drawn. For one terrifying moment, as the leader shoved the barrel of a high-powered assault weapon in my face, I thought they were going to shoot us.

"We're unarmed," I said, holding up my uninjured hand. "And we're on your side."

The leader eyed me with a spark of recognition. "Search them," he called, and two men stepped forward as the others fanned out inside the manor. While Hannah bowed her head, I held mine high, looking the leader in the eye. Instead of focusing on me, his gaze drifted over to Hannah.

"Ah, a Mercer. Just what we've been looking for." He gestured to the soldier searching her. "Bring her to the holding facility."

"No," I said, and fear shot through me. I struggled to stand, but the second soldier held me down. "She saved my life. She killed Mercer—"

"She's still a criminal," said the leader, and Hannah stumbled across the marble floor, turning enough to look at me.

"I'll be fine," she said. "Look after yourself."

"Hannah—no—let her *go!*" I shrieked, but another soldier joined the first, and together they pinned me to the ground as the others led her out the door.

"We're not monsters," said the leader, peering down at me. "We won't hurt her until we receive our orders."

"*I'm* telling you to let her go," I spat. "Don't pretend you don't know exactly who I am."

"I do, and I also know you're not authorized to give those kinds of orders, Miss Hart."

I scowled. "I want to talk to Knox Creed."

"He might be a bit busy right now—"

"Then I'll wait."

The leader stared at me, and I refused to avert my gaze. At last he mumbled something into his sleeve, and another half dozen guards joined us, surrounding me while the others searched the manor. I couldn't tell if they were protecting me or holding me captive, but either way, at least they weren't Mercer's men.

As soon as the leader called the all-clear, the soldiers pulled me to my feet. "Take her upstairs," he said. "Creed's orders. Be gentle."

"What?" I struggled against the hands that held me in place. "Where is he? I need to talk to him."

"He'll be by as soon as he can," said the leader. "In the meantime, take her upstairs."

No amount of fighting, kicking, screaming, or biting made the soldiers release me, although I found some amount of dark satisfaction when it took four of them to carry me to the Augusta Suite. As soon as they deposited me on the bed, they filed out, locking the door behind them.

I scrambled across the room and banged on the door. "Let me out!" I yelled. "Please—I need to talk to Knox!"

But no matter how loudly I screamed or how hard I pounded on that door, no one answered. Eventually, after what must have been an hour, I stumbled to the bed and collapsed, burying my face in one of the pink pillows and struggling not to cry.

If anything happened to Hannah, I would kill Knox. And this time I meant it.

I didn't know how long it took me to fall asleep in that pink-and-gold canopy bed. Minutes, maybe—or hours, or maybe I never really fell asleep at all. Vaguely, as I drifted on the edge of consciousness, I felt cool hands touch my temples, and a flash of bright light appeared in my eyes. Distantly I heard the low murmur of two men speaking, and while I could have sworn one sounded like Knox, when I finally managed to open my eyes, they were gone.

The next time I awoke, weak early morning light filtered through the stained-glass window, giving everything in the room a strange shimmering feel. I groaned as I tried to move, but something heavy weighed me down.

"Get off me," I mumbled, not yet entirely conscious. Instead, the weight only grew worse, and something shifted on the mattress beside me.

"Five more minutes," mumbled a voice into my ear, and my heart nearly stopped. Benjy.

With more energy than I thought I had left in me, I rolled over. He lay beside me, his eyes closed and his red hair sticking up all over the place. His freckled face was scrubbed clean, and he wore a fresh change of clothes that looked a size too big for him. But he could have been caked in mud and smelled like a sewer, and I would have been just as elated to see him.

"Okay," I said, snuggling up against him. "Five more minutes."

He kissed my forehead and cracked open an eye. "I'm still mad at you, you know. You swore you wouldn't leave."

"I'm here now." I nuzzled his collarbone and inhaled his scent. "I'm sorry."

Benjy sighed and ran his fingers through my matted, dirty hair. "Me, too," he whispered. Together we closed our eyes, and surrounded by his warmth, I fell asleep once more.

The Battle of Elsewhere raged on for two more days. Booms rattled Mercer Manor on the hour for thirty hours straight, and as I curled up with Benjy in the darkness, sometimes I wondered if we were already dead.

The door to the Augusta Suite unlocked three times a day for meals, and once for a doctor to check on me. "You're healing well," she told me as she dosed me with another painkiller, and by the time she slipped out the door, I was already asleep.

I dreamed of war. I dreamed of bullets and blood and neverending gunfire, and when I woke up, there was no relief. Benjy remained with me every moment, talking to me and whispering stories in my ear through the worst of it, and in the middle of the night, we clung to one another, both of us knowing that no matter how often Knox promised to keep us safe, some things were beyond his control.

"Sometimes I wonder if it was all worth it," I whispered in the darkness. We were intertwined so completely that I had no idea where I ended and Benjy began.

"What do you mean?" he murmured as he kissed my hair, now clean thanks to the bathroom that connected to the Augusta Suite. It wasn't very big, but it had a bathtub deep enough for me to soak in. No matter how hard I scrubbed, however, I never felt as if I'd washed the blood off completely.

"I mean—all these people dying." I flinched as another spike of muffled gunfire filtered into the room. It grew farther and farther away as the battle raged on, but it was only another reminder that I had dragged countless innocent people into this fight without ever asking if they'd wanted to be involved in the first place. "What if we don't win?"

"And what if we do?" Benjy's fingertips danced across my cheek, leaving trails of warmth wherever they went. "What if every single prisoner in Elsewhere is freed because of your bravery?"

"I'm not brave," I said. "I'm just trying to make sure the wrong people don't win."

"Sometimes that's all bravery is." He brushed his lips against mine, and I responded in kind automatically. "You're the bravest person I know, Kitty. You did everything you could to make this happen. Even if we fail, it won't be because of you. I promise."

"I don't deserve you," I mumbled. He chuckled.

"Probably not, but you're stuck with me anyway, so you'll just have to find a way to deal."

I poked his stomach. "You know what I mean."

He sobered and slipped his hand underneath my shirt, pressing his hot palm against the small of my back. "What I know is that I love you, and I will do anything to spend the rest of my life with you, no matter how long or short it may be. But I also know how important this war is, and I know how important you are to the war, even if you don't see it yourself."

I stared up at him, trying to memorize the look in his eyes. They were full of something I couldn't name, but I would have happily drowned inside them if it meant being closer to him. "It wouldn't mean anything if you weren't there with me."

"And I will be," he said. "I always will be. But the things

I made you promise—" He shook his head. "You're not just mine anymore. You never were."

"I'm always yours. No one else's."

He smiled faintly and brushed his lips against mine again. "You're theirs, too. They need you. Not Lila Hart, but you—Kitty Doe."

I licked my lips, dried and chapped from all that had happened. "I can't give them anything they don't already have."

"Don't you see?" He smiled, but it was a wistful smile that made something inside me ache. "You already have. You gave us hope, and you gave us the will to fight. And no matter what happens, no one—not the Prime Minister, not Knox, not even you—can take that from us. Promise me you'll remember that, okay?"

"Okay," I said softly, countless thoughts swirling in my mind, each one shattering the moment I tried to touch it. "I love you."

"And I love you," he murmured. "More than you could ever possibly know."

But I did know, and I kissed him again, molding my body against his. "Benjy?"

"Yeah?"

"There's no Blackcoat meeting tonight."

He blinked. "What?"

"And Knox isn't here. No one's coming to check on us for hours."

Benjy frowned. "I don't understand—"

I cut him off with another kiss, deeper than the one before and filled with every promise we'd ever made one another. "I think it's about time we get out of these clothes, don't you?"

At last realization dawned on him, and his eyes widened. "You're serious? Right now?"

"Right now."

His mouth opened and shut several times, and he glanced nervously at the door. "But what if—"

"It's the middle of the night. No one's coming, and there's protection in the kit the doctor left us." I propped myself up on my good arm. "Please, tell me you're not actually going to fight me on this."

"No! No, of course not," he said hastily, and he sat up long enough to pull off his shirt, revealing his bare chest. "See? There. Shirt off."

I grinned. "That's it? That's all I get?"

He looked down at his chest, running his hand over his pale skin and nonexistent abs. "Admittedly it's not much, but I would've thought you of all people wouldn't get hung up on looks," he said, though he couldn't hide the smile tugging at the corners of his mouth.

"I've seen you shirtless before, you jerk." I pushed myself up and toyed with the hem of my oversize top. "But you haven't seen what the Harts gave me. They're a damn sight better than my old ones, you know."

His expression softened, and he cupped my jaw. "Impossible. You were perfect just the way you were, and you're perfect now. You always will be."

I closed the distance between us, leaning in until my forehead rested against his. "You're wonderful," I whispered. "And I can't tell you what that means to me. But don't you dare pretend you're not going to enjoy the hell out of these, too."

He laughed, his low chuckle sending shivers through me, and he slid his hand underneath my shirt again, his fingers creeping upward. "So will you, if I have anything to say about it."

Together we leaned back into the pillows, his warm weight

settling over me as we both set out to prove we meant everything we'd said to one another. And in that moment, I forgot about the rebellion. I forgot he was kissing Lila Hart and not the real me. I forgot about Knox and Scotia and the Mercers and every terrible thing that had happened over the past few days. I lost myself in him—I lost myself in *us,* and for the first time since this whole mess had begun, I remembered what it was like to be me again. I remembered what it was like to be loved.

I wish I could say that night was perfect—that it was straight out of one of the romances Benjy had read to me, full of fireworks and grace and everything a first time should be.

But it was awkward. And we fumbled. And neither of us knew quite what we were doing. And afterward, once it was over and we lay tangled together underneath the sheets, we both watched each other as if we couldn't quite believe what we'd just done.

"All right?" I whispered, running my fingers through his hair. He nodded, his brow furrowing.

"I'm good. I'm really good," he promised, tracing an invisible pattern on my arm. "Are you okay?"

I nodded in return, and for several seconds, we were silent. At last I couldn't take it, and I blurted, "That was weird."

An odd, strangled chuckle escaped him, as if he'd been trying to hold it in and failed. "Really weird."

"Is it always supposed to feel like that?"

"Really? You're asking me?"

I looked at him, and he looked at me. And together we burst out laughing.

This was what I'd missed—happiness that wasn't weighed down by grief. Enjoying all the moments together we could steal. Looking into his eyes and knowing that no matter what happened, I would always have him, and he would always have me. This was what I was fighting for. This was what we were both fighting for.

I laughed until tears stung my eyes, and even then, Benjy's unintentional snort only egged me on until my stomach ached and I could barely breathe. That night may not have been perfect, but it was ours, and I wouldn't have traded it for all the romance novels in the world.

Somehow, miraculously, by the time cheers echoed from every side of Elsewhere as the Blackcoats declared victory, Mercer Manor was still standing. Even the guard outside our door let out a whoop of triumph, but it was another six hours before the door to the Augusta Suite finally opened.

Benjy and I were curled up on the bed as he read a book to me, both of us fully dressed now, but we sat up when a soldier appeared in the doorway. It was the same one from the foyer—the leader of the squad that had taken Hannah away. "Miss Hart," he said gruffly. "Mr. Creed wants to see you."

"It's about time," I said, and I glanced uneasily at Benjy. He kissed my temple.

"I'll be right here when you get back," he said, and I squeezed his hand.

"You'd better be."

The soldier led me through the hallway and down the familiar grand staircase. I expected him to open the front door, and I was just about to mention the fact I wasn't wearing shoes when instead, he opened the doors to Mercer's office.

Knox sat behind the desk, his reading glasses perched on his nose as he sorted through several files. In the background, a television monitor displayed a twenty-four hour news channel, and I briefly saw a picture of what looked like a bird's-eye view of Elsewhere.

"This close the whole time, and you couldn't bother to say hi?" I said, crossing my arms. The soldier shut the door behind me, leaving us alone.

"I was a little busy winning the battle," said Knox. He finally looked at me, and even with the ten feet between us, I could see that the lines in his face had deepened, and the skin underneath his eyes had turned purple.

"Is Hannah alive?" I said, and he nodded.

"She's being held in an underground facility right now with the other prisoners of war."

"She's not a prisoner," I said. "She's my mother."

"I know." He removed his glasses and pinched the bridge of his nose. "I'm doing my best here, Kitty. The prisoners want someone to blame, and there's a chance she's going to take the fall."

My stomach tightened. "If that happens—"

"It won't." He straightened, and his dark eyes met mine. "Tonight, during shift change, Hannah is going to disappear."

I opened my mouth to object, but before I could utter a single syllable, he continued.

"She'll be alive, and she will be moved to a safe location only I know," he said. "Everyone else will be told she was executed. Do you understand?"

I clenched my jaw and nodded. If nothing else, at least Hannah would be safe. "Why didn't you tell me she was my mother?"

"I only found out when I read your files. She was no one to you until you arrived in Elsewhere, and once you were here, it was safer that you didn't know. I only showed her who you really were when I thought Mercer was going to kill you."

"He was," I said, my skin going clammy at the memory. *Teeth or toes.* "And you left me."

"I had no choice. If I stayed, Mercer would have caught on, and then we would have both been dead."

For a long moment, I was silent. He was right, of course, but no amount of rationalizing it would ever make me forgive him. "I needed you," I said shakily, "and you were off playing soldier instead. Mercer had us in the cage—Benjy and me. We nearly *died*—"

"Did I or did I not tell you not to go after the codes?"

I faltered. "If I hadn't—"

"I would have found a way," he said. "Sometimes you need to trust me, Kitty."

"I would, if you ever stopped using me like another piece in your damn game," I said. "I'm not your toy, and until you start trusting *me,* there's no way in hell I'm ever going to trust you."

Knox sighed, and he reached into a drawer, pulling out the picture frame Greyson had given me. "Here. I thought you might want this back."

I took it, gazing down at Greyson's face. No matter how this ended, his life would be another casualty of war one way or the other. "Did you know the whole time?" I said, the words sticking in my throat.

"Did I know what?"

"That Greyson and I—" I swallowed hard. "Did you know the real Daxton was my father?"

Knox grimaced, and he folded his hands. "No."

"Why didn't you tell me after you found my file?" I said. "I had a right to know."

"You did," he agreed. "And I would have if things hadn't

happened the way they did. But who your father is—it was never important."

"It was important to me. Even if I never tell you where the impostor's file is, holding back something like this—you should have told me."

He rubbed his eyes wearily. "Yes. Probably. But you know now, and that isn't the reason I called you here anyway."

"Then what is?" I said. "I know we won the battle. I'm pretty sure the entire country does by now."

"We won the battle, but we haven't won the war," he said. In the background a newscaster flashed a picture of Knox across the screen. There was no going back for either of us now. "We have the weapons, but Daxton still has the Ministers and the military on his side. This is an uphill battle, and I need people I can trust. People I can depend on."

"I've risked my life for you so many times that I've lost count."

"And I'm grateful for it, but right now, I need teamwork and respect, not willful disobedience whenever you don't agree with my decisions. I need an army, Kitty. Not someone who's unreliable and doesn't listen."

"I—" I stared at him. "If you just *trusted* me and told me things—"

"But I don't," he said. "Not yet. Maybe not ever at this rate. I'm keeping my promise to you. You and Benjy will be shipped off with Hannah, and the three of you will remain in a safe, undisclosed location for the rest of the war. No one will find you there, I promise, and once it's over, you'll live the rest of your lives in peace. Isn't that exactly what you wanted?"

It was. Peace, a life with Benjy, a chance to know my biological mother—he was giving me a future, one I would never have otherwise. But my mind drifted to the conversation I'd had with Benjy in the dead of night as we listened to the sounds of war and death, and before I could stop myself, I blurted, "No."

"No?" He raised an eyebrow. "I'm only going to make this offer once. If you refuse—"

"I'm not going anywhere. Whether you like it or not, these people need me. And I'm never going to earn my freedom by letting others die for me instead. I've done enough of that already."

His mouth formed a grim line. "Kitty—"

"Why are *you* doing this?" I blurted. "You're the son of a Minister. You're a VI. You were going to live in a mansion. You were going to marry Lila Hart. You were going to be one of the most powerful people in the entire country. Why bother supporting the Blackcoats at all, let alone leading them and throwing away your future?" I paused. "Are you really in love with Lila? Is that it?"

Several long seconds passed, and finally Knox sighed. "People like you hold their loved ones above ideals. They'll do anything to protect them, no matter what it costs. But me—I hold ideals above people. No single life is as important as this revolution, not even mine."

"Why?" I said again. "People don't just wake up one day and decide to lead a rebellion."

"Sometimes they do," he said quietly, "but that's a story for another time. I need you gone, Kitty."

"And I already told you, I'm staying." I twisted around, sweeping aside my hair to show him the X scarred into my skin. "You see this?"

"Yes," he said, and I turned back to face him.

"I'm one of them now. There is no hiding, and there is no going back. I'm not giving up just because you're too proud and arrogant to trust me. I know these people better than you ever will, and like it or not—"

A tone on the television cut me off, and both Knox and I focused on the monitor. The camera switched to a live feed inside Somerset, where an empty podium stood.

Knox swore. "I was wondering when Daxton was going to address the public," he muttered, and he pushed a button on the monitor to record the speech.

But instead of Daxton stepping up, a girl with wheat-blond hair and eyes the color of the ocean stepped into view.

The real Lila Hart.

"What—" I started, but Knox shushed me, and I fell silent.

"Good afternoon," she said in a voice I could mimic in my sleep. "As I'm sure you've heard by now, the restricted territory known as Elsewhere has fallen into the hands of a violent terrorist organization known as the Blackcoats, led by my mother, Celia Hart, and my former fiancé, Lennox Creed."

I glanced at Knox. His expression hardened.

"These extremists have taken our lands, they've captured and tortured our people, and they've killed countless innocent men, women, and children, all in the name of their own ideals that destroyed the very foundation of our society less than a century ago," she continued, looking straight into the camera. "My uncle, Prime Minister Daxton Hart, is working tirelessly to secure the country from the dire threat they pose, and he will stop at nothing until he has ensured the safety of every last American life.

"I'm not here today to appeal to the Blackcoats," she added.

"We cannot reason with the irrational, and there are no words that could possibly express our sorrow and grief over the losses our people have suffered at their hands. Rather, I stand before you today to ask for the support of everyone watching right now. If you or someone you know has information leading to the identification of those who supply or support these terrorists, we ask that you step forward. We need your help to stop this senseless violence and bring people like Celia Hart and Lennox Creed to justice. Not only will we reward everyone who comes forward with information that leads to the eradication of these criminals, but you will also gain our eternal thanks and the thanks of your fellow Americans.

"The time has come for us to fight for our freedom, our safety, and all we as a nation stand for," she said, holding her head high as if she were speaking to a stadium full of people instead of a single camera. "Stand with us, and together, we can overcome this dark time in our history. Together, we can defeat these radicals who want nothing more than to destroy the peace and prosperity we've worked so tirelessly to create. Together, we can prevail."

Somerset faded away, replaced by the newscaster once more. Knox turned the television off, and for several seconds, neither of us said a word. Silence smothered me as the weight of what had just happened settled on my shoulders, and I replayed her words over and over again in my mind.

There was no hidden message. There was no secret meaning.

Somehow, someway, Daxton had convinced the voice of the Blackcoat rebellion to speak for him instead.

"A Lila on each side. This should be interesting," I said coolly. "Guess it's a good thing I'm not going anywhere, isn't it? You're going to need me."

And without waiting for Knox's reply, I turned around and walked out the office door, heading back upstairs where Benjy was waiting for me.

★ ★ ★ ★ ★

Turn the page for a sneak peek at
QUEEN,
the exciting conclusion to The Blackcoat Rebellion
by Aimée Carter,
available now from Harlequin TEEN!

I

SPEAK

I gazed out across the gathering crowd, my heart in my throat. The citizens of Elsewhere shifted restlessly, their red and orange jumpsuits bringing color to an otherwise gray winter landscape, and I could feel them growing impatient.

They weren't the only ones.

"Knox, everyone's waiting," I said from my corner of the stage the Blackcoats had constructed over the past several days. It was made of whatever materials they'd been able to salvage from the buildings that had been destroyed during the Battle of Elsewhere. Two weeks later, they were still pulling bodies from the wreckage.

Knox Creed, one of the leaders of the Blackcoat Rebellion—and my former fake fiancé—looked up from his spot at the base of the stairs. His forehead was furrowed, and the annoyance on his face was unmistakable. "I'm aware, thank you," he said. "There's only so much I can do to hurry things along."

I hopped down the steps to join him and the other Blackcoats who lingered nearby. He'd made no secret of his distaste for my less-than-obedient attitude, and though I'd done my best to play by the rules after the battle ended, we were still on shaky ground. I wasn't so sure our friendship would ever be mended completely, no matter how the rebellion turned out. But right now, we both had more important things to worry about: he had a rebellion to lead, and I had a speech to give. As soon as the cameras were ready for me.

"Benjy said the test run this morning went fine," I said. "Is there a problem now?"

"There's always a problem," said Knox. Turning away from me, he spoke into a cuff on his wrist. "What's the holdup?"

I waited in silence as he listened to the reply in his earpiece. He muttered what sounded like a curse, and it was my turn to frown. "How much longer?"

"They're having trouble breaking through the network's security," he said. "Something about encryptions and passcodes."

In other words, nothing I could help with. Or Knox, for that matter. "Why don't we just record the speech and broadcast it once they've found a way around it? Wouldn't that be easier?"

"If it comes to that, we will, but we can give them a few more minutes." As if realizing for the first time that I was standing next to him, he did a double take, his dark eyes looking me up and down. "Did you bathe?"

I blinked. "Are you joking? I spent an hour letting them do my hair and makeup."

"What did they do, stare at you the entire time?" He ran his fingers through my hair in an attempt to do—something. I didn't know what. "You look nothing like Lila anymore."

Lila Hart—one of the founders of the Blackcoats, who also happened to be Prime Minister Daxton Hart's niece. Four months ago, on my seventeenth birthday, I'd been kidnapped and surgically transformed to look exactly like her in order to take her place. She had been Knox's real fiancée. I was only playing the part.

But now, after the dust had settled, the entire world knew there were two of us. Lila was working for Daxton, who had to be holding something over her. Whatever it was must have been a matter of life or death, because the Lila Hart I knew, while not particularly brave, would have never openly supported the government that had murdered her father and turned her mother into a fugitive rebel. Not like this. Not unless there was a gun to her head—or someone else's.

There was little we could do about Lila's sudden change in allegiance now, though, and in the meantime, I was working for Knox and the Blackcoats. He had plenty to hold over me, but none of it mattered, because Knox didn't want me here. I was in Elsewhere because I wanted to be. I was about to speak in front of countless Americans because it was the right thing to do. And no matter how many times he tried to intimidate me into leaving, nothing would make me change my mind.

"I look exactly like Lila, and everyone in this damn place knows it," I said firmly. "You're just beginning to see the differences more clearly. There were two boys in my group home—they were identical twins, and no one could tell them apart at first. But the more we got to know them, the easier—"

"You can spare me. I know how telling twins apart works." His scowl deepened, and I wondered what I'd said to upset him. But it was gone as soon as it came, and someone must have talked in his ear, because he stopped fussing with my hair and touched the piece. "All right. Kitty—they're ready for you. Remember your talking points, and for once, would you please stick to them?"

I shook my hair out, letting the shoulder-length blond bob

fall wherever it wanted. "Do I get to tell my version of events, or yours?"

"I want you to tell the truth," he said. "The entire truth. We can't afford lies and misdirection anymore, not when Lila and Daxton are the ones feeding them directly to the people."

The corners of my mouth tugged upward in a slow smile. "Really? The entire truth?"

His dark eyes met mine, and he leaned in until I could see the gray that ringed his irises. "Every last bit of it."

Whatever his reasoning was—whatever he was using me for—I didn't care. He was giving me permission to be myself for the first time in months, and I wasn't going to turn him down.

Someone had fixed a bright light over my spot behind a makeshift podium, and I climbed back up the steps and walked over, my boots thumping against the wooden planks. Hundreds of faces stared up at me expectantly, but the more I focused, the more discontent I saw in the crowd. The people of Elsewhere, who had not only survived the battle, but in some cases an entire lifetime of captivity, were less forgiving than most. During my few days here as a prisoner, I'd been beaten up and threatened more times than I could count. They were hostile, merciless, and quick to protect their own skins above all else.

But this was different. The government had cut off several of Elsewhere's key supply lines and destroyed most of the stores in the battle, and the more time that passed, the fewer resources Knox and the Blackcoats had to take care of everyone. They were going hungry, slowly but surely, and if I didn't do this—if I couldn't convince the people to listen—then we would soon starve. And they knew it.

I cleared my throat. The microphone hooked up to the podium amplified my voice, making it echo through the square. Two weeks ago, a cage had stood in the center, and every evening, insubordinate citizens had been forced to fight to the death for a second chance. Now only a twisted lump of melted steel remained.

Things in Elsewhere weren't easy, and they wouldn't be for a long time. But at least that ruined cage was a reminder that they were marginally better than before.

In my peripheral vision, Knox stood with his arms crossed, giving me a look, and I didn't need to hear him to know what he was trying to tell me. They wouldn't be able to hold the broadcast channel open forever. If I wanted the five hundred million people who lived in the United States to hear me, I had to start talking.

I pushed the number from my mind and held my head high. This wasn't about me. This was about the rebellion, about freedom, about doing the right thing for the people—I was just the mouthpiece. Nothing more.

"Good afternoon," I said, and for the first time, I used my own voice and accent instead of the dialect I'd painstakingly learned in September. "As I'm sure you've put together by now, my name is not Lila Hart."

A murmur rippled through the crowd, and Knox took a deep breath, his shoulders rising and falling slowly. His lips were pressed together, and even from twenty feet away, I could see the fear and anticipation in his eyes. We were both keenly aware of how much was riding on this.

"My name is Kitty Doe, and seventeen years ago, I was born here, in Section X of Elsewhere," I said. "My biological mother is Hannah Mercer, and my biological father was Prime Minister Daxton Hart."

These were facts I had only become aware of two weeks

earlier, when Hannah—my mother—had confessed her affair with the Prime Minister. The words stuck in my throat, and even after repeating them countless times to myself, they still didn't feel real.

"I was lucky," I continued. "Because of who my father was, he had the power to make arrangements for me outside Elsewhere, in a group home for Extras and orphans in Washington, D.C. I am, as far as I know, the only person to ever leave Elsewhere."

Once someone was convicted of a crime, no matter how innocent or small, they were sent to Elsewhere for life. Population control, I'd been told by Augusta Hart, Daxton's cold-blooded bitch of a mother. In reality, it was just one more way for the government to assert control over the people.

"I was raised in a group home with thirty-nine other children," I said. "I thought it was a relatively normal life. I went to school. I played with the other kids. We dodged Shields, snuck into markets, and imagined what our lives would be like after we turned seventeen, when we would take the test and become adults. But there was one thing no one had ever told us—that the freedom we'd imagined, getting to make our own choices and deciding what our lives would be like... that was all an illusion.

"We were naive to believe it, but we never knew to question it until it was too late," I added. "We're all given ranks based on that single test. Compared to the rest of the population and put in our place. A low II, a high VI—it doesn't matter. Our lives are never in our own hands. Our rank dictates everything. Our jobs. Our homes. Our neighbors. Where we live, what we do all day, the amount of food and care we're allowed—it can even decide when we die. Some of you have been lucky enough to have easy jobs, ones that don't take an insurmountable toll on your body. But others aren't so lucky.

"I wasn't one of the lucky ones." I turned around and swept my hair aside, revealing the VII tattooed on the back of my neck and a scarred X running through it. I let the camera linger for several seconds before I turned around. "What you see now is a VII, but the ridges underneath will tell you my real rank—a III. I was assigned to clean sewers far away from my home and the only family I'd ever known. It's good, honest work," I added. "But it wasn't what I'd dreamed of doing. I was one more cog in a machine too big for any of us to fully comprehend, and because I couldn't stand the thought of leaving my loved ones, I chose to go underground and hide in a brothel instead."

At some point while I'd been speaking, Benjy had joined Knox on the side of the stage, his red hair fiery in the sunlight and the look on his freckled face relaxed and encouraging. I flashed him a small smile. He was the reason I'd risked my life and entire future to stay, but he was mine—he was private, and while anyone in Elsewhere could see the pair of us walking around together, working on target practice or tending to the recovering victims of the battle, I wasn't going to tell the world about him. He was the chink in my armor, and I wouldn't give anyone the opportunity to use him against me.

"If you'll bear with me, I promise this all has a point," I said as more and more people began to shift and glance at their neighbors. The revelation that I was really the Prime Minister's illegitimate daughter was only good for so much rapt attention, and I was rapidly burning through it. But the Blackcoats wanted me to tell my story. I wasn't the only victim of the Hart family, but I was the only one who the people already cared about, without even realizing who I truly was.

"At the brothel, Daxton Hart bought me. But instead of—well, you know—he offered me a VII." The highest rank in our country, one you had to be born into in order to receive. "I had no idea I was actually a Hart at the time, but even then, no one turns down a VII. No one. A VII meant luxury, enough to eat, and what I thought would be a good life—it was an easy choice, so of course I said yes." I leveled my stare at a painfully thin woman in a red jumpsuit. I didn't recognize her, but I needed to look at someone. "On the way out of the brothel, my best friend saw us together by chance. Daxton Hart had her murdered in the alleyway, and while I was screaming, he gave me something that made me black out. When I woke up, it was two weeks later, and I had been Masked—surgically transformed into an identical version of Lila Hart, whom her family had secretly assassinated days earlier."

More murmurs ran through the crowd, and the woman I was watching held my stare. I had their attention again. Good.

"I was given a choice. Pretend to be Lila, or die. It wasn't a real choice at all. It never is when you're staring down the barrel of a gun and waiting for someone to pull the trigger. And I thought that was what my life was going to be—a series of dodged bullets until one day, I wasn't lucky anymore.

"But when I agreed to impersonate Lila, it opened up an entirely new world to me. Not just the unparalleled luxury of the Hart family's day-to-day lives, but a real opportunity to change things through a revolutionary group called the Blackcoats. As soon as my education on becoming Lila began, Celia, Lila's mother, and Knox, Lila's fiancé, made sure my education on the Blackcoats did, too.

"They didn't have to tell me about the injustices our citizens face day in and day out. How Shields often kill and arrest innocent people in order to meet their quotas, or because they're having a bad day and have the power to take it out on us. I already knew that—I'd been dodging Shields since I was a kid. But Celia and Knox did tell me how IIs are given rotting food, houses with leaking roofs, and no respect or support from anyone above them. How most extra children born to IIs and IIIs are sent to Elsewhere, to be raised inside a prison, and never see the outside world. How our *entire lives* are dictated by a single aptitude test that only caters to one type of intelligence, and how children who are lucky enough to be born to Vs and VIs get certain advantages. Tutors, inside information—in fact, every single one of the twelve Ministers of the Union received VIs, not on their own merits, but because of the family they were born into. They never took the test, and neither will their heirs.

"Before I became Lila, I believed the lies the government feeds us—that we're in charge of our own lives, that if we just do well enough on the test, they'll take care of us. They'll tell us where we belong, and that every single one of us has a place in society. I believed them when they told us we were all important and needed. I may have rejected the life they wanted for me, but I still *believed* them.

"The first lesson in my education came the day I was finally declared ready to impersonate Lila. Daxton Hart brought me to a wooded area for a hunting trip. But we weren't hunting deer or quail," I added. "We were in Elsewhere, and we were hunting humans."

I let this sink in for a moment, and the crowd stared at me with slack jaws and pale faces. During my few days as a prisoner, I'd quickly discovered none of the other citizens of Elsewhere knew why so many of their ranks were plucked without warning, never to be seen again. Now they knew. Now everyone knew how VIs and VIIs had hunted humans for sport, all because there was no one to stop them.

"All of the VIs and VIIs took part in these hunting trips, and as Lila, I was expected to shut up and go along with it. And I did, because while I hated watching innocent people die, I knew that blending in and doing what was expected of me then meant a chance to help others now.

"America is supposed to be a fair meritocracy. We're all supposed to receive what we deserve based on our skills and intelligence. But unlike the rest of us, there is a small section of the population that is born into a life of luxury that they never have to work a day in their lives to earn. The Hart family included.

"But being born into a life of privilege isn't the only way to get a VI or a VII. I received a VII after I was Masked, for instance. And I wasn't the only one." I gripped the edge of the podium so tightly that I felt a splinter wedge its way into my palm. "Over a year ago, another citizen was Masked as a Hart—a man named Victor Mercer. Except he wasn't Masked as a background figure like Lila, too many steps away from power to be anything more than a pawn. Victor Mercer was Masked as the one and only Daxton Hart—Prime Minister of the United States."

An audible gasp rose through the crowd, and they began to push forward in their eagerness to hear more, jostling for a better position. Victor Mercer had been a high-ranking official who ran Elsewhere with his brother for years, and no doubt many of the former prisoners remembered his particular brand of sadism. Several shouted at me, demanding proof, and I shook my head, my voice rising.

"I've felt the V on the back of his neck myself. But he's done a masterful job of destroying nearly all of the evidence that he was Masked. Some still exists, though. And when the time is right, the Blackcoats will release it and prove that the man who calls himself Daxton Hart—the man dictating our lives, the most powerful man in the country—is an impostor."

I had to shout the last few words into the microphone to be heard over the audience's roars of outrage. Out of the corner of my eye, I saw Knox give me an approving nod, though he still didn't smile. Either way, it was enough. At last we'd agreed on something—that telling the truth, the full truth, was what would eventually help lead the rebellion to victory.

"This country belongs to the people, not to the ruling class," I called above the noise. "We're the majority—we're the ones their policies and decisions affect, while they constantly hover above the law. They kill the lower ranks for sport. They live in luxury while IIs and IIIs starve. And *we* have the power to stop them. Yet not once, in the seventy years the Harts and the Ministers of the Union have been in power, have we risen together to face these injustices. But now we can. It's our *responsibility* to stand together against these monsters—against the impostors that rule our government. This is *our* country, and we need to take it back before the man who calls himself Daxton Hart destroys it completely."

At last a rousing cheer rose from the crowd, and I exhaled sharply. My hands shook, and my heart pounded, but I felt as if I were floating. I wasn't done yet, though, and the next portion wouldn't be so easy. I'd gone back and forth with Knox, arguing about it for days, but ultimately telling the truth meant telling the entire truth—and that meant calling out the real Lila Hart.

"Daxton will try to tell you that every word I say is a lie," I said. "He'll ask for proof. He'll call this a trick to gain sympathies. He'll insist I'm only acting as a puppet for the leaders of the Blackcoat Rebellion. But the real puppet here is Lila Hart. I've seen the speeches she's given since the Battle of Elsewhere. I've heard her cries for peace. And we—the Blackcoats—will do all we can to make sure no more blood is spilled in this war. But when peace means lying down and allowing the government to execute us, for standing up for our freedom and for those who can't stand up for themselves, I'm afraid we can't do that. Peace without freedom is imprisonment. It's oppression. They can try to scare us. They can try to threaten our families and our lives, but ultimately we won't *have* lives if we can't decide for ourselves how we live.

"I don't blame Lila," I added. "I know that, if she could, she would be here with me, giving this speech much more eloquently than I ever could. And I say to her, right now—" I looked directly into the camera. "You are not alone. Whatever Victor is holding against you, whatever he's doing to make you obey—we know those aren't your words, and we know they aren't your beliefs. And we will do everything we can to help you, the way we're doing everything we can to help the people. You are one of us, and we will not forget you."

I paused to allow that to sink in. While the citizens of Elsewhere couldn't have cared less about Lila, the rest of the country did, and they had to know she was a puppet. It wouldn't completely cut off Daxton's counterpoints, but maybe it would be enough to plant the kernel of doubt.

"This isn't about Lila, though," I said at last. "It isn't about me, and it isn't even about Victor Mercer posing as Daxton Hart. This is about *you*—every single person watching right now. This is about *your* future, *your* family, *your* health and happiness and hopes. All our lives, we've been living under a dictator masquerading as a friend, with no way to overthrow him and take back the freedom Americans enjoyed a hundred years ago. But the Blackcoats have opened the door of possibility. They've paved the way for real change, and it's up to us to take this opportunity and turn it into a reality. *Our* reality. Not a dream, but something we can *live*. The chance to choose our own paths in life. To be *more* than the numbers on the backs of our necks.

"The Blackcoats have crippled the military and seized control of their main arsenals. They have infiltrated the government, and they have worked tirelessly to give us back the inalienable rights that were stolen before any of us were born. But it's up to us to finish the job. We need to stand together against the Shields, the Harts, and the Ministers of the Union. We need to remind them that *we* are the ones in charge, not them—that this is *our* country, and after all they've done to us, our families, and our friends, we are revoking their privilege to rule. Because it *is* a privilege," I added fiercely. "*Not* a right. A privilege *we* gave them through our compliance. And the time has come to take back what is ours. Together, we *will* prevail, and we *will* be free."

The cheers from the former prisoners were deafening. I could see it in their faces—for these few moments, they forgot about their hunger and their despair. They believed in what I was saying. They believed in hope, and that alone had made everything I'd been through worth it.

Knox joined me on stage, but instead of saying anything to the audience, he set his hand on my shoulder and led me away. "Good," he said. "Lila couldn't have done it better."

High praise, considering she had managed to rally the initial support for the Blackcoats from nothing but mild discontent. "Do you think they'll listen?" I said.

He pressed his lips together as we descended the stairs toward a waiting Benjy, the crowd's screams ringing in my ears.

"They'd better. We can't do this alone."

And if we didn't have the support of the people outside Elsewhere, too, then we were already dead.

COLLECT THE COMPLETE SERIES!

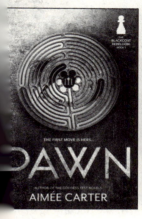 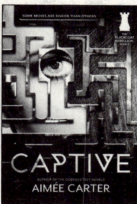 

The world is supposed to be equal.

Life is supposed to be fair.

But appearances are deceiving.

And Kitty Doe knows that better than anyone else...

Full series available now!

www.HarlequinTEEN.com

Find Harlequin TEEN on

Discover a thrilling modern fantasy saga:
THE GODDESS TEST NOVELS by Aimée Carter

Available wherever books are sold!

Kate Winters's life hasn't been easy. She's battling with the upcoming death of her mother, and only a mysterious stranger called Henry is giving her hope. But he must be crazy, right? Because there is no way the god of the Underworld—Hades himself—is going to choose Kate to take the seven tests that might make her an immortal...and his wife. And even if she passes the tests, is there any hope for happiness with a war brewing between the gods

Also available:
THE GODDESS HUNT,
a digital-only novella.

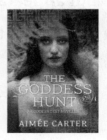

www.HarlequinTEEN.com

Find Harlequin TE

From the *New York Times* bestselling author of
The White Rabbit Chronicles,

GENA SHOWALTER

"*FIRSTLIFE* is a nonstop thrill ride that will stop your heart... and shock it back to life."

—#1 *New York Times* bestselling author P. C. Cast

Firstlife is merely a dress rehearsal. Real life begins after death.

ONE CHOICE. TWO REALMS. NO SECOND CHANCE.

Look for Book 2 in the ***Everlife*** series, *LIFEBLOOD*, coming February 2017!

HARLEQUIN®TEEN
www.HarlequinTEEN.com

Find Harlequin TEEN on

HTGSFTR5

From the limitless imagination of *New York Times* bestselling author Julie Kagawa

THE TALON SAGA

In this groundbreaking modern fantasy series, dragons walk among us in human form.

Long ago, dragons were hunted to near extinction by the Order of St. George, a legendary society of dragonslayers. Hiding in human form and growing their numbers in secret, the dragons of Talon have become strong and cunning, and they're positioned to take over the world with humans none the wiser.

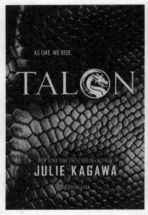

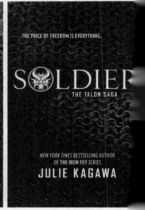

Read books 1-3 of the epic *Talon Saga*!

www.HarlequinTEEN.com

Find Harlequin TEEN